MORTAL

BY

REBEKAH MCCLEW

DEDICATION:
TO MY DAUGHTER,
THANK YOU FOR
GENUINELY LOVING
THIS STORY, YOU
GIVE ME HOPE.

BEGINNINGS

I never thought this would end. Such a happy moment. I looked forward to it all my life. Every year the same tradition, not much had changed other than the fact I was older now. I never wanted to start my birthday any other way. Nothing else could start until this event happened. If I had known this would be the last time I did this, then I would have appreciated it more. Surrounded by nothing other than meadows, yellow wildflowers, and the little farmhouse behind me, I had stood there waiting in the middle of the field as I always did on my birthday. Waiting for the sun to set just enough behind the clouds for them to show up. I knew they would never leave me waiting there for too long. My father's childhood friends would come to visit.

They had started this ritual with me from the point I was dropped off at my father's door telling him he was a father. I was only three years old at the time. After my mother passed away my father made it a consistent tradition on my birthday when they would come to visit. As far as I knew I had the most average life possible just with several unusual people who loved me. Each year I would wait here and as I grew older and taller; I could finally see over the tall weeds in the field. Now I was finally at eye level with the two that had become very important in my life. Only two months out of the year my father would leave and come back without explanation. Just before that, they would spend two weeks with me for my birthday and then take off. I always spent the night at my best friend's house when they left; at least I had until she moved away. I had been so young when this started that I never thought to question where or what my father was doing during those two months. When he was gone it felt like an eternity until I had grown older, and I understood exactly when they would be back.

Eventually, our neighbor would babysit me since my father felt he not only trusted her but felt she would protect me as vigilantly as she did her children. When I had turned fourteen, I was finally allowed to stay at home alone even though the neighbors were always there in case I needed anything.

Now standing out here watching as the sun slowly began to get sheltered by the clouds leaving less light out, I looked across the field as I saw two tall dark figures walking their way towards me. If I hadn't known them it could have been rather scary except, I knew it was only Voncha and Jasper coming to visit us. Voncha as calm and gentle as he was, you would never know it by his looks, he was never concerned with his appearance. Always scruffy and sometimes he was even a little dirty but then I assumed it was from his lack of coordination. He couldn't seem to be outside for long without attracting dirt somehow. Jasper was the complete opposite. Always clean in appearance, not one hair out of place and I doubt I ever saw a speck of dirt on him. His face was always shaven looking nice, both looked like very nice young men despite Voncha's rough exterior. As much as I loved Voncha I was very close to Jasper. Voncha was my partner in crime; we would explore everywhere and usually came home with a few bumps and bruises. Jasper taught me everything from playing classical music, reading, and world events encouraging me to be my best. To think for myself.

I never thought about the fact that they or my father hadn't aged much; they simply explained they had good genetics and aged well. I accepted this only because of a few teachers. I had later when two of them were the same age and only one looked so much older than what she truly was. She always said it was the environment, that she was stuck in a classroom with us kids. I almost felt sorry for her.

As the two men came closer, I could see their smiling faces, I couldn't help but feel excited to see them here finally. Every year it was the same, first, they would greet me with a hug and a birthday wish, and then we would follow Voncha as he led the way and Jasper placed his arm around my waist. Jasper used to carry me around until I had become a teenager then he gave me more respect by either guiding me or simply holding my hand. The dynamics had started changing, not that I paid attention to this either. I will admit I am sheltered and naïve. Dad was always happy to see his old friends. Whatever they did when they were gone, dad always acted revived and ready to face the world again once he came back home.

Standing in the kitchen with Jasper, with his arm around my waist, we watched as father had just finished lighting the candles on my cake. This year I was turning twenty-one. After the candles had been blown out and I made the same wish I had for the last four years. Dad and Voncha had sat down at the table to talk about boring business as usual. Sitting in front of the television relaxed on the couch, Jasper chose the corner to sit as I laid against him the same as I always did since I was able to crawl. When I was little I would fall asleep in his arms. This time dad's voice had sounded different than he used to, and I noticed Jasper had smelled my hair. I washed my hair this morning so there shouldn't be anything bad to smell.

"Emma, could you check on the dogs, make sure they have food and water for the night, and make sure their pens are locked." I knew from the way he spoke he wanted to discuss something that he felt he hadn't wanted me to hear.

"Sure." Getting up from my comfortable spot, only half of my program was over.

As I Walked outside, they were waiting until the door had closed behind me to make sure I didn't hear them. I hadn't minded going outside since I was starting to feel strange again. I knew dad would be leaving soon and I hadn't wanted to worry him. If it didn't go away, I would see a doctor when he came back or worse have our neighbor Jenna take me in. I never really liked telling her that I was feeling sick, or something was wrong, she was always wonderful taking care of me except she seemed to worry a little more than normal and tended to go overboard taking care of me. I guess I was fortunate to at least have someone care so much for me than not.

"I can't risk leaving her alone right now. I know she's hiding something from me, I just can't figure it out unless it's a normal teenage thing. I noticed you had a strange look on your face Jasper, did you notice something? Did she tell you anything?" My father had paced back and forth with a worried expression on his face as he asked Jasper.

"She hasn't said anything to me. I did notice a scent; she used to smell of it before I just assumed it was because she played in the honeysuckle when she was little. Now it's much stronger, is she wearing perfume?" Jasper wondered what would worry him since she seemed just fine to him.

"Emma isn't wearing any perfume and only three have noticed the scent from her. It's the same scent her mother had." Shaking his head letting out a deep sigh.

"What is bothering you? A scent can't be it, especially if it reminds you of her mother. Is there something you're not telling us?" Voncha had been the first to ask.

"As far as she understands we are all very normal, it's why I've always had you two walk when you approach the house. She simply thinks that we are all rather eccentric, especially the two of you. Being an artist has helped make this look more legitimate for her; except I'm worried someday I won't be around or be able to shield her from the truth. She has no idea what I am, she has no idea both of you happen to be the same. Her mother could do some rather unusual things except she stopped as soon as she had our daughter. She left all of it behind when she wanted to be what she considered to be a normal mortal, she wanted life to be different so neither of us talked about it, we just tried to live a normal life blending in with everyday mortals. It was hard to do when she passed away. I have no idea what to expect, what characteristics our daughter will inherit from both of us, but she's twenty-one now and I have no clue how to explain any of this, especially now she's at the age her mother was when she had full use of her gifts. I can't imagine how she will react if she ever found out she's had these gifts already." Finally sitting out of frustration Thomas could only shake his head.

"I could stay behind and watch her if you're so worried. I'm sure she's fine but then if I do stay if any of us do, she will be suspicious why suddenly one of us is staying behind." We all knew Jasper was right when he pointed out what we were all thinking.

"Emma will see through anything I do; I've never been able to keep a secret from her." A slight smile crept up on Voncha's face.

We all know how many times he's tried tricking her not being successful even though he's managed to trick other creatures who should have been able to spot his hijinks much easier.

"I'll stay behind; I know what to say to make it sound as though I have a sound reason for staying. There are things in town that I can keep somewhat busy with and still keep an eye on her without it looking as though I'm babysitting her." Nodding his head Thomas had agreed.

"I'll go see if she needs any help." Standing up Voncha made his way out of the house leaving Jasper to talk with Thomas.

We only had six dogs except it always felt like so many more with the amount they ate. It had taken me a while to drag the two bags of dog food up from the storeroom. Filling the water first I had left the dog food for the last. All eyes had been watching me waiting to be fed. They had several acres to explore and run around in but once they heard the food, they knew exactly where to wait, they each had an open kennel with a long walkway where their food bowls were stored. With three Great Danes and three English Bullmastiffs waiting the space in the kennels was rather limited for standing. Almost being knocked over I felt an arm circle around my waist catching me before I fell and hit the ground. Not that it would have been the first time I had fallen in here. Most of the time, the dogs thought I was playing and would stand over me until they realized I wasn't playing.

"I thought you might want some help." Smiling at me Voncha knew it was an understatement.

9

Before I could say anything more Voncha picked up the dog food filling the dog bowls. No one had made a move over near him as they watched from a distance.

"If I had been filling their bowl, they would have knocked me over-eager to get to it." I wondered how he was able to do this; even dad had no problem feeding the dogs. It must just be me."

"I grew up with dogs like these, so I'm used to it, besides I ignore them when I'm in here." Picking up the empty bags we both made our way out of the pen as the dogs ate.

Without having to look to confirm it. I knew we were being watched from the house. I just couldn't figure out why.

"Is there something going on that I should know about? Dad's been acting unusual for the last couple of days, he's not good at hiding things when he's worried." Not bothering to make a move towards the house I stood there hoping Voncha would tell me something.

"There's not that much I can tell you; your dad is more worried about you. He said you have been acting differently and are worried about leaving if there is something wrong or if you need help. He didn't want us coming right out and telling you, but it would be easier talking with you if there is something we can help you with." His voice sounded so gentle and sincere.

At least I don't think it will be as bad as I thought it might. But then how do I explain this?

"I don't know how to explain it without sounding crazy. Besides, I'm pretty sure it's just another growing-up girl thing, kind of like puberty." I could feel my cheeks flush, not wanting to explain the changes I was feeling.

It was difficult enough when I had to explain to my dad when I was younger that I had started my period.

"You know I would never judge you for anything, I just want to help." Voncha had never once taken his eyes off of me.

"I know you want to help. I just don't know for sure myself. If there is anything you can do I'll tell you. I still have the neighbors to call if I need anything while dad is gone." Giving Voncha a hug hoping to reassure him I was fine; I didn't want any of them to worry about me while they were gone.

10

"Did you want to finish your movie? We put it on hold." I knew Voncha was trying to keep me talking.

Usually, he seemed to ramble when he wanted to get me to talk, not that I minded.

"I need to figure out what outfit I'm wearing. While everyone else is gone I'm going to a friend's wedding. Maybe I can get your opinion." I knew it wasn't exactly what he was hoping for but then Voncha hadn't fought it either no doubt still not convinced enough I was fine.

Grabbing his hand, I led him inside past the others, and into my room with the door open. I could hear slight whispering since I was sure they wondered what I was showing him.

"At least I'm not in the wedding so I won't look as hideous as the bridesmaids, but I can't decide which one to wear. From a guy's perspective, which one do you like better?" Pulling out two dresses from my closet I held them both up next to me so he could see both.

After looking from one to the other I could tell he wasn't sure what to tell me. It had looked more like he was gauging what I had liked before saying anything. Keeping my face as expressionless as possible I could tell Voncha was having a hard time. He was always good at judging my emotions, exactly how I was feeling, and sometimes thinking just from his gazing at me. This time I wasn't going to make it easy for him.

"It's hard to tell with them on hangers. They both look nice, maybe a little short; don't you have anything that would at least touch the floor?" With a slight smile, I knew it was more of a father-type comment than what I wanted.

"No, I only have shorter. Besides these two are fine, I like both I just can't decide. Guess it doesn't matter since I won't be dancing anyway. I'm sure a few of the girls won't be bringing dates with them either." Before I could put the dresses back in the closet Voncha reached out for the black dress.

"If you must choose, I like the simple dress. The red stands out too much, when I was young, a lady didn't wear red unless she wanted to give the wrong impression." After his comment, I couldn't resist.

11

"Black is usually reserved for funerals. Maybe if I look depressed it will keep the guys from looking me over?" I could rarely make Voncha feel uncomfortable.

"I would prefer wearing black and appear to be mourning then wear red and be associated with whores." As much as I had wanted to respond to his comment, Voncha had been called out by my father no doubt to plan whatever they were doing over the next two months.

I was looking forward to having the house to myself again. Coming out of my room I could see the three sitting around the kitchen table making plans the way they always have. Resuming my movie, I sat down on the couch with popcorn watching the last of it. A couple of times I had tried to hear what they were saying except they always talked rather lightly. No doubt knowing, I was curious enough to eavesdrop. Finally feeling tired and not falling asleep yet I made myself get up from the warm couch.

"I think I'm going to turn in early." Trying to sound calm I faked a yawn and stretched.

"Did you want to go anywhere in the morning?" I knew Jasper was trying to delay me.

"I think I'm just going to sleep in, I don't get the chance to do that too often now that I'm working full time." As I spoke, I made my way over to the stairs.

"When's the wedding? I could help you go shopping?" I could hear the discomfort in Voncha's voice.

We all looked at him with shocked expressions on our faces.

"Don't worry, that part is covered. I'm going dress shopping with Beth around noon. We plan on eating lunch and shopping, so I'll be gone all evening. I'll probably spend the night at her place." Taking a few more steps up I quickly turned down the hallway before they could ask any more questions and bolted up the stairs.

I probably didn't need to rush that fast, but it was the best way of avoiding any more questions or getting stuck with any of them tomorrow. Normally I would have loved to stay with them except I had felt so lousy I just wanted to be alone. I knew I wasn't going to get much sleep tonight. It almost seemed as if they were checking on me trying to be quiet walking back and forth in the hallway in front of my bedroom door.

Slipping my feet out of my warm bed I decided to take a shower, and I was going to insist that I have carpet installed. I loved the old wood floors, but I was tired of having them so cold. It felt great in the summer but not as winter approached. I felt so frustrated laying here not able to sleep. At least I didn't have to share my bathroom. At least I wouldn't have to leave my room. The water felt so good on my muscles. I just knew I would regret it once I was out. I couldn't figure it out. My entire body felt overwhelmed, some muscles more so than others. At times it hurt to walk. My feet felt bruised almost as if I had been beaten up just no bruises to show for it. When I was vacationing with my family, I had fallen twelve feet from a cliff. I scared poor Voncha, he thought I was dead since I hadn't moved or made a sound for several hours. I was amazed I was alive, but I was lucky. There were still several more feet to go down, at least I hadn't fallen all the way. The pain I had now was far worse than that and I was finally at the point I couldn't hide it anymore.

I had already taken six ibuprofen and five acetaminophens in the last twenty-seven hours to help relax my muscles and hopefully to help with the headache. I had the heating pad in bed; the heat seemed to feel much better. Ice packs only caused the pain to increase. I found that out the hard way. Normally I would never stay in the shower this long; usually to make sure I didn't dry out my skin. I know I should care about the environment; it's not as if I littered or wore animal fur but occasionally it felt good being doused with hot water. Finally, feeling relaxed I stepped out of the shower. I was tempted to sleep nude except when Voncha and Jasper stayed I always wore sleepwear. My father never woke me up but occasionally Voncha would if we were going to go hiking or Jasper found something interesting. Walking into my bedroom I was very glad I decided to get dressed in the bathroom. Voncha was sitting in my computer chair waiting for me.

"I could have come out nude!" They really must have wanted to know what was wrong with me.

I had never seen Voncha look so worried before.

"Yes, but you didn't. Tell me exactly how you're feeling." I knew what he meant but I was tired and wanted to be left alone.

"I feel just fine, I felt like taking a shower." Placing my towel over the hook on the bathroom door to dry I made my way over to my bed and pulled down the covers.

"You were in the shower longer than normal and I thought I heard you make an odd noise." Voncha was serious.

"So now you're spying on me? When did you start doing this? It's not a crime to stay in the shower longer than usual. Excuse me for having my period." For the first time, I was upset with him.

"Your father said you already had your period, is it normal for a girl to have it twice?" Voncha seemed surprised.

"Get a girlfriend and ask her. Now out of my bedroom so I can sleep. I probably won't sleep since I'm angry now." Sitting down on my bed I watched Voncha nod his head in agreement, not saying another word he left my room.

The pacing outside my door also stopped. As soon as the morning came, I was careful not to run into the others. Packing a bag with several items I had planned on staying away for a few nights, not just one. I made sure to spend the night at Beth's apartment at least once. She was acting so strangely and talking about her sculptures all night almost as if they were alive. I didn't mind that she took that much pride in them except it's all she would talk about. We used to talk about anything, she was just acting so differently that I was thankful to go back to the hotel and be on my own. Occasionally I had something strange happen along with the pain, the pain would ease up and most of it was strange.

Standing up in the hotel room I could hear two men arguing on the street. I hadn't wanted to attract attention by looking out except it had gone on for quite a while before I heard police cars. Turning the television on to see if anything was playing, flipping from channel to channel I wasn't finding anything to watch. I had heard a loud thump come from the balcony. Standing up looking at the sliding glass door for a brief second it had been moved back by a hand. The man standing there looked grizzly, bloody, beaten looking, half of his skin torn away with blisters. If he had told me he had been in a fire and burnt. I would have believed him. Then he raised a gun pointing it directly at me.

"I have to kill you. Because of you, we will all die. You don't understand what kind of monster you are, it's why we've spent years trying to stop your kind." I could hear the click of the trigger.

I thought it was all over, I had raised my hands to shield myself even though I knew the bullet could shoot straight through my hands and kill me. I didn't want my father or the others to find me this way. He was an insane man. Why would he ever think I was dangerous? Without knowing how I had done it, the sheer panic and deep feeling of being sick I had felt myself fly across the room slamming into the wall behind me leaving a huge dent. Opening my eyes when I realized I was still alive I thought maybe my pain was worse than a bullet. Looking my hands over and checking the rest of my body I hadn't found a wound anywhere. Did he miss? I looked up at the wall for a hole of any kind and there wasn't any. Looking back the man had disappeared except the glass from the sliding door was now smashed to pieces with a few that look like they melted, the curtain was torn, the bed covers slightly burnt. I wasn't sure what happened, what would have thrown me back so far if I hadn't been shot? It was moments like this I was beginning to think I was losing my sanity. Walking over almost feeling numb I hadn't felt any pain of any kind. I hadn't even felt it when I had glass puncture my skin as I stepped on it to look outside. The man was laying on the ground with several people standing around him. The police were trying to control the situation by making the people back up. One was collecting the gun using gloves and a bag. I had looked down at the carpet and finally saw footprints leading up to me in blood. Feeling sick again I walked over to the bed. I had planned on taking the pieces of glass out except I had passed out instead.

No one ever came to my room, no one asked and apparently, they didn't realize he had flown out of my room. My feet no longer had glass in them, and they were already healing. The bed beneath me was already made and the blood stains were gone from the carpet. Did I imagine this? Then I noticed something. The only person I ever knew did this. Everything in the room was straightened, even the bath towel I had left by the television. It had been folded and put away. The room wasn't this clean before he burst through, and I never folded a towel after I used it. At most I would hang it up. When I looked at my feet it almost looked like I had candle wax on the bottom of them. Jasper used to use candle wax to close bleeding cuts or protect cracked skin on heels. Someone was up here. I couldn't have imagined it if this was on my feet, could I?

One of the nights I swore I had seen Voncha standing across the street. I had to take a second look to see if it was him. Whoever was standing there wasn't there anymore. Unfortunately, I couldn't stay away forever, and I had no idea when this would be over. At least work was much closer; I could even walk there from the hotel. Staying gone for the last five days I finally went home. No one was there now so I could slip into my bedroom without being noticed.

Setting down my bag I could see one of them had been in my room while I was gone, not snooping but there was something left on my bed. Walking over to the bed there was a note and my favorite white roses.

"Emma, I hope you find these roses before they wither. I'm sorry I made you feel that you had to stay away. I wanted to make sure you're alright. If you need anything you know I'll always be around for you.

Much love, Voncha"

Picking up one of the roses and smelling it, I felt guilty for losing my temper with Voncha. I wasn't angry, and I would have been concerned with him if he was acting differently. He was used to taking care of me. There was already a vase on my dresser with more white roses. Adding the ones from my bed I placed them in the vase with the others. There was still strong sunlight outside so I knew they wouldn't be back for a few more hours. I had passed the time playing with the dogs outside, later, the computer, and then reading a book. I had finally fallen asleep on the couch when I felt the slightest brush against my skin. Someone was placing a blanket over me. Opening my eyes, I looked straight up and there was Voncha. I think I took him by surprise for once when I reached out and grabbed him. Holding on I had given him the tightest hug.

"I'm sorry I woke you up, I thought you might be cold." I knew he wanted to ask me if I was alright.

"I'm fine and no I wasn't cold. I wanted to let you know I loved the flowers. I wasn't gone because of you; I just wanted some privacy. I'm going through some feminine things and didn't want to discuss it. It's difficult growing up with only men raising me. I know you do your best and I don't regret it. I just wish there was a girl sometimes now that I'm older. That's one of the reasons I had stayed at Beth's." I knew I could at least get away saying that since I had hoped to talk with her, unfortunately, she was preoccupied with her current obsession. At least this time it wasn't a man.

The rest of the time had gone by rather quickly. We did our usual camp out by the stream and went hiking. I knew they would be leaving soon so I pretended to be perfectly fine. I knew they still questioned it, but I did do a pretty good job at covering the pain. I knew even for a second if I let them know they would have stayed. I didn't even know if it was serious, and I didn't want to risk telling them the strange things that would happen. I wasn't sure how they would react or if they would think I was crazy. Finally, the last night came, staying up extremely late we had all watched a movie together relaxing inside the house. We even let all the dogs in. Not that there was much space left on the couch when an English mastiff decides she was sleeping there, we had been on the love seat or the other smaller chairs the dogs hadn't taken over. I always felt sorry for my Persian cat, she was the only kitty and she thought she was a dog even making attempts at barking when the others had. I almost felt like sleeping down here on the loveseat laying against Jasper except I had work, and I knew I would be very sore in the morning. Besides, they always left extremely early, and I wanted my sleep.

"I need to get off to bed, I probably won't see you in the morning; you usually leave early so I'll say my goodbyes now." Smiling I hugged and kissed dad on the cheek.

17

Making my way around the table giving both Jasper and Voncha a hug goodbye, they had been so quiet when I closed my door almost as if they were listening for something. They hadn't said anything more to me about how I've been acting, not that I noticed a difference in myself. I guessed the next two months would be the same as always. Before sleeping I had taken a hot shower hoping it would help me relax. Pain meds and hot showers were starting to help less and less each time.

Morning came far earlier than I cared for. All I could feel had been the tightness in my muscles almost as if I either had the flu or was dehydrated. The shower I had taken the night before really hadn't helped relax the muscles. Getting out of bed rather slowly and deliberately, I had stalled as long as I could before I finally forced myself out of my nice warm soft bed. I was never a morning person. When I was younger my father pretty much had to pry me from my bed to get me to school, sometimes I still feel I need his help getting myself out since I still didn't like waking up in the morning. I liked staying up late at night and for the next few weeks I would be able to do exactly that, I couldn't wait to start my vacation. I hadn't been feeling well for the last three months so I had decided to take my paid vacation that I earned from work. I didn't say a word to dad since I was sure it would worry him even more than he already was. It was a good thing he hadn't seen the bruise on my back from hitting the hotel wall. It was almost healed but now it was that ugly yellow color before it left. At least it wasn't the dark black it had been before.

Placing my feet into my slippers I made my way out to the kitchen. All the curtains had still been drawn closed. Both dad and I preferred having the house rather dark, we were able to sleep much better that way. We lived out in the countryside, which helped, no light from streetlights or cars driving by. I loved the privacy we had out here, especially when I had the place to myself.

Grabbing a banana and a bottle of water from the fridge was all I had been in the mood for. Taking just as long to get dressed I finally left for the hospital, this would be my last day before I took off for my vacation and today was one of my lighter workdays. Monday never had too much paperwork; I had worked in the medical records room for the last three years. I think they only hired me because they knew I would be an intern here soon. At least now I will finally start my vacation that I've been looking forward to since I requested the time off last week. It might not seem like long except the last few times I had put in for a vacation I hadn't been allowed to take time off, others were taking their earned vacation time that had seniority and had the first choice over dates. That didn't bother me, they certainly earned their time off, what irritated me was having to justify using the time I earned to take time off that no one else was occupying. This time I didn't care about the dates. I just wanted time off.

After spending what felt like an hour finding a parking space, it equally felt as long navigating my way through all the hallways and different floors, finally making my way to my office I could already see my desk was piled high with papers just waiting to be entered into the computer. Today should have been my easy day. There was a sticky note on the corner of my monitor in bold letters stating the papers had to be done and which ones had to be sent to another hospital. Before I could even get started with the paperwork my boss had already seen me before I had a chance to get started. No doubt to state what he had already written out for me. At times I wondered why he even bothered leaving me notes if he was always going to tell me verbally later? Maybe he thought I couldn't read? If that was the case it was sad I worked in the medical records room where reading was more than just important, not a place I would want to make a mistake with so much personal medical information.

"I need the papers on your desk done before you leave. The ones in your blue bin are not immediate; the other intern can finish those while you're on vacation unless you get a chance to finish them. The others need to be placed on a thumb drive and sent immediately down to Vincent's Hospital. If I don't see you before you leave, enjoy your vacation." Watching my boss leave he was always telling me the obvious, but then I wondered if it was because he had nothing else to say other than wanting to say something.

Sitting for the next few hours at my computer inputting information on patients for results of tests or other reasons, I couldn't help yawning; sometimes my job would almost put me to sleep. Trying not to yawn while the unit clerk walked by. As soon as she was out of sight I let go of the yawn feeling a slight snap in my jaw. It's not that I disliked my job, it was rather Monotonous sitting here for hours only typing with no change. When lunch break finally came, I was happy to get away from my desk. Leaving for the cafeteria. I stopped to pick up Janice on my way, we usually took our break around the same time. I knew the topic of conversation would be over her wedding but then that was better than discussing patient ailments and possible reading errors. Grabbing a jello and a boiled egg before I sat down with the others.

"Is that all your having for lunch?" Janice seemed surprised my appetite hasn't quite been the way it used to.

"My stomach isn't exactly feeling that great so just having a light lunch for now." I might not have wanted to talk about work, and I certainly didn't want to talk about how I was feeling.

"Hasn't it been quite a while since you've been feeling sick? I know I sound like a broken record, but you need to see a doctor, heck you're surrounded by enough of them and you're here every day, you don't have any excuses for not making an appointment, this could be serious." I understood Janice's concern; her father seemed perfectly healthy, mildly sick one week, and then suddenly passed away.

Since then, she gets overly concerned when someone gets ill.

"It's nothing to worry about, I'm just overly tired, after today I'm taking my vacation and planning on nothing but resting and taking care of myself." I was so happy not to finish my sentence any further or ask any more questions. As both Natalie and Joanie sat down.

"I just picked up my dress yesterday; I can't wait to wear it. Plus, I won't be the only one without a date; I'll be bringing Brian with me." I hadn't thought for a second Joanie would go alone.

"Does everyone have dates? I felt bad I was bringing my boyfriend, but I guess if everyone has dates, I don't feel bad anymore." Not wanting to correct them I guessed I was the only one without a date for the wedding.

Not wanting to be the center of attention or risk getting set up on a blind date. I just listened to the others as they discussed the wedding details. Not paying too much attention I was more concerned with the way I was feeling. I had only taken one bite from my jello and never once touched the egg. There were days I wished I had more time for lunch but today I was glad that time went a little quicker. Not wasting time, I had made it back to my office to finish putting the information into my computer, I hadn't wanted to get stuck any longer inputting information than I had to. As soon as the last piece of paper had been finished, I looked around to make sure no one else was making eye contact or needed me for anything. Grabbing my purse, I took the stairs down instead of the elevator hoping to avoid anyone. I only came across one person and he was already pretending not to notice me, no doubt using the stairs for the same reason I was.

Making my way out to the parking garage I let out a deep sigh as I sat in my car. Looking up from my steering wheel I could see I hadn't gotten very far without being noticed. Walking over to my door the man motioned for me to roll down my window.

"Sorry to bother you, I heard you start your car and no one else has been in the parking area for a while, I can't get my car started and hoped you could help me with a jump. I have the cables; it would only take a minute." He looked nervous but there was something about him I felt a little strange about.

I don't remember seeing him before but then there were a lot of people who worked for the hospital.

"Sure, where is your car?" I hadn't seen him when I walked through the lot to my car.

"Just at the end of row three on the other side of that blue truck there." As he said this, he was pointing towards an ocean blue-colored van.

Walking around to the other side he sat in my passenger seat. I couldn't help but feel a moment of panic. He was wearing the right uniform for working in the hospital except I just kept getting this strange feeling. Starting up the car I drove around the side and stopped next to the truck he had pointed out earlier.

"Which car did you say was yours?" As I went to turn to face him for some reason, I had the urge to duck, which I had done without really giving it much thought until I could feel the breeze of his arm sail directly over me.

Pushing my door open quickly not bothering to grab my keys out of the ignition, I got out as fast as I could. I didn't have my seat belt on yet, so it was much easier to exit. Sliding across the seat he tried to grab my skirt. As he did, I slammed the door shut on his hand tearing the corner of my skirt. No one was around that I could see. I doubted he even had a car in here as I turned to run for the hospital. If anything, I could get help from inside. I could hear his footsteps running behind me as I ducked behind a car hoping to lose him that way. The doors to the hospital were much further away and he was already catching up to me rather quickly. I kept hearing these strange sounds from him. His breathing alone gave him away. I kept moving carefully between the parked cars working my way down to the lower level. I had left my purse in the car; I hadn't a chance to grab anything so I couldn't use my cell phone to call the police either. Leaning against the wall I kept looking for shadows or his breathing which both had stopped. I doubted he had left after attacking me like that; I could describe the way he looked. Moving over to see around the next car I found where he was, the hard way. Something rather cold and hard-hit me from behind.

All I could remember had been falling to the cold cement ground. My eyes were rather blurry as I had expected him to finish me off with whatever he had hit me with, only he hadn't. I kept waiting for that final blow, another pain to be added to my already throbbing head. All I could see was a dark blur. Not sure what exactly that was since he was wearing light-colored clothing. The muscles in my body were tightening up making it difficult to move. I tried to push myself up with my arm but just did not have the strength to. Then I felt myself get lifted off the ground with quick ease. Barely able to see who it was, all I could hear was the voice.

"Who are you?" I wasn't sure if I had sounded coherent or not.

"Don't worry you're safe now." That was the last I had heard before I passed out.

As I was finally coming to, I could feel the soft bed beneath me with equally soft sheets until I recognized the scent. It was my bed. Opening my eyes, they were still blurry, but I could see much better than I had earlier. Looking around I was the only one in my room with the door open to the living room, this is when I realized I was in the guest room and not my personal bedroom. Pulling the covers off from me I tried to sit up when I felt the room spin on me. Looking over at my dresser with the mirror. I could see a huge cotton bandage across my forehead where I had bled. Vaseline was peeking out around the corners, no doubt to keep it from scarring. Looking down at my shirt I should have been covered in blood except I wasn't, I hadn't even been wearing the same shirt. Slipping out of bed still holding onto the side I stood up still feeling dizzy. Walking over to the door I just hoped not to see my attacker again. Not that I was sure how he would know where I was living unless he had watched me for a while. Even if he had looked at my driver's license, I hadn't taken the time to update my address. I was going to stay at the college except after the first year I moved back home. Too many strange things happened making my choice to move back home much easier.

Peeking out slowly, I still hadn't seen or heard anyone. Walking out into the living room I could see my purse sitting waiting on the table. Someone brought me back here and went back for my purse. Walking over to the window I looked out and there was my car parked outside in its usual spot.

Checking the rest of the house no one seemed to be inside with me, who spoke to me? I know I heard someone tell me I was safe; someone must have said it. There was only a small burlap bag in my dad's study which I knew wasn't his. Looking through it there were only two shirts and a pair of slacks, pair of socks, and a few dollars inside. Closing it up before the owner found me looking through it, I left the study and went directly outside. The dogs were barking so I could tell someone was over near them otherwise they were normally quiet. I was wishing I had one of them walking beside me right now. I could see a figure standing near them covered by the shadow of the tree. Whoever it was had been filling the dog bowls. Who would bring me home and feed my dogs if they intended on harming me unless they loved animals? This person must have saved me from the person who first attacked me. Walking closer to see who it was I knew immediately without even seeing him in the light. Just the shadow of the person standing there alone gave him away.

"I thought you left with dad?" Not that I minded but I was surprised to see him standing there.

"I thought after the day you had I would help you with the dogs." As he said this Maddy my English Mastiff made a run for the house.

"I guess that's her hint she wants to sleep inside tonight." Walking over to Jasper I put my arms around him leaning into him.

I was so happy to see him, I was happy not to be alone. Still leaning against him we walked towards the house.

"I had some things I needed to take care of back here and I'm glad I was. I missed seeing you inside the hospital, I was going to get a ride from you, but they said you were already in the parking garage and that's when I saw that man running after you. Sorry I didn't stop him before he hit you. You lost quite a lot of blood. How are you feeling?" As I went to reach for the door Jasper reached out quicker, grabbing it, opening the door for me still helping me as I walked in.

"I feel sore but most of it was previous, only the headache and slight dizziness came from getting hit." Walking over to the fridge I grabbed an orange juice and then closed the door to find Jasper standing directly behind me.

"You never said anything about that yesterday, Voncha said you were fine. When did this start, what exactly are you feeling?" Jasper immediately reached out to help me almost as if I had been crippled.

"I can walk fine on my own now. As I told Voncha I was experiencing some muscle cramping. I'm sure it's just a girl thing and will pass. I just want to go sit down and relax. What happened with the attacker? I don't know how to explain it but there was something different about him. That and I don't know how I knew to duck the first time, next time I'm going to follow my instincts, I kept getting this strange feeling." As I said this, Jasper followed me over to the couch, sitting down next to me.

"I think you should call into work, after today I don't think it's safe for you to be there." As I picked up the remote, I looked at Jasper.

"I wasn't planning on going into work for a few weeks, I'm taking vacation time. I didn't want to tell dad since he was already worried about something even though now, I know it's about me." Leaning back against the wall, Jasper seemed surprised that he didn't know I was taking time off.

"Why didn't you tell Voncha when he asked you? We are all worried about you." Jasper had a hurt look on his face almost as if I had betrayed them.

"I'm not always going to tell you everything, that's part of growing up and not needing to. Not everything needs to be turned into a family discussion. I am thankful you came when you did, that's a rare thing that happened but I can take care of myself. I wasn't trying to keep something important from you. Besides, you know if it's serious I always tell you." This was my turn to give him the hurt look.

Jasper had sat back against the corner of the couch the way he always had. Sitting back leaning against him I rested my head on his chest. He felt colder than he usually did. Not that I needed the throw blanket I only grabbed it and covered us since he never seemed to complain about being cold. Not really in the mood for anything on television I flipped through the music stations with the other remote until I found a station I liked. Jasper never complained about what I listened to but then at times I wondered, if he had disliked something would he ever tell me?

"You said you had things to work on? What were you working on in town? Are you staying here?" Looking up at Jasper he had been staring at the window almost as if he was expecting to see someone.

"Just boring business." There was a strange sound to his voice.

"Are you waiting for someone?" Shifted slightly placing my left hand to rest it on his shoulder, looking down at me he just smiled.

"Who would I be waiting for?" Leaning down and he kissed me on the forehead.

"I can't help it but all three of you have been acting strange and I know dad is keeping something from me. I just wish you would tell me." Trying to sit up Jasper had reached out to prevent me from leaving until he realized I was only fully turning around to look at him.

"Sorry I thought you were getting up." Now he was sounding nervous.

"If there was something wrong with dad, would you tell me?" I hoped he understood just how serious I was.

"Yes, I promise I will tell you. Your dad is just fine and so are Voncha and me. We were only worried about you. I had some business to handle so I told your father I would check on you and I'm glad I did. It's getting late so I should get to the hotel. People seem to look at me strangely when I check in late at night for only one night." Attempting to slide out from under me I still had the feeling he was hiding something.

"Only one night? Do you have to go? You can stay in the guest room; I highly doubt dad would mind especially after what happened. Maddy may protect me to a point but she's still a huge coward. Please stay." I barely whispered the last but meant every word of it.

"Yes, just one night. I never stay longer than one night at the same hotel, a personal preference of mine. I have my bag in your dad's office, I'll put those in the guest room but tomorrow night I will be staying at the hotel. I'm sure by then you should be fine." Excited he was staying I reached up putting my arms around his neck hugging him close.

"Thank you for staying, by the way just a minor hint, cut back on the cologne, it doesn't smell bad. I like the scent but you're starting to put more on, it's much stronger now than it was yesterday." Looking surprised I wasn't sure if he understood right away.

"I'm not wearing any cologne?" Jasper was still surprised by this.

"Then I guess we have the same problem then. I'm not tired since I thought I was out for a while. Maddy looks like she could go for a walk. I usually prefer her to go out for a while, if she's sleeping inside tonight, otherwise, she tends to leave me a present I don't want. Want to come with?" Before I could say anymore Maddy was already at the door waiting with her leash in her mouth.

I never had to convince her to go for a walk.

"Emma, there is no way I'm having you walk in the dark this late at night alone. You were out for quite a few hours; you had me worried; I can take the dog for a walk while you stay here and relax." The concerned expression came back to his face.

"I've walked late at night before and been perfectly fine; my head doesn't hurt at all. Besides I'm much safer with Maddy, a person sees her, and they won't try anything." I could tell I wasn't convincing Jasper for a second.

Letting out a sigh he followed me outside. Watching me let the other dogs loose from their kennel, they were all excited to be out of their cages. As soon as the other dogs were out of their kennel, Maddy and the others raced for the trail stopping for a second looking back to see if we were following. They all ran in the same direction since they were used to the path we took. The slightest warn path had shown in the field as we followed it. Heading towards the tree lining I had my hands in my pocket and Jasper still walked rather closely to me looking around almost expecting something. He still hadn't told me what happened to the attacker other than the fact he had taken care of it.

The weather was chillier but then that was to be expected with winter coming. After walking through the tall grass and finally the woods I could hear the stream in the distance. We always stopped at the little bridge that was built over it, and then we would make our way back after the dogs were done playing in the water. Most nights the path we took was lit up by the moonlight.

The dogs did something I hadn't expected, they bunched together rather closely almost as if they were protecting each other. I could hear a deep low growl at first as they were making it clear there was something on the path they did not agree with, apparently felt the need for the combined support of each other. Jasper grabbed me by the arm preventing me from moving further. I wanted to see what was upsetting the dogs as Jasper moved forward to check it out.

"Take the dogs back to the house with you; I'm going to look around. I don't want to risk you if the dogs have picked up on something." Jasper made his way around the dogs not that they gave him a problem.

They were backing up stopping just in front of me. They were determined to defend me against whatever it was. Only taking a few steps in front of me it looked as if Jasper had been swallowed by the ground. Not wanting to leave him alone there I walked forward quickly to see where he had disappeared. There was a hole just in front of the little bridge. I couldn't see or hear anything. I knew if he fell there, I would find him if I followed, which I did. Jumping down not sure how far down it would be or how this hole wound up here. Hitting the ground with a thump I could barely see anything as I tried to let my eyes adjust. I could hear movement; there was an awkward grunt and loud thud. I could slightly see two figures in the distance as two others were about to attack the one laying on the ground. I wasn't sure what I was going to do other than grab the stick from my pocket I had for the dogs to chase after, I threw it at one of the standing figures. Now I had everyone's attention, not that I knew what to do. Leaning against the wall I could hear Jasper groan; he was either upset I had followed or from pain. I was hoping I hadn't just thrown the stick at Jasper but then he wouldn't be standing with another person, I had hoped my reasoning was correct.

Feeling along the wall I kept moving not that I thought I could get away somewhere, I was lost in the dark let alone couldn't tell how huge or long this tunnel was. Moving back. I fell flat on my back there was another room and it had slanted downward which I wasn't expecting. I didn't want to leave Jasper but at least this way they were following me until I backed myself up against the wall again. I had all five dark figures standing in front of me; I just wished I could have been able to see more. Right now, all they looked like were dark blurs walking towards me. At least I could make out the outline of each body. All I could see was something glistening in the dark coming at me, as it came, I raised my hand to protect myself when the strangest thing happened. I had that moment of panic, my anxiety kicked in, again when my hand felt almost as if it was on fire. I felt so much force being pushed against my hand I wondered if it was the shiny object I was trying to shield myself from. The room temporarily lit up with such a huge flash of light it was almost blinding, I couldn't see anything other than to hear so much screaming and a reddish-orange glint right in front of me as the shiny metal object looked as if it exploded.

My hands felt like they were burning as I saw a brief glimpse of the ones who were about to attack me. As the light disappeared into the darkness all I could see were the shadowed men lying on the ground no longer moving or making any signs of breathing. Getting up making my way over to Jasper trying not to step on the bodies. I kept expecting one to reach up grabbing me on the leg, not one of them moved at all.

CURSE OR GIFT

"Jasper?" I tried calling out hoping he might make a sound.

I could barely hear him breathing.

"Are you alright?" At least he was able to respond to me

"Yes, I'm fine, I can't see down here." Kneeling on the ground I felt around until I could feel his clothing.

"Did you see what caused that flash of light?" Jasper barely breathed his words.

I could feel his flesh, sticky and wet. I could only guess he was bleeding.

"I don't know what caused the light, I think your bleeding, we need to get you out of here." Looking upward I could hear the dogs barking outside the hole with the slightest light shining through.

Walking over to the hole I looked straight up, it was a way up and there wasn't anything to grab onto, no strong roots or wall near it. Someone had scooped this out on purpose to trap something or someone, maybe us? I could hear the leaves below me crunching as I stepped back. I knew the dogs would stay there until we got out. Their dog pen was open with their food still in there; at least they would be fine if they were hungry. One strange thing I noticed was the muscle pain went away, not that I knew what exactly burned my hands unless it was because I was protecting myself from the shiny object, I was possibly very lucky, and the light only burned my hands and nothing else? Making my way over to Jasper I knelt next to him again. Feeling for his hand, once I found it, I held on tight almost as if I feared he might fall further away.

"Don't worry, I'll get you out of here, I just need a few minutes to heal. Hopefully, those people won't come back in here before then." Taking a deep breath, just from the sound of it, I could tell he was in pain.

"I'm only worried about you. The others won't be bothering us, at least not from the way they looked. I should be looking for another way out, if they were able to get in then there should be another way out." As I tried to stand up Jasper gripped my hand pulling me back down.

"Don't go. I don't know if it's safe and I don't want anything happening to you, especially right now when I can't protect you." I didn't need to say anything.

I hadn't wanted to risk leaving him, but then could I afford not to? I couldn't tell how injured he was since it was so dark. Holding his hand tightly despite my burned hand, I wasn't sure if he could even tell I was injured.

"I'll stay, but I do wish you would let me look. I don't know how injured you are, and you might need emergency care." I started feeling my pocket for my cell phone when I finally found it.

Pulling it out, I had the tiniest light from it. Taking the cell phone from me he flipped it closed.

"Trust me that I will be just fine, why didn't you tell me you hurt your hands, did they do that to you?" I could hear the concern in his voice.

He was always putting me first even though we should have been thinking of him. He might not have wanted me to see it but now I knew he was covered in blood.

"I think the light burned them, they don't hurt, and my hands should be fine. Why did you take the cell phone, I could have called for help." Still holding his hand as I placed my other hand over his chest.

"I didn't want you to see me. We don't need to call anyone; just give me a few minutes and I'll get us out of here." Jasper was trying to sound determined.

"I've never known you to be vain before. I will see you once we're out." Jasper seemed nervous, for which reason I wasn't sure.

"I'm not being vain; I didn't want to upset you. Help me up." Sliding my hand and arm under his arm then slid it slowly behind his back pulling him gently upright trying not to cause him any more pain. As I did, I could feel a twinge in his side as he stopped for a second.

"Did they break a bone?" Now I was getting worried, and I didn't bother hiding it in my voice at all.

"They might have, after all, they had the advantage of starting first. I'll push you through the hole and I'll find another way out." Sounding as if this was the best plan.

"I'm not leaving you any more than you would have left me. Besides they could have someone outside the hole waiting. I'm coming with you." I knew there wasn't anyone waiting outside, or the dogs would have been barking.

"You're as stubborn as your father." Smiling he knew he wasn't going to win with this one.

Standing up Jasper started walking in the opposite direction of the hole, and away from the little room that I had fallen into with the others. Holding his hand so that I wouldn't lose him I wondered how he wasn't walking into the wall or knew to go this way? Could he see well enough in the dark? If I were to put my hand out in front of my face, I never would have seen it. Stopping abruptly, I could hear the slosh of water. The ground underneath us was turning muddy; I could guess we were close to the lake. I just hoped that this area wasn't getting flooded since the tunnel wasn't naturally here. We stood there for a few minutes before Jasper said something.

"We need to turn back, there's water up here and I don't know how deep or how long it goes. I can't swim, the safest way back is through the hole. I'll figure out how I'll get out once I get you out." Walking back towards me I hadn't moved at all.

"I can swim, I want to find out how far or how deep it is. If they came through here, it wouldn't be too bad. I won't stay gone long. If it's short I can help you get through it, you won't need to do any swimming. I've helped dad when he fell out of the boat. I don't know why the three of you refuse to learn?" I was always curious, for living so close to the lake and the fact dad loved watching the waves he never did learn how to swim.

It was like forcing one of the dogs in the water, but then once they were used to it, they loved it. Unfortunately, it's much harder to force an adult into the water.

"No, it's not a good idea, if you end up in trouble, I can't help you and you can't even see." Letting go of his hand I was determined to test it out.

We didn't have a ladder or anything or I would have gone out the hole for it. I doubted I was strong enough to pull him out and I didn't want to leave him in here so if going through the water was faster then I needed to try. I might not have seen him, but I swear I could feel his frustration as I walked away from him towards the water. One thing that was confusing me had been the fact I wasn't getting wet. The further in that I had gone with the water up to my knee I was still dry. If I hadn't heard the typical sound of water sloshing as I walked through it, the feel of the water moving, I would have sworn I wasn't walking in water. That's when I stopped walking waving my hand over the very cold surface trying to see if I would get it wet and I still hadn't. I had heard his voice echo behind me.

"Are you alright? Why have you stopped? You're not too far I can come to get you if you're stuck?" I could hear Jasper making his way towards me.

I knew he hated the idea of going into the water which meant this must be scaring him seeing me stop not explaining why.

"How could you tell that I stopped? The water isn't normal, I'm not stuck but then I'm also not wet either." I continued to swish my hand around feeling the water move around it, almost more like a light breeze than anything.

Walking much quicker now that Jasper realized he wasn't getting wet either had taken hold of my hand again as we both

33

walked forward. Jasper still hadn't answered my question. Following the rest of the tunnel, it was lit well enough for me to see from the fake water, it had a light blue glow emanating from it. The water hadn't started to get cold until we were at the very end where I had reached out to touch the dark blue water that my hand did get wet. Guessing I would say this was finally the lake and whatever this fake water was, somehow it was keeping the real water from entering it. Nothing I had ever seen before was anywhere near this.

Having Jasper wait behind I went out into the water, as I expected the lake caught me swiftly moving me downstream as I swam straight up to only getting my head out of the water for now. Getting close enough to the shore which thankfully I hadn't been pulled out too far, I could see exactly where it had come out, now the trick would be to swim back down against the current. It was much harder swimming against the current, after struggling; I had made my way back down to the opening I had first gone through. At least Jasper wouldn't have to hold his breath for too long. The only problem I hadn't expected and wondered if the others had a secret for re-entering the fake water. I went out with no problems but couldn't make it back in. The only way I had to encourage Jasper to come out had been to motion for him to come towards me. Thankfully he trusted me, holding his breath I grabbed a hold of him around the waist before the water carried him away from me. Swimming as hard as I could to bring both of us up to the surface, thankfully people were lighter in the water. I wasn't sure if it was from adrenaline or something else, I had suddenly felt so much stronger, we submerged much faster than I had on my own. I wasn't the only one that was surprised by how strong I was at the moment when I was able to push Jasper out of the water. I had always been on the short side assuming I had taken after my mother. Jasper was rather tall like my father and Voncha.

"When did you get so strong?" I knew I had surprised him just as much as I was.

"A second ago." As I said this Jasper lifted me out of the water without any effort, I was used to him being strong, even Voncha and my father were much stronger than I had been.

34

"Mind me asking when these strange things started happening or has it been a while? This is something you really should have talked to your father about. We have no clue who else might be after you or if those guys down there are going to come after you again." We were dripping wet on the way home and unfortunately the wind had decided to kick in making me feel colder.

"I hadn't noticed anything strange; I had no idea the man in the parking garage was going to attack me or that the hole was there. I've walked here so often, and it had never been there before. How was I supposed to know all of this would happen before dad left? I was occupied with my muscle cramping. Oddly enough I thought I was having another growth spurt, at least I was hoping I was." Smiling, I was hoping I might grow unfortunately it hadn't happened.

"You're handling this much better than I thought you would. Not that I expected you to be a wreck but at least a little scared, it's why I keep asking you if this has been going on for a while." I had to admit he was right, there was a lot I was keeping from him, I just didn't want him to think I was a freak or misunderstand things before I could figure out myself what was going on.

"You know that I trust you right? At least I hope you do, I'm just not ready to talk about some things even though I'm still not sure how they fit in with the rest of this. All of this feels as if it's unreal and I'm going to wake up at any moment." I hadn't wanted to say anything but then Jasper had been the one I used to share everything with.

I never had to hide anything from him.

"I've never pushed you; I've always let you come to me when you were ready, but this isn't something we can wait on after seeing what we have so far. I would be more worried about what might happen later." Stopping me in my tracks Jasper stared at me letting me know how serious he was.

"I just don't know how to explain it or if it's coming from me. The last thing that happened was the flash of light. This has only happened one other time, both times my palms burned and there was this strange flash of light, both times extremely bright it

35

blinded me for a few seconds afterward. I think I'm causing it." Watching his reaction he hadn't taken it the way I thought he might.

"Let's get home first so that no one listens to us. There is something you need to know that your father hasn't exactly wanted to share. If he gets mad at least it will be directed at me, I feel you should know, I've never kept anything from you except for this." Not wasting any time, we walked faster, whatever he wanted to tell me was important.

The dogs must have assumed we were not staying in the hole, they were already in their pens eating their food reacting perfectly normal. Maddy was at the front door waiting to be let in. Once we were inside the house I was beginning to wonder if I would ever find out what was on his mind or what he was going to tell me. Jasper kept pacing back and forth almost as if he was formulating what he was going to say. Having me sit on the couch figuring out how to explain it to me, as he did this my cell phone started to ring.

"While you decide what you're going to tell me I'm going to answer this." As I did there was nothing on the other end, they either changed their mind or were disconnected.

"Who was that?" Jasper seemed rather anxious.

"A friend, but they must have already hung up; she butt dials me a lot so she might not have even planned on calling me." At least now he had stopped pacing.

"Butt dials? That doesn't sound good." Jasper had a strange questioning look on his face.

"She tends to leave her phone on and in her pocket so if she bumps against something or sits it calls the last number she dialed." Looking over the phone, on the caller ID, it was her number that just called me.

"At least tell me what you do know so far?" Jasper knelt in front of me getting closer to my level the same way he used to when I was little.

"I thought you were going to explain to me what father should have told me?" Not that I wouldn't tell him since he's asked but I was still curious what we had to rush back to the house for to tell me in secrecy.

36

"I don't know how to start since there is so much and if you were aware of this growing up it would have made it so much easier." At least I wasn't the only one having a hard time explaining it.

The phone started ringing again only this time it was the house phone. I could tell from the expression Jasper was giving me he would prefer that I didn't answer the phone. I was guessing he was worried about who it was and if they were checking to see if I was home. Going over I picked it up as Jasper watched my every move.

"Did you just call me on my cell phone?" Waiting for an answer I knew something was wrong just from the way Beth was breathing.

"I don't know how to tell you this and you're going to think I'm crazy. I don't want to end up in the psych ward, but I had to tell someone, can you meet me at my condo in town? Preferably now, it's really important." I wasn't sure what was in the background, but I was guessing she wasn't alone.

"I'll be there as quick as I can, I'm only ten minutes away." After hanging up I knew I would have to make an excuse since Jasper had already stressed himself out about telling me some big family secret.

"You're not honestly thinking of going are you? It sounds like a trap. If it's serious enough let her call the police when it happens, you don't need to take care of it." Jasper seemed positive of his accusation.

"I doubt whoever attacked us earlier would use Beth if they wanted to set me up for a trap. She's my friend and she needs me right now; besides it also sounds like you could use some time to figure out how you're going to tell me this big thing." Grabbing my keys off from the counter I made my way to the door.

Just before I could leave Jasper blocked my way.

"If you're going then I am coming with you, to offer protection." Not giving him any problems with it I agreed, and we both got into my car. I couldn't help it, but it always felt as if he was uncomfortable being in a car.

I wasn't sure why I hadn't thought about this until now. Jasper had been bleeding badly when we left. I was guessing one of them had hit him with a knife. There was a tear on his shirt still except where the skin showed through there was no longer a cut or blood. There weren't any of the scratches or deep cuts anywhere on him anymore. Bringing my attention back to my driving I sat there silently for the short drive. At least we hadn't lived that far outside of town. Parking my car on the side of the street, Jasper was out opening my door rather quickly making it clear he intended to come up along with me. Most of the condos here were locked, there was a locked lobby before you were able to get inside the condos. I had an extra set of keys to her place in case she lost her own again. She lost her purse quite often.

It was rather quiet but then it was still too early for anyone to wake up. Skipping the elevator I took the stairs, ever since I was little, I had a nightmare that I was stuck in the elevator when it plummeted to the ground. Since then, I have refused to use one. I felt perfectly fine until I was standing in front of her door, why was she even up this late? Beth never liked staying up past ten in the evening. She liked to go to sleep early otherwise she was cranky at work all day. This was the first time I felt a moment of panic and was thankful to have Jasper with me.

Her door was left slightly open. Jasper insisted on going in first and I hate to admit I let him. As we entered there weren't any sounds, no lights, and no signs that Beth was even here. As Jasper went in further, we found out we were wrong when a huge baseball bat came swinging at him as he ducked out of the way. Thankfully I was standing just far enough back. It was Beth and I didn't blame her since I hadn't told her I would be bringing anyone with me. As soon as she saw it was me, she ran over grabbing me.

"I swear I'm not losing my mind; it keeps happening." Whatever it was she was terrified of it, she was trembling trying to hold her composure.

"What keeps happening?" I was beginning to wonder if anyone was going to share anything they knew.

"Stay the night and it will happen in just about an hour. I called because I wanted someone else to witness it, so I knew I wasn't crazy. Out my window in the living room is the alley between the two buildings. These strange creatures come out. I think I will end up going crazy since I can't get any sleep." Placing my arm around her I just wanted to reassure her.

Helping her get comfortable Jasper and I had agreed we would wait in the living room, neither of us would sleep, that way she could finally get to sleep herself. Not waiting long, I heard her breathing relax as she drifted off. Closing her door slightly I walked out to the living room where I could see Jasper sitting out on the fire escape watching down below. I found I had stood there just staring at him for a while until he turned to see why I had stopped. Feeling embarrassed I made my way over to him.

"Is everything alright?" Reasonably worried.

"Beth finally fell asleep; I was just thinking how this evening seems chilly out." Not wanting to tell him the real reason.

For the first time, I had paid attention to the clothing he wore, the way his hair was, the expression on his face with the darkness of the night setting in.

It's not as if I hadn't seen or looked at him before, just this time it was different somehow? I felt as if I had been taking something for granted and seeing it for the first time.

"I can keep an eye out here on my own, it's not too chilly for me, stay inside that way you won't catch a cold." Still climbing out to join him I sat down next to him.

"I'll be fine, if this thing happens tonight, I want to know what Beth is talking about. I am curious if it has anything to do with those that attacked earlier on our walk or the one who came after me in the parking garage at work." Looking down at the alley below, Jasper had gone inside for a moment returning with a throw blanket from the couch.

Wrapping it around my arms he sat behind me wrapping his arms around me. He was still worried about me being warm enough. There were a few people who had walked along the alley only to take the back way into the other apartment building. Leaning against Jasper feeling relaxed there wasn't very much going on this early in the morning. I was beginning to wonder if anything would happen tonight; maybe Beth had imagined whatever it was or being paranoid since she hadn't been very trusting. Even though we were supposed to be watching out for what Beth had described I was more curious about something else.

"Will you be joining Voncha and dad soon?" I wanted to know when I would be on my own, not that I minded Jasper being here, just helps to know if I'm alone, no one else is supposed to be there.

"I won't be joining them this time. Are you already tired of me?" Smiling, I knew what he meant.

"Other than the attacks, I've been spoiled having you here." Which is exactly how I felt.

"I'm glad I haven't been too much of a nuisance." Giving in to a shiver Jasper held me closer.

"Are shadows supposed to move that much?" Something at the corner of the building had caught my attention.

"I believe that's what we are supposed to be looking for. Stay up here and I'll check it out." As Jasper stood, he looked back at me in surprise as I was already following him.

"I'm not staying behind, not that I'm afraid; it just won't hurt you to have some backup." Smiling I knew he could handle it himself I just didn't feel like waiting to find out from him.

"This could be dangerous, I would rather have you stay here, and it's easier if I only have to watch out for myself." Jasper seemed rather serious.

"I'm sure it is easier for you but I'm not staying, I'll look after myself. That way I don't have to watch for you." Not waiting any longer or risking the shadow from disappearing I made my way down the fire escape.

Making my way down to the alley with Jasper close behind me, we followed the trail made by the shadow. It had led us behind all of the buildings to the other side of town near the lake where it had stopped all of a sudden. Guessing it had gone into the water, not that either of us had wanted to follow it, this water was real and very cold. As we were about to head back, we saw in the distance a flash of reddish-purple spiral up into the air almost as if it was a private signal for something. Hiding behind a tree trying to cover our tracks from the frosty ground, it wasn't quite winter yet but with mornings getting as cold as they have been it won't be long now. Several others had run past us, almost running on water; they were running so fast I thought maybe the speed kept them up out of the water until we had realized there was a pad slightly under the water that allowed them to stay above. There had been a group of them; we guessed this was their way of possibly knowing when and where to meet. Watching as they passed, I still hadn't recognized any of them yet. Now that the platform disappeared making it harder to catch up, we had to find another way of crossing the water without being seen. Taking the long way, we worked our way around until we saw a small plastic board slightly under the water raised just enough leading to a tunnel downward, I knew he hadn't cared for the fact there was water surrounding us, but he still forced himself to follow down the tunnel that was no doubt hollowed out by hand.

There were voices not far from us as we stopped to listen. One of the voices had sounded familiar. It was a voice I would never forget since it had such a distinctive ring to it. My boss was talking to the others making plans for a ritual using the old, abandoned state hospital. Normally I wouldn't have a problem with any of this until I had heard him say my name and sacrifice in the same sentence. Even Jasper was uneasy as we heard this. They were moving around heavy-looking objects no doubt not wanting to draw attention to themselves with a forklift. At least we knew who was after us but then if he was human how could they be so strong and fast? Working our way back out hoping to leave unnoticed the same way we had when we first came in, feeling we heard enough, I didn't want to risk getting caught by them. My only guess had been that Morris was bothering Beth and perhaps said something disturbing or maybe showed her something, perhaps not the whole thing? As soon as she woke up, we had a few questions to ask her. That's when we noticed not too far that her window was shattered, most of the glass on the ground. The wind had picked up except we both knew we had been careful to close the window securely. I was beginning to think I should have stayed to make sure she was safe. Did they know she would tell us? Making our way into the condo, the entire living room was trashed; even the couch was ripped through with stuffing all over the floor. Every room looked the same way with the front door torn off its hinges. Strange they would bother with that if they were going to exit the fire escape?

I didn't need to search her room to know she would be gone, I just wished I knew who exactly took her and where. We didn't see them take her where we were but then someone must have been watching us when we left to break in unless they didn't know we were here? Now I wasn't sure what to do. At least there wasn't any blood anywhere.

TRUTH

"They have Beth, but we don't know if it's my boss who has her or if another group has her and where?" I had started to pace back and forth when Jasper grabbed my shoulder to get me to stop.

"Do you know where your boss lives? Maybe we can search his house for clues, maybe find out what they want with your friend and why they want you?" Jasper was feeling hopeful.

"I don't know where he lives but I can find out from work, they would have it in the employee listings." The only problem would be going to work without anyone noticing, to interrupt our searching.

After all, it would look strange that I finally took a vacation and then showed up searching his office for his address, there was also the risk that he might be there.

"As long as we search in the evening most from my regular shift would be gone, so less to question my being there." Grabbing my purse, I had intended on taking off right away.

"I think you should stay here to stay safe. I can sneak in without you; you're not going anywhere near that place for a while. I don't want a repeat of what has already happened." Trying to be protective, Jasper had yet to remove his hand from my shoulder.

"I know you're only trying to keep me safe, but you don't know where his office is. The way the offices are set up it would

43

take too long for you to find it on your own. You can come with and keep me safe; I just have to come up with an excuse why I'm letting a non-employee in a restricted area if we get caught." Grabbing Jasper by the hand I walked out to the car throwing my purse in.

I had only lived a few miles outside of town; the hospital had been rather busy when we did arrive. Being careful when I parked to make sure no one was watching, we took the stairs up to the third floor where all the offices had been. No one even bothered looking at us unless they were worried they might get stuck working on another project. Most kept to whatever they were working on usually engrossed in their projects. We made our way through several corridors until we were down in the lowest basement where only employees were allowed. Our door was always locked to protect patient records. Using the keypad to punch in my numbers the door unlocked allowing us in. As I had thought most that would be here during my normal shift were gone, except a few that were notorious for staying late not that they noticed we had come in. Being quiet we worked our way over and past my desk. When we went by I noticed quite a few of my office file folders were gone. Nothing personal of mine was in them other than information on patients. There wasn't anything someone couldn't get if they had looked it up on the internet. Otherwise, I would have had them in the locked filing cabinet. Jasper stuck rather close to me; a few times he kept bumping into me.

Searching around my boss's desk I noticed quite a few of his folders were missing. Not finding anything that would give us a clue I had to search through the main files on his computer and still nothing. My boss had removed his address from the employee listings. Then Jasper had been paying attention to an area I had not, something very simple, the floor.

"At least we caught this before the cleaning crew came in. We don't have red clay in town, the closest area that you could find it is on the other side of town where the factories used to be before most of the mills closed. When we were out earlier following the group of people from your friends' condo. We were close to the old industrial park that's since closed, just past the storehouses. I'm not sure if it's flooded right now since no one has been around to bag during this season, otherwise the lake might have crested. It used to slightly flood the parking areas not that it ever really affected the trucks that went in and out of there, I'm going to venture a guess and say our next clue will most likely be over there somewhere." I couldn't help but picture Sherlock Holmes when I heard the way Jasper described his findings.

I have to admit I was rather surprised that no one noticed I entered the hospital let alone with a non-employee snooping around the head boss's office. Leaving we were just as unnoticed. Driving through town there were a few cars out, not very much happened here at night. We lived in a very simple, quiet town. Something I knew my father preferred, no one bothered you unless you wanted to be. I was always saying hello to everyone, so I was used to being stopped when I was out. This just felt weird almost as if no one even noticed I was there.

I was watching Jasper fiddle with his seat belt, he always looked rather uncomfortable when he rode in my car but then maybe he was used to driving or my driving made him nervous? I did tend to have a lead foot, not that I've ever actually seen him drive. There have been a lot of changes to the town and not many that people were happy with. The old town, which at one time had been on the verge of becoming a small city now had almost been forgotten unless you had to drive past it, the only thing still running in the old industrial park had been the old train and salvage yard.

Jasper tried to persuade me from coming, saying I would be safer if I stayed at home and waited for him. At least I convinced him I would be safer with him in case Morris my boss was to look for me at home. I was trying not to shiver, or Jasper might suggest that I stay in the car. I could already see the crystals forming on what was left of the dried-out grass. With it so cold out I was thankful not to walk again, instead, we had taken the main road leading out to the park. There were huge potholes in the road, one I swear I could have stood in; it was deep enough it would come up to my knees. The walking bridge that had connected two of the buildings was now split in half, laying on the ground. The only area we had a difficult time with was the small bridge going over the water. Since it hadn't been maintained I wasn't sure if I should even bother trying to drive over it. Slowly driving on the right side, I could look down from my window and see one huge chunk missing from the bridge.

Nothing else was out here, no people walking around and no other cars on the road. It had only taken us about thirty minutes to get there. Driving up to one of the buildings, there was just enough space for the car to fit. It would be hidden in case anyone was to walk along here not that there were any hints of anyone being here for a very long time. The old buildings looked incredibly run down and dilapidated. Jasper had been watching the ground to see if there were any footprints of which there hadn't been any. There hadn't been any sign of the buildings being used. The old industrial park had been surrounded by the lake except for one side. There were trees on the north side of the buildings that grew out of the swampy water. Walk far enough and you pass the trees into an opening where there is the slightest little sand beach. No one ever came here except maybe employees who used to work here.

Walking further and closer to the swamp we had finally found a few footprints which led directly through the deepest part, something I knew Jasper hated. I never understood or had been told his reason for hating the water, all I knew was that he would do anything he could to avoid it.

Taking that first step, I prepared myself for the water to soak my shoes. At least it wasn't as bad as I had thought it would be. Taking another step out further, the ground had been as solid as the paved road was and it was only slightly wet. I might not have been standing in deep water, but my shoes were already drenched. As I kept going Jasper followed behind me. There hadn't been a path or anything to follow, I could only guess how far they had gone since most of the ground was now covered by an odd fog. It had gotten to the point Jasper was now holding my hand so that he wouldn't lose track of me. I kept hoping I wasn't going to trip or run into them before we found out where we were. Or in the worst-case scenario, find the object we're walking on, ends and fall into deep water. I had finally stopped causing Jasper to run into the back of me. I heard a voice not that far ahead of us and I hadn't wanted them to hear us walking through the water. Listening to the voices they were not that far away from us. Then I heard Morris, my boss speaking to the others. Straining to hear I could only make out a few words. At least I could tell they were speaking about Beth, but then I finally heard her voice answering back and she hadn't sounded worried or scared the way she reacted when we had come over to her condo. Then the next went rather quickly, I felt a sharp thump on my head, and I passed out. I wasn't even aware of what happened to Jasper other than the fact he was no longer holding my hand.

Out of habit, I went to rub my head where it hurt when I realized I couldn't move my hands since they were above my head. Still feeling groggy I looked around to see an almost empty room. My hands were bound together above my head hanging from a hook with my feet on a platform. I had such an intense pain through my shoulders and arms, my hands were bright red and swollen. I felt I could barely breathe. The little box underneath me was sturdy enough, as soon as I was alert more, I stood straighter taking a little pressure but not much off my wrists. There was a second rope that was tied around my waist, if it wasn't there holding most of my weight, I'm pretty sure my lungs would have collapsed on me. Jasper was on the other side of the room in the same position only his feet were bound together attached to a hook in the ground as well. His mouth was also gagged. How can he possibly breathe, that's when I noticed he wasn't. I felt the worst panic hit me. That's when I heard the footsteps. The only door leading in opened as Morris came walking in with a few other people I hadn't recognized.

"You're finally awake, I guess we won't need the smelling salts. I'm sorry about messing up your vacation but then you did take it at the best time. At least it was at the best time for me." Pulling out a syringe, taking a sample of blood from me I wondered what he wanted it for. He had done the same with Jasper.

"We needed to experiment first, to see if it would even work. A personal project that I've been working on with Morris for quite some time. Unfortunately, it's so hard to get your hands on a vampire and I wasn't sure if you were one, so we had to make sure we caught both of you just to make sure we did get at least one." Beth lowered her hood so that I could see her. I swear she had lost her mind.

"Did I hear you right? Did you just say, vampire?" Maybe she was hysterical and brainwashed Morris to go along with her insanity.

"You've known this man your entire life and you didn't know he was a vampire? Do you seriously think I'll believe you? You are more observant than anyone I've known and you're going to tell me you don't even know what you are? You're a very important key to all of this." Morris scoffed at me as the others left the room with him following and slamming the door shut behind.

I don't care what they think; I know I'm not a vampire. With the strange things going on I might be something else but definitely not a vampire. Except how would they know? Looking over at Jasper he hadn't looked me directly in the eyes. I wondered if it was possible. I had shared everything with my family, especially Jasper of all people. How could I not know something like that but then it would explain a lot of strange things? Even for those times, the three would normally take off without saying where they were going, or where Jasper and Voncha had spent most of their time when they were not with us. Jasper had always protected me, why would I question him now? I seriously hadn't believed in vampires. But then there was that strange thing I had been able to do lately, maybe my keeping it a secret was the same reason he kept his? Fear he might think I'm crazy or dangerous?

Looking around the room there hadn't been anyone else in here and I certainly didn't want to find out what experiment they were working on, I just wished I could have talked to Jasper to see what he thought we should do. We couldn't have been here for too long since I still had some feeling in my hands, otherwise, they would have been numb either from nerve damage or lack of blood flow. Right now, they had that burning feeling mixed with numbness. At least I finally could use all those years of doing stomach crunches and gymnastics classes. Bending at the waist lifting my legs upward wrapping my legs around the rope, I had seen girls do this from a rope at a circus; I was hoping to do the same thing. The best I could do was get my feet around the long rope that held the hook. Gripping tight I bent at the knees so that the rope that bound my hands and waist would be able to slide up and over the hook. I've never had pain like this before, it made the pain I was dealing with before almost nothing compared to this.

Once I managed to get my hands free from the hook, I flipped my legs back hoping to land on my feet. Unfortunately, I wasn't that coordinated and landed flat on my back momentarily knocking the wind out of my lungs. My arms had finally given out and I wasn't able to lift or prevent myself from hitting the floor with such a loud thud. I could see that Jasper was watching the whole time. The moment I hit the floor he had a painful expression on his face.

I was getting feeling in my hands but not enough to loosen his ropes, at least I could grab his gag with my mouth pulling it away from him. My hands were still tied together, which I could deal with; it was the suspension that hurt the worst. Looking at Jasper I couldn't help but notice how sad he looked.

"I'm sorry about all of this, I wish I had known they were after me and I could have done this differently that way you would have been safe." Now he looked directly into my eyes.

"You had no idea they were crazy and wanted us, right now we just have to figure out how to get out of here. Any ideas?" I was hoping he had one.

"I doubt you're going to like the sound of this, slide the rope on your hands against my tooth, the same way you would against a filing board, at the ends. My teeth are very sharp." With the last few words, Jasper had slightly hesitated to watch for my expression.

"You're right. I don't like that idea; I doubt your teeth are that sharp. Please tell me you haven't lost your mind as they have?" I couldn't help but wonder if he did believe in vampires or that he was one?

"Do you trust me?" As soon as he asked I didn't hesitate for a second with my reply.

"Of course I do, I always have." Jasper was the one person I had trusted without explanation it just felt strange trying to cut my rope on his teeth.

I did exactly as he asked rubbing the rope against the upper part of his teeth. I wasn't sure why, but I hadn't noticed until then that his teeth were shaped differently. The rope was slowly getting cut until my hands were free. Struggling with feeling in my hands I managed to grab the rope on his feet. I was able to unhook him, the only part that kept him hanging had been his hands. Kneeling on the ground so that he could step on my back as a stepping stool I hoped he would be able to unhook himself.

"I'm not stepping on you." Making his feelings very clear.

"You might not like it, but I've already done something strange, just do it quick so we can start working our way out of here. Besides, I can handle your weight, I've held cheerleaders during practice." Even though I had to admit Jasper was much larger than any of our cheerleaders, I knew this would be our only opportunity.

Moving as quickly as he could, stepping on me only as much as he had to so I could remove his loop from the hook and drop down to the floor. Removing his ankle restraints and then working on his tied wrists we could hear voices coming back in our direction. Wrapping the rope around my wrist to make it appear I was still hooked. I held onto my hook and dangled there for a second as the door opened. Surprised and rather shocked they looked over at me almost relieved that I was still here until Jasper grabbed them both from behind the door yanking them into the room knocking them into each other, and then they proceeded to drop to the floor in an unconscious heap. Leaving the door opened Jasper leaned out making sure no one else was coming with them. Checking their pockets, they both had a few vials and two syringes no doubt planning to collect more blood.

Motioning with his hand to follow I stayed as close to him as I could, even as he had before I bumped into him, looking back at me when I did the slightest smile would show. I was beginning to think he was amused by my bumping into him and thought for a second, he would stop or slow down just so that I would. Looking around I guessed we were in one of the warehouses from all the crates that had been left behind, even some of the machinery. In the far corner, we could see the glow from a huge fire with several robed figures standing around it. There was also a huge table with large shackles lying on top. I wasn't sure what they were working on, but I certainly didn't want to stick around and find out. As we made our way out, we were finally spotted.

"Hop up on my back, hold on tight and no matter what happens don't let go, trust me with this." There was a look of desperation in his eyes but then I was sure I would have had the same.

Placing my arms around his neck, Jasper lifted me, and before I knew it, he was off running with the wind whizzing through my hair, my eyes started to tear from being windblown. Racing through the fields and woods to make sure no one would see us going this fast we were home faster than I would ever have assumed. Unfortunately, we had left my car behind. Once we were there, he set me down on the ground with a look of concern on his face, not sure how I was going to take this.

Feeling overwhelmed and not sure how to take it. I let my legs buckle underneath me sitting down rather quickly. Scooping me up in his arms, Jasper carried me to the house; I was too much in shock to even pay attention when he had. I was in too much shock to notice how badly my arms were burning, although Jasper noticed having to move his skin away from me since I seemed to be burning him. Almost as if I had set him in the sun. Setting me down on the couch Jasper kneeled in front of me placing one hand on my cheek.

"I know all of this is hard to absorb right now and later when we're safe you can ask me all the questions you need to, but we can't stay here, it's not safe. Your boss knows where you live and I'm sure they are on their way to find us here. Pack what you need and then we'll take off as quick as we can." Offering me his hand helping me up, Jasper followed me to my room to make sure I was still alright.

Grabbing a bag from my closet he tossed it on the bed as I grabbed a few pieces of clothing. I wasn't sure how long we would be gone but at least I would be prepared for a few weeks. Grabbing my little red bag, I had emergency items in it, something dad always had me pack telling me someday I might need it. Now I was beginning to wonder if he knew this would happen. Now I

51

was worried about dad and Voncha, curious where and what they were doing right now. As soon as my bag was full, I had grabbed the handles while I followed Jasper outside. We could hear the engines of a car and a few motorcycles coming in our direction. They were making their way for us since I wasn't expecting anyone else. We lived on a dead-end road; there wasn't anyone else for them to come out here to see.

Climbing up on his back again holding onto the bag, Jasper took off again heading north underneath the glow of the full moon, at least it illuminated the sky enough to see. I felt too dizzy trying to watch as everything flew by. Closing my eyes holding on tight. I trusted that Jasper knew where he was going. We had gone much further this time than before; I wasn't even sure where we were when we had stopped. Nothing looked familiar. We were on the outside of a rather large city with the lights shining from a long distance away. We had only stopped for a moment, Jasper wanted to make sure I wasn't too tired from holding on. Once he saw I still had a firm grip, and I was alright he took off again taking us closer to the city until we were just on the outskirts of it. Stopping a safe distance, we started walking towards it. Holding Jasper's hand, we made it to the beginning of the downtown, as we walked on the sidewalk only a few people even bothered to look in our direction.

The sun had already started to come out from the morning, it was rather bright, and Jasper was squinting his eyes to see. Spotting the first hotel we walked in as I made reservations which I always did for my dad. Using cash, I reserved a suite on the top floor with two king beds. It was a good thing I had just been paid before I took off for my vacation; I hadn't had time to deposit it yet. Taking the key from the hotel employee, he had looked at us rather strangely and I certainly hadn't bothered explaining our relation to each other. I used to say I was staying with my older brother but this time I was just too tired, in pain, and out of words to try to explain anything. My dad and his friends always looked rather young, and I never gave any thought to it even though in the last few years they all had aged a little.

Instead of taking the elevator, we both took the steps up. Opening the door not that anyone was expecting us to be here,

Jasper still searched the room in case someone followed us or guessed we would stay at the first hotel we had come to. Not bothering to unpack just yet since I wasn't sure how long we would be staying here. I tossed my bag next to the bed sitting down at the end of it as Jasper began to pace.

"Are we going to find dad and Voncha to let them know what is happening or something else?" I hoped he might tell me what he was thinking while he paced.

"I'm not sure, eventually yes but right now we need to figure this out, what they want with you and how to keep you safe." Still, in deep thought, Jasper had continued to pace.

Quite a lot of light had still been coming in the far window as Jasper was too busy being lost in his thoughts. I got up and pulled down the blinds then pulled the curtains closed as tight as I could keeping out as much of the light as I could. Then placing the do not disturb sign on the door so we wouldn't be bothered. We had paid a small fee for checking in early but then it helped they had also had empty suites. It was rather nice, and I would have enjoyed it more if it wasn't for the current circumstances. Standing still for a moment I looked around the room. It was rather nice for a suite, a little living room in the center with two standard-sized beds off to each side. At the far end of the living room was another room which I had guessed was the bathroom. Jasper had stopped pacing for a moment when he watched what I was doing. Smiling a little, he looked down when I noticed he was staring at me.

"I thought closing out the light might make it easier on you, I've noticed you squint when it's too bright." I wasn't sure if the light would bother him or not since I had never been outside during the daylight with either Jasper or Voncha, they had always made excuses why they were staying inside.

"We always wondered if you would question that someday. I wasn't sure how I was going to answer if you had." No longer pacing, Jasper had walked into the bedroom. Grabbing my bag off the chair I tossed it onto the floor and sat down on the edge of the bed.

"I have a few questions, I'm sure I'll think of more later if you're ready now to answer the first ones?" I think it's why he finally sat down; Jasper knew my questions wouldn't be waiting for too much longer. Gripping his hands trying to relax Jasper waited for my first question.

"How long have you been a vampire, are dad and Voncha vampires also? Why keep it from me? How does your being a vampire make you different than what I've seen in the movies, is that why you always consider them comedies?" I knew I launched a few questions at once I just wasn't sure which one, I wanted to know first. Either way, I decided to start with the more direct questions.

"I've been a vampire since I was twenty-two. That would have been about two hundred years ago when your father changed Voncha and me. As far as the movies are concerned, being a vampire isn't the same as they portray, I find them rather humorous but certainly interesting to see how mortals view us, many different ideas. We do drink blood; it's difficult to explain. It's not as desperately sought after as it is portrayed in the movies except there are certain ones who prefer the taste of human blood over an animal, a few who are tainted or are Ill will go on a blood craze. Blood is all the same no matter what source you get it from. We don't kill people and many of us can eat regular foods, the ones who eat solid food still age only extremely slow. Not that much different from when we were human, but we need more nutrients than we used to." Jasper had been careful exactly how he was explaining to me, never once looking up at me.

Getting up off the bed, I walked over to Jasper. He still hadn't looked at me almost as if he was depressed or saddened that I knew now. Without a word, I sat down on his one leg, leaning in I rested my head on his chest, wrapping my arms as much as I could around Jasper. I wanted him to know I wasn't upset, and I understood there reason for keeping it a secret, but I was curious.

"Why have you kept this secret from me? You've always told me everything?" This question was more important to me than anything else.

"Emma, your father wanted you to have as normal a life as he could give you. Keeping this from you he hoped it would be easier for you to blend in with the other mortals. This is the only secret we have ever kept from you. I know we have always had a special relationship and I understand if you hate me for not telling you before." This time Jasper had looked directly in my eyes, almost as if he was trying to find the answer before I gave it.

"I don't hate you; my opinion of you isn't any different. I just wish I had known. I still could have blended in with everyone knowing the truth, I would have been able to explain some of the strange situations better or at least made better excuses than I had when unexplained things happened, or dad acted strangely. At least some of it makes sense now." For a second, I had forgotten my second question, I was still trying to think of Jasper being a vampire not that I could picture him drinking blood.

"Do you have any other questions? If you think of more questions later, I will always answer them." Jasper had yet to take his eyes off me never diverting his attention for a second.

"Was mom mortal? How could mom have been pregnant with me if dad is a vampire?" Sitting forward-looking at Jasper waiting for his answer, I was completely lost in my thoughts with all the questions I had wanted to ask.

"We're not sure. She was killed by people she had trusted; they wanted to use her for her gift. When they found out she didn't agree with what they were planning on doing, she was leaving when they had killed her. A friend of hers dropped you off at your father's, your mother had requested it if she didn't make it. She felt you would be safer living with us than with the others in the colony. She had very special gifts, something a shade or a very powerful Witch would possess. Your father was very close to her for a short time." Placing his hand over mine, for the first time I had noticed how cold it was.

I've held his hand or even laid against him before so why now? Why does it seem that much colder to me than it ever did in the past? Maybe I would look at him differently?

I thought about the many stories' dad told me about mom and what kind of relationship they had. For the first time, it hit me that they were never really married, all of it could have come from a dating situation. Odd to think of him inheriting me never knowing she was pregnant until she was dead, maybe that's why they were finally after me now? That is if it had been the same

55

group. Folding his fingers over mine holding my hand, Jasper knew I was letting the information sink in as I thought over memories. Right now, I wasn't sure what emotion to be feeling, I almost felt numb. Knowing there were people out there that might want to kill me and finding my family had a rather huge secret they had been keeping from me. My past was still the same only in the same essence very different than what I grew up believing.

"I don't want to know anymore right now." Almost whispering the words, I had stood up with Jasper still holding my hand rather firmly.

Any time before I would have crawled into Jasper's lap when I felt depressed or just wanted to feel safe, right now I wasn't sure what I wanted to do. I wasn't angry but I wasn't happy either. Standing up behind me Jasper pulled me back, turning around to face him I leaned into him resting my head on his chest as he hugged me close. I know Jasper always told me that he only wore cologne occasionally and I always knew the difference. I loved it when he hadn't worn it, his natural scent was so much better, no matter where he was if he had been out of eyesight or just within range enough I could smell him, I knew it was him, and no one else. I must have been breathing in much more than I normally did but the scent alone always helped me feel relaxed. Running his fingers through my hair until I felt his hand slide back into place with his other hand on my lower back, I felt so comfortable I could have stayed here forever. Letting out a small sigh I felt tired.

"It's going to be a long night; we're going to meet up with your father and Voncha. First I'll have to speak with them since they will be with other vampires, they need to be warned of your coming before you come in. Go get some sleep and we will leave as soon as the sun starts to go down." Running his fingers through my hair again I hadn't wanted to let go or move away from him. One thing I had noticed was his scent getting stronger. Leaning back for a second I hadn't given thought to this yet.

"Will you be sleeping?" I never remember seeing him sleep before.

"No, I don't need to. I'll stay up and wait for you to wake up." Jasper still hadn't made a move away from me but then neither had I.

"Sit with me while I sleep." Backing up, holding his hand I easily led him into my room with no protest.

Propping himself up against the back of the bed leaving his shoes on the floor. Not bothering to change, I laid against him with my head resting on his stomach. My arms wrapped around him in a tight hug, I hadn't done this since I was ten and afraid of thunderstorms. But then I had always sat on his lap or goofed around with him as I grew older. That I had always noticed, he was always affectionate with me but as I grew older, he backed off from me. That's when Voncha seemed to get closer to me or at least he tried.

"How do you think dad is going to react when he finds out that I know?" Looking up at Jasper I could see him wince for a moment.

"He's not going to be happy, I'm sure he would have preferred my finding some way of covering it up or making it sound like they were insane, but it was the only way I could get you away from them fast enough. I didn't want to risk you getting caught." Jasper had started playing with my hair again twirling it around his finger.

"He doesn't have to know you told me; we could keep this secret between us. I don't want him taking his temper out on you." I knew how angry he could get; he might have held back because I was his daughter, but he might not in this case and with his friends.

"You've seen his temper?" No longer moving but staring down at me with concern.

"Why do you think our kitchen table gets replaced so often? I used to think he was just abnormally strong when he was angry but now, I'm rethinking that. It's impossible for me to grow up around him and not see it at some point. His temper is something he hasn't been able to hide." Not looking at Jasper I hadn't wanted to go into an explanation of the times he lost his temper.

Dad never laid a hand on me but at times he certainly terrified me which he always seemed to apologize for later. I just learned to be much more careful around him so I wouldn't upset him. In a way, I had learned to keep my secrets. I could feel Jasper squeeze me tighter and closer to him.

"Don't worry, I've dealt with your father for a long time, I can handle this. He won't stay angry forever." The tone of his voice wasn't very reassuring, and I still didn't want him to deal with the brunt of my father's anger, if he lost it. I kept hoping he might handle this better than I thought, but then most likely I was going to be wrong for thinking that.

"I still think it's worth trying, tell him what happened just leave me out of it and say I was out for a walk with the dogs when they were scared off by something, that they made it clear they were coming after me, so you hid me at the hotel until it was safe. Just leave out the fast running or anything that would make it obvious that I could figure all of this out." Looking up at Jasper I was hoping he would at least try.

"I guess we could try, it would be nice not having him blow up, at least much safer. We still need to travel; I don't want to leave you at a hotel this close. Once we are further away, I'll go get Voncha and your father. Besides if he doesn't believe it, we already have an idea what to expect." Now I had to hope it worked.

As much as I loved my father and I knew he would do anything for me, unfortunately, he had problems with his temper. Something I admit he has been working on.

Laying there feeling more comfortable, I was finally warming up no longer feeling chilly from the weather outside.

"I love you, Jasper." Barely saying it above a whisper, laying against Jasper still as he patiently waited for me to fall asleep, I could feel my eyes getting heavier as I drifted off to sleep.

"I know. I love you too, my angel." Kissing me on the forehead Jasper thought I hadn't heard what he said, I was just awake enough to hear him still.

HIDING

Waking up I wondered if it was nighttime or not, with the blinds drawn I could hardly tell, but the view was wonderful. Looking up Jasper had stayed with me the entire time I had slept, not risking moving at all since he hadn't wanted to wake me up.

"Did you sleep well? You were mumbling quite a lot, but I couldn't understand what you were saying other than the fact you said my name twice. I was hoping you weren't having a nightmare." Brushing my cheek with his hand I could hear the concern in his voice.

"I didn't have one nightmare the entire time, I felt great." I did feel slightly embarrassed because of the dreams that I did have.

"It's good you're finally up, we need to get moving." Leaning down to give me a morning kiss on the forehead, the same way Jasper always did except this time he kissed me on the lips and lingered longer but then so had I.

Turning more into the kiss I could feel Jasper pull me closer to him as he completely covered my lips with his. Without losing touch with his lips, he slid out from underneath me so quickly now on top of me pressing his body against me. Pressing more firmly with his lips, kissing me, I could feel my blood rushing as my heartbeat faster. Wrapping my arms around him pulling him in close, it had felt better than any of my dreams had been. As quickly as he had moved on top of me, he slid down off the bed just as fast. Moving away from me with a worried expression on his face.

"I can't take advantage of you; it wouldn't be right. Let me know when you're ready to leave, I'll be in the other room waiting." Walking out of the room I could hear him pulling the curtains back.

I had laid there feeling stunned for a moment. Feeling numb now, I sat up leaning over the side of the bed, I grabbed my bag which was never opened. Standing up I walked into the room with Jasper. He was staring out the window not looking back. No other light was coming in from the window other than the moonlight.

I guess when I had the chance to ask questions, I should have asked Jasper how he felt about me. It wasn't something I had even thought about until now. Jasper kissing me in this way brought back memories of when I was younger. Jasper and I shared an unspoken friendship. I've known he's had a crush on me since I turned eighteen. The first time I had even noticed or thought about it had been the night before the three of them left. I was standing outside when Jasper came to say goodbye. That he would be back as usual. Instead of kissing me on the forehead he had accidentally kissed me on the lips. It was the first time I had ever seen him act shy and fail miserably trying to cover it up with an excuse.

That was the first night I dreamed about kissing him. Even at nineteen he never spoke another word about it except when I noticed little things that were different. The way he touched or spoke to me was much gentler. Not that he was ever rough with me but certainly the way you would treat someone if you had a crush on them. He always treated me like a princess, now he treated me like a queen. His eye contact was even more intense.

"I'm ready to go; I'll stop by the front lobby to drop off the keycards." Not waiting for an answer, I had already turned walking out of the room.

Jasper hadn't caught up to me until I was already down in the lobby checking us out of our room. I walked with my hands in my pockets as we made our way through most of the town. The city this time was larger than I had cared for; several times we walked along an expressway being careful as cars sped past us. I knew once we were far enough or in a safe spot to take off, Jasper would be our transportation at that point. Once we reached the forest edge where the lights from the city now dimmed greatly leaving us in the dark, I looked back at Jasper waiting for him to stand in front of me. Looking me in the eyes I hadn't wanted to keep eye contact.

"Emma, I should have handled that better; I just didn't want you to regret it. I feel like I'm taking advantage of you at a time I should be someone you can trust, instead, I felt I was using you. I never asked if it was something you wanted and I knew for a fact your father would be against it, he made it clear to Voncha and me that you were off limits, that we were to stay away from you. I'm sorry I hurt you." Placing his hand on my shoulder I still felt numb.

"Do you have feelings for me?" I didn't want to wait to find out later, I wanted to know how he felt.

"We can discuss that later; we need to find the others first." This was the first time Jasper had broken eye contact with me.

"I'm not going anywhere until you tell me. I'm tired of secrets, especially from you. You said you wouldn't keep anything from me anymore." Standing my ground, I refused to move.

Not answering my question, he swooped over picking me up in his arms now swiftly moving across the countryside. The surroundings were a blur like before. Laying my head down on his shoulder putting my arms around his neck I just laid there waiting for Jasper to get us to our new destination. I was starting to get cold letting into a shiver. Making a sharp turn Jasper stopped at the top of a hill. As I looked down there was a small town down below that we now made our way to. On the outskirt of town Jasper finally set me down.

"I won't be far, there's a hotel for you to stay in, don't go out until we come back for you." Kissing me on the forehead I felt like a little kid again.

"Be careful." There were so many other things I had wanted to say only these were the only words I could get out.

61

"I promise I'll be back for you." Placing his hand under my chin, at first, Jasper kissed my forehead again, then the second kiss on my lips.

As he backed away I watched him take off quickly. When he had I made my way over to the hotel, checking in as I had at the other hotel only using a different name in case my boss were to check around asking for me. It was something they wouldn't guess except my father, Voncha and Jasper. I had chosen Molly Tipper. Both were the first names of my oldest dogs. I didn't know how far away from home we were until I was inside the hotel room. There was a complementary television guide with a guest pad; on the bottom of the pad, it had the city's name. We were one state over, far enough from home. Leaving my bag on the end of the bed. I sat there with the curtains open watching the light outside flickering. My dad had always been overly protective of me so I knew it wouldn't be long before he was here. The more I watched the clock the slower the time ticked by.

I had paced back and forth, taken a shower, and watched a couple of boring shows, still, time felt like it was standing still. Jasper had said he wouldn't be very far away, I just hoped dad would have accepted our story. Hopefully, he wasn't giving Jasper a hard time, I just wished I could have gone with him but to make it believable I had agreed to stay here. I could hear the music drifting upstairs from the bar next door. Dancing in place I listened as the music played, I was glad I had slept earlier, with all of this noise there was no way I would have been able to sleep. After another hour, I desperately needed something to occupy my time with. I was going to give myself an ulcer if I kept worrying about Jasper and watching the clock. I had always listened to Jasper when he told me to do something; rarely he would tell me what to do, but when he did there was always a good reason for it. This time I figured he could just be upset with me. Leaving the room making sure the door firmly closed behind me with my keycard in my pocket. I made my way to the bar.

The bar was packed as a live band played. Standing inside for only a few minutes someone had already grabbed my hand pulling me onto the dance floor where several others were crowded around dancing. The last time I had been to a bar, or a party had been with my friend Beth. Just the sudden thought of her and what she had done made my stomach drop. The person who had pulled me out onto the dance floor seemed to be dancing with a group. I felt more relaxed when he no longer seemed to be singling me out from everyone. It felt good to relax and not worry about anything for a few brief minutes, to forget the horrible things that have happened in the last week. I was completely absorbed listening to the music until I had felt someone touch me bringing me back to reality.

I hadn't been in the bar long, just about an hour when I felt an arm wrap around my waist, the sudden panic of who it might be flooded back almost instantly. Looking back to see who it was, I knew it wasn't Jasper. I knew before he was ever close by. For a second, I worried and panicked until I had seen Voncha. Voncha was smiling out of relief, a look I was familiar with since I had wandered off once and my family had no idea where I had gone. So many horrible things could have happened, they were just happy to find me alive and safe. It was the same look he was giving me now.

"You were supposed to wait for us in the hotel room; your father is up there worried. I thought you might have checked this place out." Nodding since I couldn't get my voice heard over all the noise, we walked back to the hotel.

"Is Jasper upstairs?" Voncha seemed relaxed but I was still worried about how my dad took the news and if Jasper was alright.

"Your father asked him not to come back to the hotel. Jasper didn't want you to worry about him. He knew after all these years your father would know if he was lying to him or not. Don't worry he's fine. When your father gets over his temper Jasper will be back." There was no way Voncha could have worded the message that would have made me feel better about Jasper not being here. I knew he was going to cover anything up, at least he told me the truth. I didn't want to go back until I physically saw Jasper safe, I hated the fact he was alone right now.

Reluctantly I went back into the motel room to face my father, as soon as I had he moved faster than I had ever seen him move before. I felt amazed; things were going to be very different

63

now that I knew the big secret. I just hoped there wasn't more that he was hiding from me.

"I was worried something happened to you, that miserable bastard said you would be in here waiting." As he spoke his voice rose. I knew I didn't have to ask since his tone of voice gave away how he felt.

"Don't call him that dad; if it weren't for Jasper, I would be dead right now. He did everything he could to protect me. You should have allowed him to come back, he promised me he would be back here and quite frankly, I feel safer with him here." I didn't want to hurt Voncha's feelings but even he knew it was true. Jasper was much stronger than the rest and quicker thinking.

"He's never to come around you ever again. Voncha and I will handle what's going on, I should have done this years ago and all of this never would have happened. I just thought the older generation had died off and there wouldn't be any worries." Shaking his head still angry, I knew my father meant well but I couldn't let him throw Jasper out of my life forever.

"Jasper is not going to be out of my life forever, if you and Voncha are going to take care of things I would like someone here with me, right now I don't feel safe being alone. Sad a group at a bar couldn't protect me but I felt safer there than waiting alone up here in the room. Jasper is a very important part of my life, and he can't just be removed from it because your lie to me was exposed. He's just as permanent to my life as you and Voncha are." As soon as I had said this a lamp was launched out through the window.

"I did this to protect you." Not saying another word dad stormed out of the room leaving Voncha standing next to me.

"It's not a good idea to test him right now; he already blew up at Jasper. He doesn't need to be taking his temper out on you also. Just let this blow over or let him take care of the problem and we can work on getting Jasper back later. Jasper will be alright; he knows how to take care of himself." Voncha tried to reassure me.

I felt so frustrated I pressed my face into Voncha's chest and started to cry. All of this had finally caught up to me and it was just too much.

"Do you know what these people want with me? One is my friend and the other my boss, I don't know all of them, but I had no clue they were ever planning anything. What could they have possibly wanted with Jasper and me? They made it clear I was a key to whatever they were working on, and they wanted a vampire also." Looking at Voncha I hoped he would tell me the truth. I knew by looking at him he was still nervous telling me anything no doubt worried how my father would react.

"Your mother was very special, she was born with a rare gift, neither your father or I know what exactly she was, but we knew of some powerful things she was able to do. Because of the gift, it's the only reason your father was able to have you, at least that was how it was explained to us. The older generation hoped to control your gift, the vampire part they use to make temporary vampires. Using your blood won't turn someone into a vampire; they will have traits for a short time before it wears out. We don't know if you picked up anything from your father or not." As soon as Voncha heard my father enter the room he stopped talking.

"I can't just stay here or keep hiding, eventually they will find me if they want me that bad. What do you plan on doing, if you tell the authorities they will only think you've gone mad or are a threat to others and yourself? Then they might find out you're a vampire. How could you keep something like that from me? I've kept secrets from you and at least now I know where I've learned that from. I have inherited all of Mom's powers. I just don't display them around you. It would have helped to know about you so I wouldn't have thought all these years I was crazy, or something was wrong with me because I was different." Feeling angry at myself I walked away from both Voncha and my father closing the door to the adjoining room behind me.

Sitting on the edge of the bed I felt so frustrated, looking out the window I had silently wished Jasper would show up on the fire escape just to see me, but I knew he wouldn't do that. Then I heard a light knock.

"What!" I roared my question.

After answering that way, I felt bad, I never wanted to be like my father in that way, there were a lot of wonderful things about him, but his temper certainly wasn't one of them.

"Mind if I come in for a minute?" Voncha had asked rather quietly.

"It's okay, you can come in." I felt bad for snapping at him.

Walking in Voncha closed the door behind him.

"Your father left, he's going to meet up with a few of his friends to find out what the group is working on and to see what they can do about protecting you. Your father asked me to stay with you to keep you safe since you said you didn't want to be alone. I know you wanted Jasper, but I promise I can keep you safe also." Smiling I knew Voncha was only trying to cheer me up.

"I know you will, do you know where Jasper is?" Shaking his head, no, I knew I didn't have to ask him again.

I just hope he had stayed close by but more importantly staying safe himself.

"I take it we're supposed to just wait around until the others figure this out. That's crazy, I have a job and I can't wait around forever just hoping they will figure this out. Since when have you ever known me to sit back and do nothing?" Smiling back at me at least Voncha understood, it had to drive him crazy thinking he was stuck babysitting me.

"Don't quit your job, just take family leave, the same way you did the second year after graduating. We could go on a long trip again, just you and I; we had a lot of fun camping wherever we stopped. It would help pass the time quicker, only this time if you get tired and we want to get somewhere faster we can do it this time, I don't have to hide my speed." As tempting as it was, I was worried about Jasper wishing he could come with me. But then I thought I would just rather be with him right now.

"I would need to stop and go into work to fill out the papers, unfortunately I can't do it over the phone. You will need to take me back there. Maybe see if we could find Jasper?" It was the first time I had noticed disappointment in Voncha's eyes.

From now on I would need to be more careful about mentioning Jasper. Grabbing my bag, I had checked out of the hotel. At least I knew dad could contact us if he needed to. My cell phone was securely packed at the bottom of my bag. We were already close to the edge of town; with the light coming up. I hadn't wanted to take too much time with Voncha out in the sunlight. I had already traveled this way with Jasper but for some reason, it just felt strange holding onto Voncha this way.

"Am I crazy for being concerned with my job?" I didn't want to lose my job, not that I wanted to work that close to my boss ever again.

I wasn't sure if I could trust others because of Beth.

"It's perfectly alright, you're planning on a future beyond all of this. It would be like saying there is hope that life will get back to normal." Voncha was right, that and I would keep my mind busy otherwise I would only be worrying more about the situation we were in.

As ready as I was going to be with my arms around his neck we took off for my hometown. Trying to avoid all the public areas as much as possible, brushing against a few trees. I used to think that Jasper was the fastest but now that Voncha was in a full run I was wrong, so far Voncha was much faster. Jasper either hid it better or was just a faster walker. Feeling winded and light-headed I held on tight as Voncha also held onto me with his arms crossed in the back the same way he used to give me piggyback rides when I was little. He was always cautious making sure I didn't fall or get hurt. Closing my eyes since I couldn't see anything going by other than blurs of different colors. I had begun to wonder if Voncha ever wore out.

I could feel Voncha suddenly start to breathe deeper; I wasn't sure if he needed to or if it had been from the sun coming out much brighter. When I opened my eyes instead of dark blurs they were much brighter now. Voncha's skin was starting to darken; his skin was badly burned during the short time we were in the sun. Rushing right up to the parking garage there would be shade inside where the sun wasn't able to illuminate. Stopping just in front of the door he tried to stay on the side of me so that the surveillance camera wouldn't catch him. This was the first time I had even thought about it, would it be able to record him, or was it a movie thing? Putting in my password I almost expected it to be changed. As it accepted me, the door opened letting us in.

The hospital was busy this morning, which was good; at least we stood a better chance of blending in without being stopped. Heading straight to my boss's office. I looked around for the proper forms to fill out, then with his official stamp I approved my own family leave, citing it for the reasons allowed, now all I had to do was drop it off to be filed. Approval was one thing from my boss but there were several steps, I just left a written message for them to leave a phone message on my cell phone when the rest of it had been approved not that I was worried it wouldn't be.

Sealing the application in an envelope and dropping it off on the human resources desk, I overheard a few people talking in the main room behind their cubicles. Both Voncha and I stood back just enough so we could listen. Both Beth and Morris hadn't been heard from for the last few days and no one knew if they were coming back in or not. Whoever they had included in their plans they had been rather selective. I just wished I knew what exactly they wanted.

I tried for so long to convince both Jasper and Voncha to get cell phones except neither seemed to like the modern technology. I had offered to pay for it; it was worth it to me if I could contact them when I needed to. If something had happened to either my father or myself, I would never be able to reach them. Most of the time they were off traveling, it wasn't until about a year ago that I asked where they worked. Both had said they were either retired, worked occasionally for my father in his mortuary when he needed extra help, or they had other friends they worked part-time with.

Taking the stairs down to the parking garage we could hear two other workers coming down the stairs. We had been just one floor above them, stopping to make sure we didn't make any noise, we peeked over the edge. They were carrying out two large laundry bags, something this hospital never did, they had their laundry facilities so what were they carrying out?

Keeping our distance making sure no one else was around to notice us, we followed them to the door. Looking out we watched as they set the bags rather carefully inside of a white waiting van. The person accepting the bags from them was Morris being careful not to get out of the van to avoid being seen on the security cameras. The others had something shiny stuck to their faces, no doubt to cast a shine on the cameras making sure not to pick up who they were. Keeping a mental note of the license plate I noticed it wasn't even a legitimate number. Holding onto Voncha we tried to follow them without being noticed. It was much more difficult to follow through a residential neighborhood. When we did get there, I wasn't sure what to expect, I hadn't thought they would be showing up at a house. I had hoped they would have shown up in a more secluded area. The home was at the end of a circular drive, rather large with an iron gate nine feet high with a locked front gate. Looking around for cameras surprisingly I hadn't found any unless they were hidden well.

The van hadn't spent very much time inside, only long enough to drop off the two bags with Morris dragging them inside. Waiting for the door to close, we kept waiting for a chance to sneak in without being noticed. Hiding between the bushes and the iron gate, we waited for the van to leave before attempting to get in. As the iron gate started to close, we rushed in quickly than finding another place to hide before moving forward. As soon as the van was gone, we moved again to the side of the house. All the windows had been closed and locked. The doors were locked also.

Voncha knew better than to ask me to wait outside. At least there weren't any guard dogs but then when you know there are vampires and other creatures in the world the protection factor from a dog just doesn't seem the same anymore. Tired of looking for a way in, Voncha made his way in, grabbing a door handle he crushed it in his hand as he pulled it out, with no mechanism in the way the door now opened with no problem. Following behind Voncha, we walked into the house slowly. The place looked like any other typical house that had been lived in; personally, no one that I knew lived here. The room we entered had been the kitchen with a little dining room. No food or anything had been out. No dirty dishes to show anyone had used anything here. But then when I opened the fridge there wasn't anything in there except for blood vials, and blood bags each was labeled with a name. I found mine and one with it listed an unknown vampire. There were more blood vials there than they could have collected the day they had us held hostage. Taking them out and placing them in my pocket Voncha gave me a rather strange look.

"It's the blood they took from Jasper and me." As soon as I had said this Voncha started looking through the rest, separating three vials he started pouring the rest of them down the sink then putting the empty vials in the garbage container. Now I was curious what vials he had taken.

"These have your mother's name on them." Not saying another word, he handed them to me and continued to scout out the other adjacent room.

Walking softly along the floor we heard footsteps coming from the stairs, careful not to make noise we listened as they made their way to a door in the hallway. Closing it behind them we could only guess that was where Morris had gone. Waiting for them to be at the far bottom and no one else to join them Voncha slightly opened the door enough to listen.

"The girls been back at the hospital, she requested personal family leave and conveniently it had your signature on it. I'm guessing she's hiding around here somewhere, should we search her house again?" At least we knew they were still looking for me.

"At some point, she's going to mess up and we will catch her then, otherwise she might give herself up if she wants her friend to live. Make sure he can't get loose." Morris had made an order to who was helping him. I looked at Voncha worried they might have Jasper.

"Beth's place has been trashed with a burnt body in the bathtub, so they won't know it's not her. Her life insurance should finish funding the rest of this. Too bad all of this is expensive." The voice sounded frustrated.

"Not as expensive as it could have been, it helped I was able to borrow some things from the hospital, I just listed them as damaged or missing." Morris let out a sickly laugh.

"I'm taking off for the lake house to get the rest of the ritual ready. We don't have that much more time to do this. If we don't get the girl, we at least have enough of her mother's blood to do what we need. The girl is just a bonus, she has something I want and it's much easier to get it from a living vessel than a dead one. We better add two more to search for the girl if we are going to have her on time, I don't want to miss our opportunity." The voice now was sounding angrier than frustrated.

"Don't worry; I have that taken care of." Moving back into the kitchen we listened to the footsteps now leading out of the house.

Keeping a look out, looking around in case there was anything else that might help us we made our way out. The front gate was already closed and locked, we had to climb over the huge gate; unfortunately, we both wound up getting scraped up from the barbed wire that ran along the top of it. Voncha dropped to the ground before I had, reaching out he grabbed me before I could hit the ground. He had landed so gracefully. If it had been me, I would have fallen flat on my face. Thankfully I had my phone on vibrate, it was already going off. The call was coming from a gas station; at least it's what showed on my caller ID. Answering the phone I guessed it had to be my dad since he was the only one out of three people who had my number. I had kept it for emergencies only.

"Where are you at? We went back to the hotel to find you, and neither of you were there, your room was trashed. Voncha better still be with you." I could hear the concern in his voice, no matter how hard he tried to hide how he was feeling, I knew my father far too well for him to be able to hide his emotions from me.

"Yes, Voncha is still with me, I had to take personal leave from work so I wouldn't lose my job. We think they might have Jasper. They said they had a friend of mine, it might not be him, but I don't have other friends other than a few I speak with at work." There was a long sigh let out from the other side and I knew it confirmed it without having to hear the words.

"He was protecting me when they jumped us, they did get him but the rest of us are fine. They are going to perform a ritual and unfortunately, they have other creatures with them. We might not be able to get Jasper back in time. We are going to move you far enough away to keep you safe, tell Voncha to meet us at the old tavern, he'll know where that is." Before I could ask any other questions, he had hung up.

"It sounds like they're already giving up, Jasper is just as important as I am. I don't want to keep hiding if there is something I can do. There has to be!" I felt so frustrated Voncha grabbed a hold of me hugging me trying to reassure me.

"Don't worry, we will get him. We will show up at the tavern since we need more help, but I won't leave you behind. This is something you will have to trust me with." Standing in front of me I knew he was ready to take off again.

Unfortunately, with all the sun exposure so far, his skin was red with a few blisters now showing. Voncha's eyes were dried out having a hard time seeing. I knew he was looking forward to being in a dark place for a while. I worried about Voncha going through all of this and for what they might be putting Jasper through. The old tavern had been on the state borderline. This way of traveling might have been faster but certainly not comfortable at all. I felt so bad since I couldn't shield Voncha's face from the sun; I tried to cover the back of his neck with my arm. Leaving the main roads, we had gone across a field leading into a thick group of trees. I could hear Voncha let out a sigh as we were now covered with shade from the trees.

Heading far out into the thick of the woods, there was this run-down old-looking shack that looked like it hadn't been touched in years, a faded old sign that read Millner's Tavern broken in half on the ground. The porch above had caved in covering below, working our way through the rubble, half of the porch underneath was missing. Voncha entered first with me following behind holding his hand. As soon as we were in, there was a large group of my father's friends waiting for us. As soon as we were inside everyone had stopped talking or what they were doing to look at me. I couldn't help but hide behind Voncha holding onto his hand tighter. These were supposed to be the vampires that they would get together with, only a few I had recognized as general friends who used to come by to visit dad but not anywhere as often as Voncha and Jasper.

"I see she hadn't changed much; she was always hiding behind Voncha or Jasper when she was little." The man who spoke I had known as Devon.

"You have nothing to worry about; everyone here wants to protect you, also to hopefully get Jasper back." Dad spoke as he walked over to me giving me a reassuring hug.

"What is this ritual thing they are working on?" Looking up at my father I had hoped he would finally tell me.

"We need to discuss that right now; I'll have Devon take you to a safer place and we will take care of that." I knew my father meant well trying to keep me away from everything, but I couldn't risk it, I kept getting this desperate feeling I needed to stay.

"I'm not going anywhere and I'm not getting left out of anything anymore, I want answers and if it means going to Morris to find out, I will. I already know to find him at the lake house." Looking shocked that I even knew that much dad went and sat down in a chair, putting his hand to his chin I knew he was busy contemplating something.

"It's time to stop hiding things from her, she's smart enough to figure this out on her own and now that she knows enough, you can't expect her to just sit still and hide while she worries about all of us." Devon had spoken with a rather calm voice.

I had almost expected my father to get angry about my wanting to stay but for the first time, he didn't. I wasn't sure if my father was being so relaxed because the comments had come from Devon who he greatly trusted or that he knew he couldn't hide this world from me any longer?

I wasn't sure I was going to get an explanation or not, Voncha thankfully never let go of my hand or moved away from me. He always knew when I was nervous or needed him. As I watched the others sit down looking from one to the other no doubt trying to decide who was going to explain the situation to me since my father certainly hadn't looked as though he wanted to. As I stood there a group of wolves from the back of the room started making their way towards us. There were at least five of them, the fifth in the center kept coming towards us as the others stopped. Voncha hadn't seemed nervous around them as the one stopped just short of him. Then I had seen something I thought I would only see in my dreams or a movie. The arctic wolf morphed right in front of us into a man.

"We've never met, my family as you can see is of an arctic descent, we knew your mother, Lily. She used to be with an eager group of witches except they started having problems when a particular one joined with his friends. Your mother's gift was passed onto you through DNA. They hope to not only inject enough from various creatures, but you and your mother also share something rare. They can take all the blood samples they want but for some reason, they cannot duplicate the energy that you do naturally. Have you experienced this at all?" I was beginning to wonder when I would be asked this. Still holding my hand Voncha looked at me to see if I was able to answer.

"I haven't needed it until recently. There was a situation that Jasper and I were in, other than that most of it I kept quiet. I have used it, but I still don't know the full range of the gift." I wasn't sure how to explain it since I hadn't practiced with it that much.

"It's very important you learn what you can do and how to use it." As the man stepped back, I wanted to ask him a question before he changed his physical form again. At least he seemed to be willing to speak.

"Do you know why they would be collecting blood from all of us, especially me if they needed more than that?" Stopping for a moment he glanced back at my father.

"They are creating a monster of their own; they need the natural energy that you should be able to create to help bring it back to life. The blood itself is different depending on what creatures they collected them from. It's also one of the things we need to find and destroy. Each blood sample brings a new life for the monster they intend on ruling with. Your blood they can make these attributes permanent unlike what they are dealing with now." As he spoke Voncha tapped me on the shoulder.

"It's safe to show them." Voncha leaned back whispering to me.

"Then I guess they can't do much without these?" Pulling the vials out from my pocket I heard a few gasps; my father had looked up to see what I was holding.

74

"How did you get those? I've searched for the last year trying to find those." A man I hadn't recognized seemed astonished as he asked me. My father was now standing, walking over to me.

"How exactly did you get these and how long have you had them?" My father's voice was beginning to rise.

I could feel Voncha's hand squeeze mine just a little. I wanted to stand between him and my father except with a firm hand he kept me behind him.

"When I handed in my slip for family leave, I searched my boss's office and I found them in the refrigerator." I knew I hadn't told him the truth but there really wasn't anything at the house they needed and there was always a way of pointing it out.

Besides, I had found it after dropping off the slip, I had searched his office and I did get it out of a refrigerator, just not in that order.

"If Voncha had even allowed you anywhere near that group or in danger I swear I would kill you on the spot." My father was getting riled up, as he did, I could see the others backing up. Everyone was afraid of my father.

"Father, you cannot protect me all the time, besides, Voncha has done everything he can to protect me, just the same as Jasper. If I have a gift that is as powerful as it's being made out to be then I should be able to protect myself just fine. Besides, I'm hoping if they want these blood vials then maybe they will trade Jasper for them?" I knew it was a stretch, but it might bring the rest of their group out of hiding.

At least it's what I was hoping for.

"You can't risk giving those to them and it's not safe for you to confront them since you're another piece they want. The two together makes it even more dangerous." Voncha had spoken to me in a rather low calming tone.

"Yes, but if they think I'm that powerful then they would all be there, and I don't have to give them the blood vials they want, I can exchange it for regular mortal blood, and they would never know it. I have access to our blood bank. We could set up our trap." Dad wasn't a fan of this idea.

"No, you're not to come anywhere near them, exchanging the blood samples is a good idea but you're not going to be a part of it. Besides, right now you might be considered a fugitive to a murder." The last part he had whispered as I barely made out the words.

"What do you mean murder? I haven't killed anyone." Now I started to think I was being used in another way, if I was to get loose or if authorities were to find me then they would hold me until the group got their hands on me.

"The group that calls themselves the Sargon's Order have made it look as though you killed Beth out of jealousy and that Morris is hiding from you out of fear. Supposedly you were interested in him, and you found out they were secretly dating. My family clan did our best to compromise the crime scene so that it would not look like you were involved but for now, we just don't know." Shaking his head, he looked frustrated.

"Wait with Voncha until we can decide what we are going to do next." Father's voice was still authoritative sounding but still forgetting to ask me what to do with my own life. Heading over to one of the other men he started discussing their new plan.

I always hated it when he did that leaving me out of plans. When I was younger and had my plans, I used to grab the back of Voncha's shirt since usually Jasper would try and talk me out of it. Most of the mischievous things I would get into, Voncha had helped. Trying to ignore me I knew Voncha was worried about what I was planning and didn't want to do it for once.

"You're going to get both of us killed. First, it's too much of a risk with that strange group and second, your father will kill me before anyone else ever has a chance." Voncha did his best to whisper to me without anyone else hearing.

"Don't worry, I won't get you killed, you know I can't just sit back and wait for all of this. It's because of me we are in this situation, and I am old enough to take care of myself. If I have this power, then I need to learn how to start using it instead of hiding for the rest of my life and hoping there will be someone else around to protect me." At least Voncha couldn't argue with that logic, at least I thought he wouldn't.

"I think for once your father is right, what if they did grab you again, you were lucky the first time and I don't mean to scare you, but Jasper could be dead for all we know. I don't want to risk your life any more than your father does." No longer watching my father, Voncha looked directly at me with a worried expression I had never seen before.

"I'll give you an option then, either come with me and help me or stay here and keep discussing things and Jasper will be dead." Not waiting for his response, I had turned walking away towards the door. Before I could I heard my father speak up.

"Where do you think you're going?" His voice boomed.

"Heading out for some fresh air, this is more than I can handle right now, I might stay at a local hotel." At least no one bothered to stop me, and no one disagreed with me either.

At least what I said was true, it was more than what I could handle but it didn't exactly look like I had a choice.

"Your father is going to notice once you're gone too long. Life is going to be very different, your father might have sheltered you from a lot except his anger now that you know what he is, he might not hold back anymore. Your father is a very different man than the one you grew up with, our culture is nothing like what you have been raised in." Voncha was determined to get me to change my mind.

"No matter how much I'm hidden, someone is going to find me, someone will want whatever power it is that I have and will be as devious as Morris to get it." I knew I didn't need to say anything else to Voncha.

FINDING JASPER

I could hear the door close behind me with a rather huge sigh coming from Voncha. I knew he wouldn't leave me on my own, especially since I returned to my workplace again. I still had the blood vials in my pocket so the first thing I had planned would be to switch the vials. As we moved, I could hear them clink in my pocket. Nothing unusual at work, thankfully it was another busy day, so no one noticed when I had come in and out. Not wanting to take too much time I had decided to fill the vials elsewhere. Keeping the original samples, I wondered how exactly they were planning on using them. Not wanting to risk anyone coming across them Voncha and I went far out into the woods pouring the collected blood vials out onto a rock setting fire to it until it had been burned away. Rinsing out the vials in the stream, I carefully used the blood bag I took from work to refill them. It took a while puncturing the bag with a needle and filling the vials with new replacement blood.

We also paid a visit to Beth's condo which hadn't changed much other than the police walking around outside asking questions to other tenants. Looking around to see who was there across the way sitting in the park as all of this went on had been Morris himself. He was no doubt watching to see if I were to show up, watching him from the rooftop of another building we decided it wasn't safe to enter her apartment. Staying out of sight we left as soon as we could. I wasn't sure how I was going to prove I was innocent if he was able to plant something, but for now, my main concern had been to hopefully find Jasper if he was still alive.

At least if my father had asked me, I could say I had stopped back at the hotel only thing was I didn't plan on staying here. Pacing, I tried to figure out our next move. I wasn't sure where to look next. I wasn't sure where the lake house was or who owned it. All I could keep coming up with involved using myself as bait to find out if they had kept Jasper alive or not. Writing a note but not signing it I was sure they would figure out easily enough who it was, also I wanted to make sure it wasn't anything they could turn over to the authorities without having to explain it. I had only wrote, I have the vials of blood from the refrigerator, if you want them and me, I'll let you know soon where to meet me, that I also needed proof that Jasper was still alive. If Jasper was dead, then good luck with collecting the vials intact, that I would empty them on the ground. Leaving the note at that, I risked letting Voncha take off without me. Not that I had a choice. He hadn't wanted to risk trying to get me in and out without being seen again. It had only taken him two hours to take off from here, deliver the note, and to get back but that entire time felt like an eternity. I was worried I had lost another person I cared so much for because of myself.

I realized I had been barely breathing while he was gone; it wasn't until he was back that I finally let out a sigh of relief and hugged him. Now we waited to see if they would panic or slip up. I just hoped they would do exactly what I had on my note and prove Jasper to still be alive. Voncha and I also had to be careful since my father and his group had decided to follow certain members everywhere to find out what they were up to and hopefully find the lake house. During that time my father was interrogating the ones they had found were close to the situation trying to learn anything they could. Each time my father would insist on me staying away. I wanted to listen to one of the interrogations, I had hoped maybe I could ask a few questions and find out why they thought my blood would help them at all, if everything has been so temporary for them so far. Voncha insisted that I not be anywhere near my father at that time. Even he gave into a shudder. My father was much more violent than I might ever know.

There wasn't anything new other than who else had been involved. Three former college roommates of mine were working with Morris. They were supposed to watch me to find out if I had known about my past or used any of the gifts that I inherited from my family. Mostly they were trying to figure out if I inherited gifts from either parent or both. Then news came that was interesting. A group outside of theirs was also looking for me. Not a group of mortals but a group that had called themselves the Rising Dawn. The only information that Voncha could find out about them had been the fact my mother was with them for several years; she had been trained with her gifts from them. My mother wasn't just a witch, she was also a Shade, she grew up in a city removed from mortals. While she was pregnant with me her gifts were not as strong, at least not strong enough to protect her. Now the Rising Dawn considers me to be the same as my mother having no vampire traits. They were against vampires existing and intended on removing me from my family. If it wasn't bad enough, I would soon have to deal with mortals if they thought I had killed someone, then trying to save Jasper and end this thing with Sargon's order but now this new group?

I couldn't hide my frustration from Voncha, at least he understood, even he was worried about keeping me safe now that we had so many after us. As far as we understood, the Rising Dawn didn't have plans to harm me, but they did with my family. I kept thinking how simple things used to be when Voncha and I would go camping, no worries but then at that time I had no idea what he was or that I was capable of anything. I always heard how life changes as you grow up, but I wasn't expecting it to be this much. Voncha assumed that Morris left me alone before all of this because he wasn't sure if I had inherited anything at all, I think it was the only reason I had been safe up to this point.

After being at the hotel for about a week we noticed the same men standing outside not doing anything, but they would exchange places with each other almost as if they were standing guard. Then I recognized one and we were right, they were keeping an eye on me. I hadn't heard from my father in a few days, he had found out where the lake house was but then we hadn't heard from them or anyone else from the group since.

Waiting for nightfall we left the hotel not exactly leaving the way I would have preferred. Upon the roof of the hotel, we could see the two men watching the front entrance. Voncha moved behind me as I climbed onto his back while holding tight around his neck. I wrapped my legs around his waist trusting Voncha knew what he was doing. I was positive this would be the last thing I did and splatter on the cement below. Probably to some thinking it was a love suicide. Holding on tight Voncha launched us across as he had run and jumped to touch the edge of the nearby building landing perfectly on his feet. All these years I used to think he wasn't coordinated only to find out he had perfect balance.

Thankfully the door on the roof wasn't locked even though we surprised a few people as we made our way down. Taking the stairs hoping to attract less attention we left the building out the back keeping an eye out for anyone that might be watching us. With my bag slung over my shoulder, we walked very carefully until we were far enough away to make a break for it. Holding onto Voncha again we went soaring through the woods at such amazing speeds, I was curious just how fast we were going. I wasn't sure exactly where we would be going but I was sure we couldn't stay at any more hotels since they would be looking for me at them. Voncha had decided to take me to his old cabin that we used to camp at and that he would share with Jasper when they were in there. We had shot through two states just to get there and as we did; I could feel the air getting colder wishing I had a jacket on. Finally, at the step of the cabin Voncha set me down as I caught my breath. The cabin hadn't been lived in for a while, so the front porch was completely covered in leaves and moss. Opening the door Voncha went in first to look around making sure it was safe. No one had been in here.

There was a little kitchen that opened to the living room, a bathroom, and a bedroom downstairs. Looking up you could see a little of the loft upstairs, that's where Jasper had his bedroom. Usually, if he wasn't here, I would stay in his room but then even if he was here, I still had his room while he slept on the couch.

Taking my bag with me I climbed the pine stairs until I caught the first glimpse of his room. Nothing had changed since the last time we were here. All three of us had gone camping after I graduated from high school. Father couldn't join us; he had legal matters to deal with. At least it was his excuse at the time. All of Jasper's things were neatly in place with a few pictures of the two of us on his dresser; I knew if I were to look in Voncha's room he had a few pictures of me also just different from these. The ones Jasper had been of me on my first day, I had refused to go until he had convinced me I was going to be safe, and he would stick around for a while until I was comfortable. The second one was where I was playing with my new dog, he bought me, and my arm was in a cast. The dog was a distraction from all the itching. I had climbed a tree and lost my balance falling and breaking my arm for the first time. Even to this day he never forgave himself for not catching me in time. The third picture was my prom picture. I had been asked by a few at school, but I was never interested in taking any of them to prom so instead, I had taken both Voncha and Jasper. They had acted as chaperones however it gave me someone to talk to and both danced with me.

Looking around the upstairs Jasper had it decorated with his oil paintings of different places he had traveled to. Some of them were just amazing, especially the arctic pictures. Jasper and Voncha had been best friends since they were little, living next door to each other, spending holidays with each other's families; they all had been rather close. Then after high school, they had bought the cabin together as a summer place but then eventually it just became a place to crash if they were in the area. All I knew growing up had been the fact their jobs made it possible for them to travel. I never did think once about why a mortician would travel or what other kinds of jobs they did. I just accepted things as they were told to me, I had no reason not to. What I hadn't known until recently about the cabin, this was where they were changed by my father. Opening the closet, I could see his clothes still hanging, he always wore the same style, one that always seemed to come back into style, nothing outrageous but very simple, tailored, and timeless for a man. Voncha's room rarely changed since he never cared to decorate it other than to put up a few baseball bats that he had signed and a few caps on his dresser that were also personally signed. His room was rather plain to look at but it was what he wanted and was happy with it.

Sitting down on the bed I heard the front door close; I knew as soon as we were here Voncha was going to check again on the note we had left. I had hoped to find Jasper still alive and hopefully safe until we were able to find out where he was hidden. All we knew was that he was being held at the lake house and the ritual was going to be conducted there in about two weeks which didn't give us very much time. No one other than my father, Voncha, and Jasper knew about this cabin so for now I would be safe waiting here for Voncha to get back.

They were to give us proof that he was alive, or I would destroy the blood vials. The first time they had given us an ultimatum without proof if Jasper was alive or not, they simply stated they would kill him if we didn't hand over the blood. We let them know if he was dead there was no point in us trying to bargain with them, knowing we had the only blood from my mother and me then we had the advantage, this time Voncha was checking to see if they could furnish proof this time. Even if they proved he was alive, and I had hoped he still had been. I wasn't sure what we would do. I felt so ill at the idea of him dying because of them.

The cabin was so quiet standing in the living room all alone I had kept expecting Jasper to come walking through the front door chatting loudly to Voncha; unfortunately, I knew that wasn't going to happen. Just to keep busy I was desperate enough to occupy myself that I cleaned all the clothes in Voncha's basket. The last time we had been here, neither had cleaned their clothes. At least the dishes had been done. Neither were chores I cared for, only when I had to.

It felt like an eternity before Voncha had finally returned. I was beginning to wonder if they had caught him also. I couldn't help but get that sick feeling in the pit of my stomach. Every second that ticked by. I kept worrying and then I started to pace. At this point, I was listening for any sound that would give me an idea Voncha was nearby. I could hear the clock ticking but not as loudly as my heart was.

As I looked out the window I picked up a scent. This was something I was able to do since I was very little. None of my friends were like this, neither were my coworkers or any of my father's other friends. It was just Voncha and Jasper. I had asked my father about this several times before I finally gave up. He was always nervous or avoiding my question, not even Voncha or Jasper would answer me but then they made it clear it was because they hadn't known. Jasper and I had tested this out once; I knew when he was about ten miles from me. Jasper was able to pick up on me as well, not because of his unusual tracking ability but because of my unusual scent, he had said once I smelled like lily of the valley or honeysuckle. Voncha always had the lightest garlic smell, funny now that I think about it and how movies associate garlic as a vampire repellant and yet this is what he's always smelled like. Jasper on the other hand always reminded me of pine and a musty mix. No matter how hard they would try to sneak up on me during Halloween or any other time. I could always tell they were coming, and it was the same for them.

"What? You're not going to look to make sure who it is or maybe hide until you know it's safe? I would be worried about leaving you alone for too long." I knew he was joking but normally anything else I would have been more careful.

"I knew it was you, did they do what we had asked?" Turning to face Voncha I could see the concerned look on his face.

Now I was worried that maybe Jasper was already dead. I could feel myself stop breathing for a moment.

"He's still alive just not in the best condition. I don't think it's a good idea that you see how he looks." Voncha had kept his hands in his pocket looking down at the floor avoiding eye contact with me.

"I need to know if we have time or not. We know they will kill him in two weeks regardless of whether we hand over the vials or not, will he make it until then? We still need to find out what happened to my father and his group." I felt so sick to my stomach worrying about what was happening to everyone that I didn't want to risk sending Voncha out on his own anymore in case he was to get caught also.

Voncha hadn't made a move to take the picture out from his pocket. Reaching in he never stopped me but from the first glance I had looked at the picture of Jasper, I knew they were serious about killing him, they were not playing around. I felt so dizzy I could barely stand. There was no way we could wait a week let alone two, there was no way Jasper would ever make it that long. I just wish I knew what their final plans were. Either way, we couldn't stay in the cabin waiting around for my father to show up, especially if anything had happened to him. We had to find the lake house and the only lake near here was a few miles away. That was the last place we had heard father, and his group were checking out before they disappeared. It hadn't seemed to matter what plan we came up with, it always seemed like I was offering myself up as bait or at least trying to figure out how to lure them out using me.

I knew my father would never like the idea and Jasper would be extremely upset if I had put myself in danger, even Voncha kept trying to come up with a way around it not wanting to risk my life. If any of the three had been in the same position as me, I knew for a fact they would risk their lives for me without question and I was willing to do the same for them.

Not that I could sleep, I slept off and on during the day while we waited for the sun to set again. Early evening when it was safer for Voncha we set out again searching for Jasper and hopefully find my father. We went to where they were last searching. There were only three homes directly around the lake. Two of them were rather large while one was small. From what we assumed they were only summer homes since most had been empty or unlived in. There wasn't anything around the outside to give a hint that my father was nearby and certainly no scent of Jasper.

Searching through the woods had even been more difficult to find any clues; it was easy to get lost in the woods let alone trying to find tracks. Heading into town being careful in case there was anyone who might be looking for us, we made our way into the bar ordering a few light snacks before we had planned on moving out again. The lake house could be anywhere. Then we had found our first clue, or rather we heard our first clue.

A group of kids that were at a table nearby were talking about how their favorite hangout place was going to be closed for a few weeks, that this bar was going to be fuller than it normally was. Even the waitresses had commented on how much busier they had been, not just with people visiting from the convention nearby, but also the fact the very popular teen hang-out was closed for supposed repairs. That's when we heard the part that made my heart skip a beat. They mentioned the lake house. Watching to see if anyone else was paying attention to them or might notice who we were, Voncha and I made our way over to the table full of teenagers.

"Sorry for interrupting, I was being rude and listening to your conversation; do you know where the lake house is?" The kid I had asked laughed.

"Are you serious? The lake house is the place to be. They have everything from Ouija board parties, live bands, and private parties. It's the place to hang out. They even have two nights out of the month that are adult nights only where no one underage gets to go, I hear it's a lot of drinking." The kid was rather animated as he described the décor and how pissed he was that they might be changing it.

It had looked like a dungeon with chains on the walls with gray rubber floors. A real unusual gothic style warehouse inside while it simply looked more like a huge old-fashioned cabin on the outside. Also, the simple fact the house wasn't anywhere near a lake was the main reason we were missing it. Getting directions from the group, we left right away not wanting to waste any more time. Not sure what we were going to do when we found it, we wanted to make sure it was the right place this time. We were only an hour away and there was a very strong scent that neither of us was used to, something we couldn't figure out what it was until we had found the lake house. The strange scent must be something they were doing inside.

Not getting too close we went around the place checking it out. While we were watching I had for a second looked down at the ground to see a piece shining back at me. Out of curiosity, I reached down to pick it up, it was a piece of glass, very small but then moving the rest of the leaves where it had laid there was more glass with my father's watch. They were here. We watched as a few people had come and gone with boxes. We didn't want to stay in this area too long or they might discover us like they had the others. Father was an expert on sneaking up on people or just plain staying hidden, I wanted to know what gave him away. Then we saw it. Two people had been guarding the outside of our hotel that was also in the little shack when we had met up with my father. Someone no doubt, he thought he could trust in the group betrayed him.

That's when my new idea hit me. Leaving we had gone back to town where I had purchased scissors and hair coloring dye. Heading back to the cabin Voncha had looked at me rather strangely but hoped I knew what I was doing. My long blonde hair that used to be down to my waist was now cut short to my shoulders and no longer blond but almost a blackened red. The color alone had made my face look a little different. Then the finishing touches. I had colored contacts that I had never worn yet. A few years back I had joked with Jasper saying I wanted to have red eyes, as a surprise he had bought different temporary contacts so that I could change my color, almost every color you could think of was available. Opening the chest in Jasper's room I put them in place. My eyes were always a light frost blue almost the same shade as a husky. Now they were a simple dark chocolate brown. Even though I had the same scent, Voncha admitted if he hadn't known it was me, he would have assumed I was someone else. Changing my clothes for dark black ones I had used plenty of mascara, black eyeliner, and lipstick, the inner ring of my lips I had used the smallest touch of red. I wanted to look like a gothic punk chic. So far, I was pulling it off. Now I just had to convince others to believe it. Heading back to the same bar, Voncha had waited at the counter in case anyone was to recognize us together but then he wanted to stay close in case he had to get me out quickly. Looking around I saw exactly who I had wanted to get information from. I was hoping to catch their attention without it sounding like I had invited myself. Choosing a table right next to them however not paying any attention to them I sat down. Ordering a drink, I started up a conversation with the waitress catching the guy's attention.

"I've been bored out of my mind since I've moved here, are there any exciting places to go other than these preppy wanna-be's? Any known events or anything at all interesting?" Taking the straw out of the glass I took a drink directly from the glass, not that I thought it would make me look hardcore but there was lipstick on the straw, and it wasn't mine.

"Usually, people who move here for excitement don't stay long, what interested you in moving here in the first place? It's a small quiet town, not much goes on here, we are more of a family bar and then you have the teen hang out at the lake house." The woman seemed rather curious but then so did the guys.

"My parents moved here, not much of a choice but in about a month I'll be eighteen so I can leave. Most of my time I study the supernatural, I'm a natural witch practitioner, just hoping to find some others like me here. I guess that's not going to happen, is it? Thanks for the info though." Going back to drinking my glass I still felt grossed out knowing there was a used straw in it and the pop tasted flat, some family bar.

Trying not to get excited or show any signs that I knew they were watching me, I sat my glass down leaning back in my chair letting out a heavy sigh. Voncha didn't need to tell me how worried he was, I could feel it. He was getting even more nervous and worried now that they had been paying attention to me. They might not know who I was, but he still didn't want to risk me being around them since there was no reason for them to keep me alive.

"You're a witch? Any kind of special powers you can show us or is it all verbal." The one facing me from the table half-joked but also seemed serious.

"I'm not wasting my time on those who do not believe, I don't have to prove anything." I had kept my voice calm and almost monotone.

Getting up from his table one of the young men had moved to sit with me at my table now, sitting back relaxed looking me over for a moment before asking any questions.

"What makes you so special?" Sounding snide but with a slight smile.

"Never said I was." I kept it short and to the point.

"Not a bad thing, you don't give too much information, I'm guessing you're more of a private person?" Now he was finally starting to ask questions that they might be interested in.

"For the most part, what I do is my business unless there's a reason for sharing it." Nodding his head in agreement I could see he was formulating his next question.

"What kind of witchy things do you do? That is if it's not too personal." With his hand on his chin, he was still testing to see how I would answer.

"I've belonged to occults, paranormal hunters and several different forms of Wiccan groups; if you're familiar with those then I shouldn't have to explain more than that." At least this way I might even find out if they were an occult group or not.

"You do realize that witches are not exclusive to occults, that they have little to do with each other?" There was a glint of light that flashed over his eyes for a second.

"It's good that you know that, now I won't have to give you a history lesson." Smiling coyly and sounded as sarcastic as I possibly could.

"Our group isn't for the faint of heart, sometimes to get the best results you have to get your hands a little dirty." As he had said this, I took a look at my hands.

"I doubt I could get any dirtier than I already am." As soon as I had said this he glanced over at his group, nodding in agreement, he faced me again.

"We happen to be a secret society, but we are careful who we admit in. You have to be able to contribute something to the group." Now at least it sounded like I might be getting an offer to join.

"The real reason we moved here had been to get away from the rumors. The group I was in was a group of girls like me. We were doing a ritual and I had written the spells we cast. We had an accident when one of our members hadn't listened and she died. It was ruled an accident, but no one believed it or forgave us. My parents couldn't handle it anymore, so they moved us. Why conjure angels when you can call forth demons that are much more powerful?" Not looking as though I was excited by what I had just said or given too much reaction.

Almost as if it was an everyday occurrence, I had poked at my black nail polish peeling it a little. I could feel Voncha cringing from my words.

I was thankful I had a scab that hadn't fully healed. I originally scratched my hand on the ground when I was knocked over by my dogs. Looking down at it now, I slowly peeled it from my skin watching the small drop of blood rolling down my skin. Smudging it with my other finger I placed my finger in my mouth licking it off. Returning my attention to him as if I had done something minor as brush a strand of hair away from my eyes, I could feel Voncha's reaction. I was just thankful I hadn't seen his face, or I would have reacted, hiding my emotions it had hurt, the skin was almost fully healed.

"She might be exactly what we need. Can you meet us here again tomorrow?" The tone of his voice had changed to a serious deeper tone.

"Sure, I have nothing better to do, at least not yet." Agreeing to be here at the same time I had watched as the group left.

Not bothering to finish the drink since I was sure she handed me a dirty glass, they had been staring at me from the moment I had first walked in the door. From the way everyone around me had looked, I definitely stuck out. Paying my bill, I stood up leaving, not with Voncha but on my own. Voncha had kept a safe distance behind me to keep it from appearing that we were together. I had only walked far enough to head towards the cabin before Voncha finally swooped in and picked me up carrying me the rest of the way. I was thankful not to walk the entire way there. Stopping inside the cabin Voncha made a double check to make sure no one was following even though he had already been doing that when he took off with me so quickly.

"I don't normally tell you what you can and cannot do but you better tell me the rest of your plan, I thought you were just trying to get information from them, not join them. If they asked you to torture Jasper or your father to prove your loyalty to them, would you be able to?" Standing extremely close to me I knew I had gone past his comfort zone.

"We have to do something and if they don't know who I am. I can at least get in there and find a way of getting them out, at least how to save them. So far this is the only opportunity we have. You're not that far behind, I would have disguised you, but the story was easier with just me, besides, you would have been too protective, and I had to give them the attitude that I just didn't care. I don't know why but I just can't be mean around you, and I hadn't planned any further." I hadn't thought about the fact they might want me to hurt Jasper or my dad.

Now I wasn't sure what I would do.

"You should have had me try to join them, I could harm anyone and walk away from it without anyone knowing my connection, and you can't afford to do that." I knew Voncha was worried, but I didn't want him hurting anyone any more than he wanted that from me.

"Could you harm me?" I was curious if it had come to it or if it were a last resort if he could do it since there was still a part of my plan I hadn't shared.

Harm yes, kill, no." A shiver went through him that he couldn't hide.

I knew the thought repulsed him.

"Voncha, I need you to trust me, especially if things seem strange or contrary to myself. I know some horrible things could happen; I realize I could even die but there's no other choice. I'm not going to wait for you to disappear also. I just really need you to trust me." Covering his face with his hands he had let out a frustrated muffled scream.

"I do trust you; I'm just scared I won't be able to stop or protect you." Wrapping my arms around Voncha, he put his arms around me just as quickly and securely.

Leaning my head against his chest I felt safe. He was right, if anything did go wrong, he wouldn't be able to rescue me but right now this was our only chance of saving the others, we couldn't keep waiting.

"I would much rather risk my life than yours, if I die there's no loss, I already know I don't get to have you." Rubbing his cheek on the side of mine as I looked back, I could see a tear forming in his eyes.

91

Placing his hand underneath my chin tipping my face upward looking at him, Voncha leaned down giving me a gentle but lingering kiss on the lips, feeling his lips slowly slide away from mine as he now stepped away. I just stood there frozen; I had no idea what to say if he had stayed. I was already surprised to find Jasper shared the same feelings with me, but I never saw it coming from Voncha. Did they know about each other? Did he know Jasper was interested and that's why he said he didn't get to have me? I felt so confused; I wasn't ready for any of this. I wasn't sure what to say and before I could he was already out the door and out of sight. I didn't know if he would be coming back or not, I hoped he would. All I could do for now was to get ready for tomorrow.

I knew it wouldn't take long to put out the makeup I needed along with the outfit. Placing my contacts into their case next to them I walked through Voncha's room. The pictures he had of me had been put away in his drawers. Walking out I climbed the stairs up to Jasper's loft, dropping my clothes along the way, not caring where they were. Getting into the steaming hot shower felt so good right now. With all the water, I couldn't tell what water was from the shower and which had been my tears. Sitting down on the floor of the shower I kept thinking over and over, what I was doing was the right thing, just a very difficult leap of faith. I just hoped when I hit the ground it wasn't going to hurt as much as I expected it to. My showers were now becoming my place of sanctuary, where I went to feel better. I had the hot water on full blast, this time I wanted something to numb my pain and something to occupy me.

Finally, feeling tired I stood up, turned the water off, grabbed my towel, dried off, and putting my robe on I made my way down the stairs. I knew Voncha hadn't come back since I hadn't sensed him. Grabbing one of his shirts out of his closet. I laid down in his bed holding onto the shirt when I had finally fallen asleep. The next several hours had passed by so quickly I panicked thinking I might have overslept. Jumping up quickly, it scared me when I noticed I wasn't in the room alone, how could I have slept that soundly? I've never been in that deep of sleep before not to notice when someone had come in the room. All I could guess had been the fact I was tired or depressed this time. Looking back at me with a smile since he had finally managed to surprise me. Voncha stood up from the chair he had been sitting in watching me sleep with his shirt.

"I thought you weren't coming back from the way you left." I could barely whisper it; I was still surprised to see Voncha back.

"I would never leave you, no matter what happens I'll still do anything for you." Walking over to the edge of the bed Voncha set down my clothes that had been on Jasper's bed along with the makeup and contacts, and then closed the door to give me privacy.

Changing quickly and placing the contacts in my eyes. I never did like touching my eyes or having anything else go near them, I needed to do this, or I would still be slightly recognizable with my natural eye color. Even if Voncha couldn't do anything for me it still felt better knowing he was here and safe. Walking out of his room still holding onto his shirt I walked directly over to him.

"Don't ever scare me like that again, you could have been grabbed last night and I wouldn't have known. Jasper may have feelings for me but that doesn't mean I care any less for you or my father." Grabbing Voncha I hugged him quickly then went into the kitchen grabbing a snack to eat before I started spewing random words confusing both of us.

I was confused over the fact my boss wants to either kill or control me, the fact my family were vampires and there's another group who wants me for who knows what reason but supposedly they don't want to harm me but would kill my family. Jasper kissed me so passionately; I admit I kissed back and felt overwhelmed with feelings I wasn't sure about. Then Voncha drops the bomb that he feels he knows he can't have me? Was there a decision made I wasn't aware of? Trying to save my dad and Jasper, I haven't had time to think about anything personal other than to panic.

Voncha didn't try to push it since he figured out, I was occupying myself before we were to leave, the last thing either of us wanted me to do was to have a nervous breakdown. We still had a few hours before I had to be there. Trying to pass the time we had chosen to watch a movie, not that we hadn't seen it many times before, I just couldn't think of anything else to distract me. We had watched my favorite Television show, Dr. Who. Voncha was already sitting on the couch. Getting close and laying against him I tried to immerse myself in the television show to temporarily forget about life for a moment. I was thankful to have Voncha's arms wrapped around me. Not bothering to discuss tonight, Voncha had planned on staying outside the bar keeping an eye on who showed up, who spoke with me, and following as much as he could. Then as I had asked him, whatever happened or wherever we wound up going, I needed him to trust me.

BLENDING IN

I didn't have to enter the bar this time; the group of guys I had come here to see were still standing outside. Walking up to them relaxed as I possibly could, I had seen Morris in the group. Only a moment of panic hit me when my heartbeat faster, I just had to be careful, if Voncha picked up too much of my panic he might not let me go through with it and whisk me away. I just hoped Morris wouldn't recognize me or that they had not already figured out who I was.

"This is the girl we were telling you about." Looking me over Morris gave me a strange look except dismissed it just as quickly.

I kept as relaxed as I could to not give in to any reactions or emotions. Something I had learned to do when my father was trying to get information out of me, or he had lost his temper, and I chose not to let him know he got to me.

"We have to give her a trial first; we need to know we can trust her and that she is capable of doing something we as a group can benefit from." As soon as Morris said that I had an image of Jasper being someone I had to harm to prove, maybe Voncha was going to be right?

"Like what?" Trying to act nonchalantly, I was hoping it wouldn't be as bad as I had thought it would be.

"Come with us." Following them to a parked van on the side street we all climbed in.

I hadn't been in a vehicle for quite a while since Voncha had been providing our transportation, now it suddenly felt like we were creeping along.

Sitting in the back seat no one had talked as the driver took us quite a distance, nowhere near the lake house thankfully, at least I hoped to rule out harming anyone that I knew. We had traveled in the opposite direction for about a half-hour just past the cabin. There was an open field with a bonfire going; the blaze could be seen from a distance with a group already standing around the fire in robes with their faces covered with mini masks. Parking near the side we all exited the car now walking over to the group.

"Group, we might have a new member depending on if she can help us out or not. Please welcome Joelle." It was a good thing he had remembered my name since I couldn't remember which name I had made up when I first introduced myself.

Observing everyone as I walked closer to the group, they seemed to be forming a circle around the huge pile of wood. None had seemed interested in me other than two of the young boys and one girl. The look on her face was almost as if she had seen a long-lost friend.

With the sound of sarcasm, Morris asked, "I was told that you write spells. I would like to see one demonstrated, are there any special, instruments that you need before you perform your spell?"

Even if they expected me to perform a miracle, I needed to know what type of effect they were hoping to achieve.

"Even a seasoned witch needs to know what you expect from them, I won't know what tools I need until you let me know what ritual or what exactly I'm doing. I tailor my spells to the situation." I just hope I wasn't getting the ritual we were trying to avoid.

"Spoken like someone who does know what they are doing, we want you to perform a fire spell, something to either influence or happen to the fire, the choice is yours." Being given free reign would help a little I just had to hide how I was getting it to happen.

Nodding my head in understanding. I tried to think of a few easy eye deceiving tricks that I used to do for school friends when I was little. I could tell Voncha wasn't very far watching me. As soon as I was ready, I asked for a piece of paper and something to write with, to my surprise they had a quill with a bottle to dip it in. The red substance was so thick I had guessed it was blood. It was an odd odor but not Jasper's. He had bled once when I was little, and his scent had become so strong I choked on the odor. So thankfully it wasn't his blood I was about to write with. All I could guess is that it might have been dove or deer blood. Writing down a spell I had always believed that the ones unspoken were much stronger than those that had been spoken for others to hear, usually, the ones I did say out loud were ones more for myself to hear to keep me from being distracted from those around me.

The only sound I had planned on making was a humming sound. As soon as I had written a basic spell of safety, not that I ever felt a spell would keep me safe when I intentionally put myself in harm's way. I had hoped this would be enough to please Morris to let me into the group.

This would be the deceiving part. There was a bush nearby; taking a long stalk from it I started to strip it into a very tiny looking nest. Writing down my spell I had wrapped the nest over the paper to make it look as if I had a reason for the nest. Truthfully there wasn't any reason for the nest other than to hide the match I pulled out of my pocket hoping no one had seen. Wrapping the items tight, I tried to strike the match against my hand leaving a red line. It lit, however, from a distance no one saw the flame until it hit the woodpile. The thin strips I had stripped off the vine to make kindling was now burning fully slowly catching the logs on the fire.

Morris handed me another piece of paper only this time it had writing on it already. The words were written in Latin. I had placed a large amount of dirt on the paper. Several people from the group were looking at me strangely almost as if they thought I was a joke, even a few had scoffed at me while waiting but Morris had just stood there waiting to see what the outcome would be. I don't think Voncha had thought for one second, I would be accepted into the group. Except he had never seen me practice spells before. I was always curious about the supernatural and even studied it for a while. Casting spells I knew I could do except most came naturally because of the gifts I had inherited.

Letting the dirt slide into the fire or at least as close to it as I could get without being burned, I then let the paper float in the air as it caught fire, while it did, I had the strange urge to say this, "show me what I need to know." I was ready for any consequences that came along with it, I had a feeling there was something else happening here.

Not just using my plan, I had let the natural smoke from the fire form itself. I had helped a little with the wind being careful so that it would appear that all of it was coming from the natural effects of the spell or rather mother nature. Amid the smoke I could see a face forming, the most I could do had been to make forms of animals or mountains and trees, nothing this detailed. I knew I was risking a lot, but I wanted to know if there was a chance that immediate danger would prevent me from saving anyone. Impressed Morris had been watching as the face appeared in the smoke. Not showing any emotions I had looked over at Morris.

"Who is this? Why would my spell be bringing this person up that I don't know? Is he part of your group?" I already knew it was Jasper, but I had to pretend that I didn't.

I knew I was aware of Voncha being close by, but I felt his reaction, he was stunned I was able to perform this trick and the fact I had just done it in front of Morris.

"He happens to be a very important part of all of this; do you speak and read Latin by any chance? How do you feel about the death of one to save that of thousands?" Displaying no emotion himself I knew I couldn't risk taking too long to answer or no matter what I said wouldn't be believed.

"Yes, I speak and read Latin, French, and Spanish. As for death, it's bound to happen, and some are just simply meant to die." I felt so sick saying this, but I had to tell them what I knew they wanted to hear.

I had to convince them or none of this was ever going to work. I didn't want to keep hiding especially if it meant it would cost my loved ones.

"Welcome to your new family." Morris turned and walked away leaving me with the others who were now impressed by what they had seen.

"Do you have a place to stay? That is after you tell your parents you're moving out?" One of the girls seemed rather excited to be asking me, the same girl who happened to be staring at me earlier.

"I wasn't getting along with them, so I moved out this morning, I don't have anything other than myself and what's on me, so I guess I'm ready." Keeping my voice calm and unconcerned sounding.

I didn't want her or the others to think I needed to go somewhere to collect my things and I certainly didn't want to fake parents if they had wanted to meet them. I didn't want to risk heading back to the cabin, I had a feeling Morris would be watching me now.

"Then you get to be my roomie, I'm the only other girl in the group. It's nice to finally have another one in our group." Hugging me, I guessed under other circumstances I probably would have liked this girl or even been her friend but right now I still have to be careful.

"Where did you learn to do that? I've tried writing my spells and I can't seem to get anything from it?" A young man was now standing beside me; he wasn't there a second ago.

"Lots of practice, I meditate quite a lot and have been writing spells as long as I can remember. The best thing to do is to relax, clear your mind, meditate, and don't rush it. It's not exactly something you can rush; it just takes time to feel natural with it." Looking frustrated I wondered if I had said something wrong?

"Everyone is always telling me to meditate; I've never been able to just sit there, I get distracted or fall asleep far too easily." Looking over his shoulder he had walked over to one of the guys who had called him.

Without warning several of the guys had shot off in a flash and for that moment I couldn't possibly hide the shock let alone the surprise I could feel from Voncha. The strange connection I had with him was so strong right now. I was just hoping no one else would pick up on it. Why would they need Jasper if they already had vampires? I was surprised they didn't have one of their own be changed by a vampire, that way they would have all the vampire blood they needed. Unless Morris preferred the temporary solution to keep control over who had power?

The girl who had been with me vanished in no time leaving me to stand there almost alone, only one of the guys had stayed behind with me. The young man who I had spoken with at the bar had stayed behind, smiling no doubt loving the expression on my face after seeing everyone take off so fast. If everyone was being injected with vampire blood, I just hoped they didn't plan the same for me?

"It takes a while to get used to that, I'm sure you've heard of vampires existing; now you get to live amongst us. Climb on my back and I'll help you catch up to the others, if you choose to, we can help you with the change, it hurts like hell at first, but it does go away." Standing in front of me I remembered how I reacted with Jasper when I first found out that he was a vampire. Putting my arms around his neck loosely as though I wasn't sure what I was doing, at least I convinced him I was new at this. Making me hold on much tighter and hinting to wrap my legs around his waist. I acted uncomfortable, not that I had to act much.

"Trust me you couldn't possibly choke me, hold on as tight as you can, and don't let go. Wrap your legs around my waist for more control. It won't affect the way I run or speed." He seemed like another person I would have liked if it hadn't been under these circumstances.

I wondered if most of these people had any idea what they were getting themselves into? We were going at extremely fast speeds but nowhere near as fast as Voncha or Jasper had gone, also not as coordinated since I had felt a few trees or bushes scrape against my skin. I was thankful I was wearing thick jeans now. When we were finally there, my legs and arms were sore from holding on while hitting things along the way. Finally settling down we were outside the lake house. I felt my heart skip a beat as I followed behind him in the doorway. Leah had been waiting for us at the bottom of the steps. Standing up she had smiled so much her face could have cracked.

"I should have stayed behind to see what your reaction was, it was a shocker for me also, the first ride is the most nerve-wracking, but you get used to it." Leah was still rather excited to have a roommate.

"They haven't made you a vampire yet?" I was curious if it was by choice.

"Eventually I will but I have to wait until after a special ceremony. I'll fill you in later once I help you settle in." Not answering my question, she had taken me by the hand leading me up the steps to the room we would be sharing.

"Does everyone live here?" There were a lot of doors down below and upstairs, if they were full this might be more difficult than I thought it would be.

"It helps not getting distracted by outside influences, plus we can be available for Morris when he needs us. Also not worrying about bills or other costs we can work on skills or anything that can better help the cause." Smiling at me Leah insisted on moving quickly.

The main room was rather large, enough for a huge party. There was one door leading off to the right and another leading to the left. One of the young men had gone through the one on the right revealing a long hallway with several doors on either side. If this had been under any other circumstances, I would have fallen in love with the large wood staircase leading up, it looked as if it belonged inside a palace. Up at the top of the steps, there had been two mini balconies to look over to the floor below. Still holding tightly onto my hand, I had noticed how warm her skin was compared to Voncha and Jasper let alone Chris who just brought me here. At the end of the steps, there was a very long hallway but then at the far end it split going in two directions, there were certainly enough rooms off the main hallway.

There were fewer doors the further we had gone; I could only guess the rooms themselves were larger. She had taken me to the furthest room on the left which hadn't been a normal door, it was slanted. The walls were painted black with fake stars fixed to the ceiling it had almost looked like the actual nighttime sky. Barely noticeable, there were larger swirls on the walls. Stepping back looking at them they had swirled into each other making up one large horse as if it was running.

"We can decorate our rooms anyway we want; I just like the nighttime sky and horses. It's so relaxing so I had my room painted to look like nighttime. Since you don't have any clothes, you can wear mine, I won't be fitting most of them for quite a while." When she said that, I hadn't noticed until now that she was pregnant, how could I have missed this?

So much for Voncha thinking I was incredibly observant. Now I understood why they hadn't made her a vampire.

There had already been three beds in the room; all three were made up except only one had personal belongings around it. Leah had sat down on her bed rubbing her belly. I didn't want to be rude except I couldn't help but stare at her belly. This had been the first time I saw her face to face without her holding onto something or standing behind something else.

"How far along are you?" Looking at her belly she looked like she could pop at any moment.

"I'm already nine months so I should give birth any time even though in two days if I haven't given birth naturally, I'm going to have a planned cesarean. I'm not looking forward to giving birth, but it is for the greater cause." Now I was really worried about what they were planning on doing.

"Everyone keeps talking about his greater cause, but no one has told me what it is?" I hoped since she was so talkative now, she might fill me in on what was happening around here.

"The greater cause is so complex it's hard to explain." This was the first time Leah had stopped smiling.

"We have time so just do your best. I just want to understand it, so I don't look like an idiot if Morris asks me to do something." I hoped this explanation would be good enough for her.

"There are vampires killing people and eventually they want to make everyone a vampire. They are killing innocent people. Morris says that people become corrupted if they have too much power. It's why none of us are fully-fledged vampires, it's to control the desire it creates, and we won't want to harm anyone." Smiling again she felt she had explained it well.

"That doesn't explain why you're pregnant for this? What does he want the baby for?" This is when I noticed her reaction changed.

She looked sad for a second and then tried smiling again to cover how she felt.

"Morris believes the baby will be easier to adjust to the change and being raised by him, he can control the rage that comes from the vampire blood by using this miracle Shade's blood to create a peaceful reaction. Her blood isn't infected like mine is. I can't heal myself or others anymore and I can't get pregnant." Leah seemed oblivious to what she was saying.

"You're pregnant now; it takes a long time for a baby to grow up. He wants to wait that long when he could use an adult and do the same thing?" I tried my best not to be sarcastic.

"I'm only pregnant because of what Morris did. He used the blood of a late Shade who died; it gave life to my ovaries, at least temporarily. She wasn't tainted by the infection, and neither was her daughter. They can heal but only to a certain degree. They can't heal disease or death; they can heal broken bones or minor things like that." She still hadn't answered my question.

"Again, why does he want your baby?" I was hoping she knew and wasn't avoiding the question because she didn't.

"He wanted to see if he could get ones who were infected just in case the tainted blood wasn't curable. The Golden Order is one of the last two Shade groups and would help out if they can be cured, or at least helped from going out of extinction." If this was it then it wasn't difficult to explain?

"Why would anyone need to die for the cause? None of this sounds like anyone needs to?" I wanted to find out what they were doing with the vampires, was Morris trying to kill them off?

"Attacking vampires isn't easy, sometimes some die from it or they get infected and turn evil from it and they have to die. Morris said we can't allow those to roam the earth, or they will start killing others also. Morris has them captured and brought to a secure place to find out where there are others. He's preserving the earth. Vampires have been lying about being immortal, all they do is doom others to a horrible painful dangerous life." Reaching over to take a snack from her side table she munched as she watched my reaction.

"Have you ever known any vampires before coming here?" I couldn't help but feel stunned.

"No, I was fortunate, I didn't learn about them until Morris had told me how dangerous the world was with them, that he was trying to save mankind. He's such a brave man." I couldn't get over how naïve she was.

Sad thing there were many more that were following Morris for the same reason. I may have learned about my family being vampires recently but even I understood that Morris was just crazy. At least now I understood why the Rising dawn was looking for me, if it had meant their extinction then I understood their searching for me. For now, I had to be careful because I was sure Leah hadn't been told everything that was going on either, there had to be more than what she knew, and whatever it was made me nervous because it could only get worse. I knew if I explained to her what vampires were like then she might tell Morris and he would no doubt find out who I am. I needed to gain her trust not just in myself but with vampires. I wasn't sure how I was going to show the others the truth unless there was a way of showing Morris had lied to them?

"Come here and feel my stomach, the baby is kicking right now, it must like the sound of your voice." Standing up and walking over to her I didn't want to upset her while she was still excited or tell her that I thought the baby might be excited over me because it's hoping I'll save its life.

She was right about the baby being active. It made sense why they were scheduling it ahead of time since it still had so much space to move around, I doubted it would be born naturally on the time limit they set. She hadn't had any Braxton hicks or any signs that she might be ready. Also, I doubted she could be as far along as she thought, from the time she had explained, it would seem she was more along seven months than nine months. I think they were keeping her blind to everything because they had no intentions of keeping Leah alive once they took the baby. They might have thought they were doing something great for others, but I highly doubted that was the same plan Morris had. At least I was right, there was a lot more to this than just collecting blood from us. I couldn't get over just how mind-controlled everyone was.

"There's a bonfire tonight, you'll hear the whole story, and it will help you understand what everyone is doing and just how important all of this is. Except, for now, you'll have to excuse me, this baby is determined to press on my bladder." Getting up from her bed she walked into the private bathroom that we shared.

I knew Voncha was still nearby; at least he was still close enough that through the house I could still sense him. I might have been closer to Jasper but somehow, I could always sense Voncha being around, I wasn't sure how it was just that matter of fact knowing he was there. With Jasper, it was his scent. Hopefully, after all of this, I'll find out more about Shades and just what I'm capable of. It would help speaking or to learn from another person like myself.

Sometimes I wondered if I had inherited any traits from my father. He's always said I took after my mother a hundred percent but then I never did have a chance to get to know her. This must be killing Voncha not knowing what was going on in the house or wondering if they had figured out who I was. Startled for a second by the knock on the door I jumped up heading across the room to see who it was. Opening the door, Zack was smiling down at me, he had to be the tallest person I've met so far.

"Let Leah know breakfast is ready. Our day is slightly flipped around; we are more active at night rather than in the morning. So, breakfast here is at twenty-three hundred, lunch is at six hundred and dinner is at eleven hundred. Leah can show you once she gets out of the restroom, get used to it she's in there a lot." Laughing to himself he started walking down the hallway.

Leah had come out of the bathroom just in time to see him leave. From the look on her face, I doubted I had to tell her why he was here. Thankfully I was already on a night schedule otherwise I would have been incredibly tired.

"Thank goodness it's breakfast, I'm starving, never thought I would be this hungry just because I was pregnant. We go by military time. I'll make a list for you in case you're not familiar with it. I took a month to memorize it." Smiling she grabbed her cardigan from the back of her chair slipping it over her shoulders.

"Have you been taking any vitamins since you've been pregnant? I haven't known you for very long, but you seem very tired, a little more than normal." I was feeling worried about her and what was going to happen to her once this was done.

"I'm fine, the house doctor had told me I'm perfectly fine without them, I get all the nutrients I need from my meals, besides the baby doesn't need the extra vitamins, anything wrong with it the ritual will cure." Smiling and completely oblivious to the truth she made her way out of the room.

The baby might be fine except it's going to suck her dry of nutrients. I felt such a sickening feeling wave over me. Heading back down the stairs we went to the left. There were a few others in front of us heading the same way. The room had opened into one gigantic room where they could hold live concerts and other private events. The signs were still up listing the last group who had performed here. The decorations were exactly as they were described, not something I would have imagined after coming in from such a neutral room before. There were chains, black and red strobe lights, and several other dark color decorations. Right now, with all the lights off and empty with the tables crammed to the far side it looked strange. At first, I thought the breakfast room was in there except we walked through the room and out another door in the far back.

The backyard wasn't exactly what I was expecting. For one thing, where was all the snow? Winter had officially hit and snowed a few inches. Right now, there was snow outside of here except in the backyard you would think it was summer. No heating devices to keep it warm, no overhead cover to keep the snow from falling in covering the ground. An extremely well-manicured lawn with weight sets, bars, lined track, and several other exercise equipment. I was guessing this entire complex was on four acres of property. There was a second building behind that we went into; it had looked more like a storage building or a barn.

Once inside, I was amazed at how it had looked. The floor was dirt, but there were rows of tables with linens and glassware already set up for everyone. A very professional-looking kitchen in the far corner with several grabbing serving plates setting them out at the tables, some were already choosing their places to sit. Leah took me by the hand as we walked through a group who had been watching me, no doubt because I was new or female. We sat in the far corner, which was nice; I could see everything going on from here.

The room was noisy as everyone was talking. They had so much food cooked for everyone; I could see why they needed a cover for this place. No doubt the club provided the money they needed for food and anything else they might have needed; minus a few things they couldn't afford that Morris stole and Beth's life insurance. By now I only had a few who would glance my way wondering who I was. Since this was the lake house I wondered where they could have been keeping my father, Jasper, and the others? The upstairs to the house itself was all bedrooms, downstairs had been the main club, and out here looked as though there was only a large room with a kitchen and eating area unless they moved the tables aside which they could do. That still doesn't explain where they kept the others? I was a little hesitant to touch the food until the others started eating it first, if it was poisoned in some way, I hoped I would know. Not grabbing much so I could pretend I had eaten; I was thankful I had a few fruit bars in my backpack back in the bedroom.

Still looking around I was rather impressed by the kitchen and those Morris had staffing it. Then I noticed finally the small room that went off to the side of it. There was a rather large cart with dirty dishes next to it and another cart that was empty. The strange door never opened once. I was curious if it had just been a back way out of the place so I hoped someone would use it except no one ever did.

"Tastes great, doesn't it? One of the guys here that handles the cooking was going to be a souse chef, but he's been busy working here now feeding everyone. He's amazing." She had loaded her plate up with a little of everything.

I hated to admit I wound up eating more than I was planning on.

"What does everyone do after breakfast?" There were so many teenagers in here I wondered why none of their parents were missing them.

"Everyone has an assignment; most likely you will help me with mine. I could use the help." Finishing her plate, she still sat there, everyone waited until they were all done for a meeting with Morris.

I wanted to ask about her parents; unfortunately, I haven't had the chance yet. The young man next to me was frowning no doubt wondering why I was asking Leah so many questions. On the left side of the room, there was a slightly raised platform where everyone could see him, Morris stood there waiting until he had everyone's attention before he started to speak. Smiling as he looked around the room, I had a chill run down my back once his eyes rested on me. I still hoped he hadn't figured it out.

"We have a new member; if she will please stand I'm sure most of you have noticed her when she walked in. Joelle will be helping Leah while she is staying here, she is a new permanent member of our family, please welcome Joelle." Clapping his hands, the others joined as I stood up.

Waving slightly to everyone feeling my heartbeat go faster I quickly sat down. I hated being put on the spot like that, but I had a feeling it might happen.

"Our ceremony will take place as scheduled; we now have a spell reader who can also perform rituals. Most of you already know from the short demonstration. Everyone has their assignments, be back here by dinner time, lunch will be served to your rooms." Sitting down in his chair that was placed behind him he clasped his hands together.

Looking as though he was giving thought to what he was going to say, he kept looking over at me. Had he figured it out or was he still planning what to do with me? I wondered how the others were given their roles in the ritual and when he intended on telling me what exactly he was expecting me to do unless he was leaving it for the last minute? Clearing his throat for a moment he finally started speaking again.

"I know many of you have already heard this and it certainly never hurts to hear it again, this is more for the benefit of Joelle since this is her first day here. The outside world has no clue what we are doing for them. Many would not have the stomach or the ability to understand what we are doing or what a positive impact this will make for generations to come." Taking a moment to let it sink in and no doubt gauge how I was taking this so far.

I kept my expression as relaxed as possible.

"There are violent creatures out there that are determined to take away our safety, to infect and destroy our loved ones and friends. They have already killed so many it's time to stop this. We as a family have found a way to do this. I admit it is not easy, especially what I am asking you to do at such a young age. No one will be killing themselves. This is not a harmful occult, but we will be calling for higher powers to help us, to help our loving family. Trust is key and I know for a fact this will all work out. The entire world will one day finally understand and accept the great sacrifices we have had to make on their behalf so that they can live in safety." Not bothering to say another word he had looked at the ground for a while before he finally stood up from his chair.

As he finished speaking, everyone stood up from the table now leaving heading off in different directions. I felt surprised that was all he said. I was expecting so much more other than a little fluff feel-good speech. Why isn't anyone questioning this? Leah was the last to get up; tapping me on the shoulder to let me know it was time to get started on her assignment.

At least now I would see where the door next to the kitchen leads to. Pulling the covered cart away from the wall, the one I had noticed was empty earlier now had food on it. Opening the door and flipping on the light I couldn't see much other than the little that was lit up with lights. A thin rim made from metal went all the way around the room with two solid planks making an x shape on the floor. There wasn't anything other than a huge hole in the ground and a huge metal contraption in the center with four chains leading downward.

Making sure the door was closed securely behind us Leah pulled the cart to the one side of the room where there was a desk along the sidewall with nothing else with it. Helping push the cart from behind, we made our way over to the desk. The pits were so dark I couldn't see down in them, I was guessing this might be where they were being kept. If so, my father was going to get a shock to see me in here, I just hoped he wouldn't blow my cover by yelling at me for not following his orders.

"What are we doing now?" With no one in sight, I could feel my heart beating faster, if we were supposed to feed the people they had captured then that would mean they could still possibly be alive.

"Since this is your first time and you haven't had much of the speech, this might be a little disturbing for you, I understand if you would prefer to skip this part. It's part of my duty and I'm used to it enough to do it; I'm not bothered by it at all. I'm just careful not to get too close." Picking up a long rod from behind the desk, I recognized it as a cattle prod.

"Explain first, then let me choose if I stay or not. Except for now please put that down, I've had one used on me before and don't want a revisit of it." Looking at me shocked she set it down right away.

I had lied but I felt she might sympathize with me more.

"That's fair enough; the creatures that I was telling you about are kept in these pits. The ritual when it's finished will be able to cure disease and several other things also. There are so many that will benefit from using the medicine that will be made as well as the one who is gifted to pass on the gift of healing. Why keep something like that to yourself, it's just selfish! We must feed them to keep them alive for the ceremony. We use the cattle prod to keep them back while we push the food through to them. Not much to it but they don't seem to do well in here. Especially the one in his cell but he's causing that himself, he refuses to eat anything we've given him." Shaking her head, she seemed angrier than anything.

"What do you feed them? Why is the cart covered?" Maybe they were not eating it for a reason? They might think you're poisoning them." At least it's what I would be assuming.

110

Did they honestly think they could cure the disease? With my gifts the most I was able to do was fall through a wall when I wasn't paying attention, manipulate energy in the air to move other things, or at best heal minor things like a scratch, I might be able to do more if I knew how or practiced more. I couldn't even heal a disease or ailment. It had to be so minor, anything that was an injury of some kind but not one from disease, and being a vampire certainly wasn't a disease. It didn't work that way. At least not from what I had read about it, not that I was sure how accurate it was so far, they were only assumptions.

"Whatever we do not finish is what they are served; besides we are not the evil ones, the good you can always trust." Removing the covering I could see the food; it wasn't any different unless they did do something we didn't see to it?

"It's safe I've taken a few bites of it myself. There's plenty here." About to pick up the cattle prod I had grabbed it from her. Not wanting to upset her I certainly didn't want to use this or see it used on anyone.

"I'm pretty sure we won't need this. Besides, I know how to handle creatures and if they are the type of creatures I'm used to dealing with, this won't be difficult." I was hoping she would trust me or at least assume I had safely worked with creatures before because I had been declared a witch by Morris to her.

There were a few buttons on the desk, pressing the blue one there was a loud thump sound in the center where it controlled the chains hanging over each corner. As soon as they were tight three cages from the ground started to rise and now hung in the air. I recognized the majority of the group while there were a few I hadn't recognized; I assumed they were vampires or other creatures as well. My father was in the second cage keeping his feelings to himself, except the second I had made eye contact with him he knew who I was. I knew no matter how much I changed my appearance he would never mistake me for anyone else. Jasper would be the same way.

Most were now standing in their cell, making Leah nervous as she quickly grabbed the cattle prod about to hit them with it. The end had been modified along with the battery being used to give a stronger shock, I was amazed they didn't simply have tasers to use. Grabbing the stick before she could do anything with it, as soon as I stopped her, she stepped back almost hesitant to be next to me.

"They are just standing; this is something you're going to need to trust me on. Do you trust me?" Nodding but still not saying anything she leaned against the wall with her eyes wide in surprise.

Setting the prod down on the ground and snapping one of the wires, I wanted to make sure it wasn't used again. Picking up the large tray I opened the window sliding it in so that each person could grab a plate, as I did when one of them asked me.

"Is this safe?" They had never said one word since they had been here.

"Yes, it's safe or I wouldn't give it to you." Nodding they took them and finally ate something.

The second cage was the same, then heading over to the third that was hidden behind the other two I already knew who they would be keeping alone in there. Leah had followed behind me, still, very silent watching, amazed none of them had even attempted to come after me. Looking down at him. Jasper hadn't even bothered to get up. His eyes were swollen shut; he was completely covered in blood. He hadn't done this to himself, they had beaten him. How could Leah possibly think he would do this to himself? Looking around to see how I could get into the cage. I felt the sides until Leah tapped me on the shoulder.

"It's not safe to go in there; Morris said he's faking it to escape?" Even her tone gave away that she wasn't sure if it was true or not.

At least I knew I could get to her mentally.

"How do we open these doors? There must be a way of getting the food to him if he can't get up, look at him, there's no way he's going to stay alive if he doesn't eat something. He has no strength to harm let alone escape." Pointing at the corner of the cage there was a pin running down the entire side of the cage.

Leah held onto the plate as I moved the pin, it had been latched the same way it would have been on a dog pen. I would have expected him to be able to remove it himself except for the lock that was made not to be broken. I wasn't even sure of the material used other than the fact Leah wore the key around her neck with the key that first let into this room. The cage moved slightly as I had stepped in upsetting the balance. Taking the plate from Leah I walked close to Jasper. Sitting down I set the plate on the floor of the cage. Placing my hand on his side I could hear Leah gasp. I figured I would explain it later to her, I just hoped she wouldn't leave the room running from fear that had been soaked into her head. Jasper did have a little strength and he had grabbed me by the neck with his hand, not crushing but squeezing hard enough.

"Your friend was right; it's not safe in here." Jasper was barely able to get anything above a whisper out.

"Jasper, I know you can't see me, but you must be able to sense me." Barely getting the words out as he finally relaxed his hand around my throat now letting go, letting his hand drop to the floor.

"You never should have come in here, they will kill you, are you helping them?" Jasper had sounded as if he had just lost all hope.

"I'm trying to find a way to save you and the others, there was very little time and no other options. Voncha is waiting outside." With my hand still on his side, I could feel my hand heating up as I tried to heal him the best I could.

At least it wouldn't show on the outside for Leah to figure it out but at least it might help him survive or endure until I could get him out. I hoped if I concentrated enough, I might be strong enough to heal him enough that he could defend himself if he needed to. I just wished I could have broken them out now instead of waiting. There were too many outside or I would risk breaking them out now.

We probably spent more time in here than Leah was used to. I made sure Jasper was able to eat all his food before leaving the cage. I hated to see them get lowered again but I knew I was here to save them. I wouldn't be leaving without them. Pulling my shirt up to cover the red mark around my neck, we took the cart leaving it in the kitchen area to be cleaned down. At least no one was around to see how late we were in there. Making our way back up to our room Leah didn't have much more of an assignment other than what we had just done. No doubt they kept it simple since she was pregnant. Sitting down on the corner of her bed Leah never once took her eyes off me.

"Weren't you afraid of him killing you? He had you by the throat, all those creatures are affected, and they aren't normal vampires like the guys here. Morris cleans the blood before they use it to keep it from corrupting them." Her voice shook a little.

"I wasn't afraid for a second; he was only protecting himself since he couldn't see me well enough. Once he found I wasn't going to harm him he let go." I had hoped that was all she would ask.

"How is it that you've had experience dealing with vampires before, you seemed shocked when you found out what we were, I thought maybe it was the first time you had ever seen vampires?" Leaning forward she waited for my response.

"There are more vampires out there than anyone knows. They are not all bad just like not all humans are bad. There's always going to be at least one that can be pointed at as horrible, but you can't judge all of them by that or vampires could assume we are all like Joseph Stalin or Hitler. Dracula himself has a bad reputation but that doesn't mean all are like him. Vampires were once humans before they were changed, the only difference is they've had years to watch and learn." Nodding her head, I knew she was agreeing but still had questions.

"What was he saying to you? I knew you were talking to each other, but I couldn't hear anything. They haven't spoken a word since they've been here." She was still amazed they had talked to me.

"I was just reassuring them I wasn't going to harm them. The man on the floor wasn't saying much, he was more mumbling than anything, he's still too weak to do anything, have you tried talking to them?" I didn't want to explain any more than I had to.

"Not really except you still hadn't answered my other question, how good are you at keeping a secret?" Getting up from her bed she came over sitting right next to me.

"I'm extremely good with secrets, I don't make promises that I can't keep so I've always kept secrets to myself. I've been around vampires before and none of them is anything like what

Morris is describing, even the ones he is keeping locked up are not at all what he has everyone believing. I would explain more but I don't know how you would handle it?" Again, nodding her head in agreement, at least she understood what I was saying.

I was curious why she asked me about secrets.

"I have a secret I've been keeping. No one else can ever know and I'm positive I can trust you after what I saw you do. You did heal him I know I saw it." I couldn't help but stop breathing for a second when she said that.

"I did what?" I didn't want to reaffirm what she said but I hoped she might take it as a mistake.

"It's alright, I won't tell anyone you're a healer, I'm a shade but I'm infected so I can't heal anymore. If I don't get infused by the girl, they are sacrificing along with the demons then my group of people will be wiped out for good. There are so few of us left. How is it that you're not affected and that I didn't know about you? You must be from the other group of shades; they are rarely even seen." She looked me over and then the expression changed on her face. Sitting back an inch I knew she figured it out.

"You might be hiding your real reason for being here, as honorable as it is, there are so many other ways it could have been done without killing innocent creatures to do it. This ritual is a cover for something else. I need to save my family, but I also need to find out what Morris is doing to help stop him from harming anyone. I'm guessing you're going to tell them about me?" I felt sick getting this close and now I could be turned over, I wasn't sure what to do now if she told Morris who I was and what I was trying to do.

"No, I'm not. Your secret is safe with me, just let me know if there is anything I can do to help you. I thought I was doing the right thing, but I still don't like the idea of killing the others to do this." Giving in to a shiver I did feel like I could trust her.

Excusing herself to use the restroom again I had noticed there were pills beside her bed. Before we left for breakfast, I replaced her other ones with vitamins from my backpack. I had packed them out of habit when I had taken off from the house the first time with Jasper.

UNEXPECTED HELP

Leah and I had gone outside during lunchtime with Zack to eat our lunch; most avoided the sun or were ready to sleep for a while. Leah was having heartburn and decided to stay up for a while. Being out in the fresh air helped me pinpoint Voncha's location. During this entire time, he hadn't left once. Making an excuse all three of us walked through the woods, I wasn't sure if I could trust Zack yet, Leah had stayed at the stream while I made the excuse, I wanted to follow some fake deer tracks on the ground to see if its home was nearby. In case he were to check, I kept kneeling over pretending to study them and I would make a few indents to make it look real. Walking off until I was out of sight from the lake house and the eyesight of Zack, I finally started walking in the direction of Voncha's scent. Walking further I knew he had been this way, but I couldn't quite find him. It was getting stronger; he should have shown himself unless there was a reason he couldn't? I started to worry he was injured, or someone might be watching that I hadn't picked up on yet. Looking around I still couldn't spot anything. No hidden cameras or people nearby. Jumping back as Voncha dropped down right in front of me, I reached out and hugged him as tight as I could. I wasn't the only one worried.

"You're not going back there, I haven't slept or moved since you've been in there. I was worried they found out who you

116

were. I hate being out here where I can't protect you." His voice hadn't hidden his concern at all. This time I knew he was really scared.

"You don't sleep to begin with, they have no idea who I am; I found dad, Jasper, and the others. I'm so close and I've also found out why the others are here, but I haven't found the real reason Morris is doing this. I can't leave yet, or it will attract attention. We can't afford to stop now; I know you're worried, even scared a little but we must do this. I'll let you know when I need you. Just stay ready; I'm sure it won't be long from now." Hugging me so tight I almost thought Voncha would never let me go.

"How did you get out without someone coming with you? Does your father and Jasper know you're here?" I knew he would be curious how they reacted.

"They know, dad noticed me first, Jasper took longer, and he wasn't able to see me. He's been hurt badly. Once he realized it was me, he was angry that I was there. Not that he can do anything about it now but I'm sure he will let me know how he feels repeatedly later on. Leah and I were going outside for lunch and Zack joined us. I should get back before they think something happened. It's the only way I could get out, I wanted to let you know I'm safe." Giving Voncha one last hug before I left, I had started to walk away when I turned back, giving him a second hug and then a kiss on the cheek.

We hadn't been back to the room for very long when Zack came to collect Leah. They were going to help the kitchen crew pick up a few things from the store, it took quite a few people to shop for the food and bring it back. Leaving me on my own for a while even I had someone come to get me, for what I wasn't sure. I had told the young man at the door I had to use the restroom first. Waiting in the hallway for me I grabbed my cell phone slipping it into my pocket, shutting the door to the bathroom so the person would think I had come out of it.

Leaving the lake house, we walked around the outside of the barn in full sunlight. At least I could guess the one I was following wasn't a vampire yet. I was finding it had been one of Morris's ways of gaining trust by not forcing the change and

117

accepting it in others. Just behind the barn was a little pond where no one was standing. For a second, I thought this person was going to walk directly into the pond, which he had. The water moved gently around him except he didn't seem to be absorbing the water as he slowly went under out of sight. Standing on the edge I wasn't sure if he expected me to join him or not? Reaching down to touch the water. I was still fascinated by it; this would be the third time at least I had encountered this. Morris likes the deception it gave. All it had been was dark blue smoke to look like a pond with a few fake lily pads propped up to make it look authentic.

Following behind I had coughed from the smoke getting in my lungs, I was now completely covered by the fake water. I wondered if Voncha was able to see me from where he was at. Looking around there was a long dark hallway leading downward and then straight out. The young man hadn't waited for me as I started walking down the hallway. Now I was worried again if they had figured out who I was. The walls were made of cement blocks, very solid and very long. When I had come to the end, three others left the room leaving me there only with one other young man and Morris himself.

Morris and the other young man had been looking at the piled-up tarp on the ground. Sliding it out there was still a large lump underneath it, seeing it caused me to panic thinking someone dead might be under it and worse yet someone I know. Before taking the tarp off the young man had gone around the room shutting off the lights and instead of lighting countless small candles that surrounded the entire room.

"Glad you could make it, sorry about not explaining about the fog up there, it's to distract those who are not supposed to be down here. I see you've been spending time with Leah, that's good but I need to borrow you for a moment." Walking over to me he had a thickly wrapped cloth in his hand now giving it to me.

"What's this?" Not sure what it was or if I was allowed to open it up yet to look.

"They are a few tools you might need for the ritual we have coming up. Practice and get used to using them, it will help later when the time comes. Also, there is a spell in Latin I need you to memorize so that you get it right for that night." So far nothing bad, I was still waiting for the bad news to drop.

"I don't want you to take this the wrong way, but you are a new member, I'm sure you've been filled in on things from Leah and you didn't seem at all shocked when you left the prisoner holding after helping out, you seem to be adapting rather well so I believe you're ready for the next step. Do you have any questions before we start? I want everyone to feel comfortable with our family." I wasn't sure I wanted the next step to happen except whatever it was I had to do it to continue blending in. Every time he used the word family, I had to fight the red flag feeling that ran through my thoughts. I held my breath for a moment wondering if I should ask a question or not?

"I noticed there aren't any other adults, does anyone get visitors here that don't live here?" I hoped it would answer my questions without causing him to question why I would ask that.

"Are you missing your parents?" Not bothering to answer my question he tried to act sympathetic.

"Not really, I just wondered. Everyone feels like family here so I'm comfortable." I had matched his sentiment not that I found out what I wanted.

I was curious to find out what happened with their families.

"That's good to hear, Robbie will pull back the tarp and we will begin, everyone practices on this one." Morris had an evil smile that appeared much different than his usual plastered one he paraded around with.

Bound and shackled on the floor, Jasper was laying there with his eyes closed. New blood now soaked what was left of his shirt. All his clothes had been badly torn to shreds and from the looks of it burned with pieces of his skin stuck to it. They weren't going to kill him before the ceremony but that didn't mean they weren't going to harm him before that. The thing I couldn't figure out was if they had other vampires trapped why single out this one? What exactly was it about him that made him different? Part of the tarp had been underneath Jasper no doubt to keep from staining the ground with his blood. I wasn't sure what they expected me to do; I was just hoping not to perform any spells on him. Pulling a chair up behind me, Morris had me sit down. Turning most of the lights off in the room other than the ones on Jasper. I was beginning to see what he was doing. He wanted to find out how I would react to someone being tortured, especially when I was the one causing the pain, Voncha was right, it had come to this. Morris wanted to know if I would still perform the ritual or not. If this had been something I would refuse to be a part of. If I had planned on saving Jasper, I would have to watch whatever they did, or participate and pretend not to care and truly hope he forgives me later.

"This creature had killed so many, we don't compare him to our vampires because ours were made to do good, to protect those who are not strong against evil vampires, and he is of tainted blood while ours are from clean pure blood. This one is so evil his only purpose in life is to kill others, he has caused such grief for your family members that we are now making him pay for his crimes." Stopping for a moment to gauge my reaction I had simply paid attention trying to react like any of the others might have.

"He is not a traditional vampire where they simply had the tainted blood festering until they turned murderous. He was created by the Shades, he's a despicable experiment. However, he will now help right the wrong. Right now, we are pouring hydrogen peroxide over his cuts to keep them from getting infected." No matter how he tried to rationalize it, I knew the truth.

Wearing gloves and a smock, the young man had picked up a bucket of liquid that I highly doubted was hydrogen peroxide, I never remembered it having that odor before. Pouring the liquid out, Morris had watched me to see what my reaction was as soon as it had hit Jasper. Not changing my expression, it was so hard to fight the urge to stop them. There were far too many outside, even with Voncha waiting we never would have been enough to get everyone out. Besides my father and the others were still in their holding cells, I would have to get past the others just to get to them and I doubted from the way Jasper looked that he would be able to move. Even if I was fortunate enough to get

Jasper out, I was positive they would kill the others immediately. I was worried about whether I would be able to move him. Jasper hadn't moved one inch other than the smallest twitch that I doubted the others noticed.

"This letter I'm giving you has a spell written for you, it's incredibly important that you devote your time to it. You must have that memorized for the ritual. So many are depending on you, it means their very lives. We can save millions doing this." The young man had been agreeing with everything Morris was saying, the look on his face had been so vacant.

"Leah and I have been busy working on her assignments, I've made sure I was ready any time you needed me. I learn rather quickly; I will have no problem at all having it memorized in time." I wasn't sure what else to tell him other than what I knew he wanted to hear.

Briefly taking a glance at the paper he had just handed me I felt sick, this was the spell to kill the others. The first two lines although won't kill Jasper, could give him enough of a shock to hurt him. The way it had been written would be giving blame or credit to the gods that if it were in their best interest let it be, however in this case it was being caused and not asked of the gods to do it. I was in the middle of the worst situation possible. This was getting much more difficult than it had started to be. I didn't want to hurt the others since they were innocent being controlled by Morris, no doubt having no idea what they were doing. I feared he had killed their parents and family to keep them here or no doubt getting to them when they were most vulnerable. I would think I finally had this figured out when I would have to alter any ideas or plans, I would start to formulate a new one.

"That is excellent to hear your bonding with Leah; it is wonderful for her to have another lady around. Now that you've looked over the spell, I have an exercise I wish for you to do." Now as he said this, a few others had come back to join us only they stayed behind me this time where there had been no candles.

I was the only one in the small circle with Morris now standing outside of it, only Jasper and I had remained. The others stood behind me blocking the doorway and I wondered if this was going to be the ceremony after all. I felt that strange prickly feeling

121

wave through my body. Standing in front of Jasper I was worried about what they were planning on having me do to him. I was positive he could sense me; besides the way that I looked, I knew he recognized me by the sound of my voice and my scent. Almost holding my breath, I knew whatever they had me do I wasn't going to like it. Handing me a small slip of paper there was simply one word written on it. Saying a word out loud wouldn't cause any harm but I had wondered if the liquid they had splashed on him was already enchanted and combined with this word.

"Now say the word I just gave you; the ritual is going to be much harder than this, we are only trying to prepare you emotionally right now. Sometimes it's difficult to do the right thing. Say the word three times slowly with a space between each." The young man patted me on the shoulder no doubt thinking he was giving me support.

"Impetum." As soon as I had said it the first time, a jolt shot through Jasper's body lifting him off the ground. In Latin, Impetum meant to attack.

As soon as it had I felt sick. I still had to say it two more times. The second and third weren't any easier. Each time the jolt seemed to increase. Morris had kept his eyes on me watching for my expression. The others were more aware of Jasper; he still hadn't made a sound no doubt not to trouble me any further and not to let the others know they were getting to him. Jasper and Voncha were the strongest people I knew. Right then and there I had promised myself I would do anything it took to make it up to Jasper. As soon as I had said it that last time Morris started to comment

"Well done, I'm sure you should be able to handle the night of the ritual." When he said this, I felt strange almost light-headed. The room temporarily became foggy.

"I'll have the rest memorized in time." I had told Morris as he put his hand on my shoulder now that the candles were blown out and the regular lights were turned back on.

"I have no doubt you will, this is very important, I cannot stress that enough Joelle. I will have someone else helping Leah in the next few weeks so that you will have plenty of time to memorize your assignment. The directions are also included. If you have any questions let me know right away." Before he left, I wanted to make sure I kept helping Leah, it was the only way I could also help Jasper and the others.

"Helping Leah doesn't take that much time. I was planning on helping her and then spending the rest of the day studying since I don't have any other assignments to do; it helps me having another girl to talk to, female issues." I was hoping I could keep helping, I doubted anyone else would have taken care of them.

"True, she would be better help to you with feminine issues than the boys or myself. Just make sure you study, this ritual will save countless people in the future. We all are depending on you." Before I realized what I was doing, almost as if my body and mind had a plan of its own, I had turned and hugged Morris.

"Don't worry I'll make you proud." Before I could figure out why I had said and done that I was already skipping out of the room.

Jasper might think it was really put on but then he might realize I was being controlled now no doubt like the others. One thing I had noticed after leaving, the fog cleared. I felt so sick that I had done that in front of Jasper, if Morris was able to control me like that then he really could force me to do the spell on the night of the ritual causing me to kill Jasper, my father, and the others. I couldn't get back to the room fast enough. Leah was sitting on her bed humming to the baby while all I could do was close the door, crumble up and drop to the floor in front of my bed and start crying. Leah was looking at me strangely no doubt wondering what had happened to make me so sad.

"I take it meeting with Morris hadn't gone well? I have good news that might cheer you up. A few of the guys are going to try to convince Morris that we need to change the date of the ritual; we have everything we need now. It might happen earlier. They caught the guy who you were speaking with outside, none of us told them that you knew him or that he spoke to you. Morris just thinks he was spying on us to get to the others. He had the blood vials on him." She seemed so excited about this as if this was good news.

"That's supposed to be a good thing. I need more time not less. Did you already go shopping earlier?" I noticed she was acting the same way she was when we first met.

"Yes, we went shopping, and then we had stopped in Morris's office before going to the kitchen the same as we always have." Stopping for a second, I could see she was finally questioning why they did that.

After shopping why not go directly to the kitchen with the food?

"They gave us pills again, they were a different color, I didn't take both, I told them I would take the second one when I got back to my room that I was more likely to throw it up because of the pregnancy and they didn't push it." The look on her face gave away how she was feeling, very confused.

Even though I hadn't memorized the spell, if Morris was able to get me to react the way I had he could get me to say anything, the same way he kept everyone here under his control especially when I knew many of them questioned his actions. I doubted any of them would even be here if he wasn't controlling them. But why did he need me to know Latin unless he hadn't understood the spell himself?

I noticed the only times Leah had started to question anything was when she saw me show her something different, I was curious what spell he had used on her and how exactly Morris was doing it. This wasn't something shades were supposed to do; he must have another witch doing it for him. There had to be something else to it. Without anyone knocking, the door had opened followed by ten young men, only Zack and Chris I had recognized out of the group. They came in and sat down looking at me no doubt wondering why my cheeks were red.

"Did you tell her the good news or was she that excited from it she cried?" Even his voice sounded doubtful.

"Yes, she told me, I'm fine I just had sympathy feelings for Leah, just a girl thing." It was the only excuse I could come up with.

"We told Morris that we would stay up here to make sure you don't get distracted, they have another vampire from that group in the cages. I think there are too many of us here right now; it doesn't take all of us to watch you." Two of the young men had left.

I was thankful even though I would have preferred all of them to leave right now.

"Does anyone know what we are going to do now that the plans have changed?" Chris looked around until they all looked at me.

"What do you mean plans?" I was curious why he wanted to know about the ritual being earlier or if there was something else he had in mind?

"We hoped you might come up with something. We don't know about the others, but we stopped taking the pill that was left for us twice a day. I've hidden it under my tongue so that I could spit it out later." Chris was sounding much clearer and without the vacant stare the others have had.

"I think by now we were all convinced by Morris it was our idea to shorten the time after last night. The ritual will be in two days now, I know I won't live through the ceremony, and neither will the baby. Morris has figured out who you are, even I did when I saw you heal that one vampire in the cage. It's hard for a shade not to see healing transfer." Leah was speaking so clearly; I think it helped her to be away from Morris unless she finally accepted the truth that the spell just wasn't strong enough to stick this time.

"Whatever we are going to do we need to do it before the actual event, he can control Joelle, so we need to bust out of here before then. I just don't know what we will do with the others who were turned into vampires? I don't know what I'm going to do with myself after a while." Chris sounded more frustrated as he spoke.

I doubted many of them thought about the long-term consequences but then it wasn't as if they were given the opportunity.

"We need to get the blood vials, but Morris will have those with him." Leah looked panicked when she first thought about this.

She knew she would never be around long enough to benefit from them.

"Don't worry about the blood vials he has if he has them with him. That might help us a little, except we won't have a lot of time." Thinking it through we had to get this done by tomorrow, maybe just after breakfast when everyone has taken off to handle their assignments and there are only a few hours before the sun comes up, with everyone spread out, that would be the best opportunity with the least amount of people around to contend with.

At least with Morris thinking he had the real blood vials it gave us more time. I had left the real ones in a cooler that plugged in under the floorboard at the cabin. I only managed to dump out one, it had my name on it. I just couldn't get myself to dump out the blood in case there was an actual need for it. I had tried except I kept getting that feeling that was telling me not to, almost as if intuition was screaming at me not to. Over the years I had learned to listen to it more often than not. For a while, we simply talked as I held the paper in my hand in case Morris wanted to check to see if I was studying and if the others were there for more of a social visit or to keep me studying.

A few of them had left to finish their assignments so they wouldn't draw attention to themselves. Tonight was going to be very long, as the time went on more had gone to their rooms to get ready for this evening. I had almost been up for a full twenty-four hours. Both Leah and I had tried to get a nap in before tonight since I had a feeling it was going to be a long one for both of us. Sleeping in the same bed as Leah. I wanted to make sure if she moved or anything happened, I would be aware first. I had this sudden fear she was going to be grabbed or worse before I had a chance to do anything.

When breakfast had come everything was the same as always. Morris gave a good morning speech to the group as they finished eating. He had called for a few to meet him in his office for early preparations. As usual, the table was left along with the dirty plates, only a few had the job of cleaning up after everyone. Our cart was waiting for us in the kitchen. Making our way over there I had a strange feeling that Morris was watching us, but I didn't want to look suspicious, so I never once glanced in his direction. We had a plan, so far, we just had to hope it worked.

126

Pulling the cart into the other room, as usual, giving the food to my father and his friends, I had made my way into the cage with both Voncha and Jasper. They had felt like hurting Voncha the same way they were with Jasper. Now I was beginning to wonder if there was something different about Voncha that they might have wanted. Voncha still had enough energy to feed himself, but Jasper still needed help.

"I'm sorry, I didn't see the trap. I wound up getting too close." I could hear how defeated Voncha felt.

"There's nothing you could have done, besides Morris knows who I am, he found out. Why he hasn't locked me up is that he needs me to perform the ritual and I found out he can control me. Not sure how but he can." As I told Voncha everyone looked at me worried.

"You need to get yourself out of here." Jasper barely whispered but was still strong enough to try to protect me.

"I can't leave, there are far too many depending on me but not for the reason Morris tries to convince others of. Besides, I learned from the best, just trust me that I know what I'm doing." I hoped this would help relax everyone a little.

"You learned from the best? Look at us, we're all in here." Giving a sarcastic laugh I knew what my father meant.

"Everyone is grouping right now in the main house. I think they are starting the ritual right now." Leah and I gasped at the thought.

Looking back eight different young men had gone into the room no doubt to collect the others, I just hoped they wouldn't do anything to them before the ceremony. Leah hadn't given birth yet and no one has tried to approach her. Everyone seemed to be extremely busy for this soon. The yard was filled with the group now placing everything into the open backyard of the club. I doubted any of these here even had a clue what they were doing, just blindly following a leader under a spell. After all, Leah slowly started to snap out of it when she stopped taking the pills and saw things that were contrary to what she had been taught to believe.

We waited in the main house as Alex had snuck in a quill to write with, blood as its ink, and I started writing a spell as quickly as I could. To make sure no one had heard it I wrote it not in Latin but a made-up language of our own, at least one my family would know. When I was little Jasper and Voncha thought it would be fun to create our language, we wound up using it quite a lot. Writing it into this spell was more to give a warning to my family and the others. Most everyone was going to be wearing dressing gowns, I just wish there was a way of doing this without harming those who were not conscious of what they were doing. There was still time since nothing could happen during the daylight, at least nothing Morris would want. We had quite a few hours until tonight when the moon would be out in full and the sky dark. We weren't the only ones watching from the window, the majority who had changed and were unable to be out in the sunlight were inside. Morris had been standing outside even though his skin was turning a brighter red color he could still see and cope well enough. All I could guess had been the shade part of him was still alive and going strong. Otherwise normally once changed the inherited shade gifts tend to either diminish or parish. Some were lucky to keep both fully intact for life as long as they were not tainted or infected somehow.

Leah kept close to me hoping they wouldn't pull her away from me early to do anything with the baby, but then when I saw the way they were setting up the ritual. I was pretty sure they intended on handling the baby tonight with everything else. Torches were being put in place along with a huge fire pit in the center. The cages were covered with thick white sheets making it impossible to see whoever was in there. So many of them looked so young, guess it was easier to pray on those who attended the club. I was curious why he chose these unless they were more susceptible to his gifts but then I would have no doubt been drawn in also since he was able to control me somehow unless these others have some sort of natural ability or gift, they weren't aware of?

Sitting back on the bed reading over what I had written I knew I didn't have to wait for tonight to start reciting it. Not wanting to upset Leah anymore I had simply closed my eyes concentrating, meditating on what I had written, and mouthing it over and over. I was only going to get one chance tonight; I couldn't risk a failure.

All day they were busy but not once had anyone come near the cages, there was no movement and now they were swaying from the wind. I began to wonder if they had already taken them out, that's when I started to worry that it might be too late. I couldn't wait for the ceremony and possibly get controlled by Morris, what if he could make me say the right words? I had to strike during the light. Taking Leah with me, we went outside, at least this was the first person I wouldn't have to worry about, I wasn't going to risk leaving her alone for one second because all it would take is that split second and I might not be able to stop whatever they planned for her fate.

Doing our best not to be seen, we went around the side of the building to make it look as if we were going for a walk on the paved trail; instead, we entered the kitchen from the side entrance. No one had been in here other than a strange glowing glass set on one of the tables, inside it held several vials of blood. No doubt the ones they confiscated from Voncha. No one had been in the room where the cages had been removed, a little blood but not enough for someone to have died. Making our way back out through the prisoner's hold we had taken the door Leah never used, it had to lead to a long tunnel underneath. I just hoped not to run into Morris or anyone else in there since it would be dark and a place most could go during this time. Thankfully we never ran into anyone. I guessed this had been for Morris if anything happened, he could use it to escape rather easily. I kept getting a sick nauseous feeling that something wasn't right. Taking Leah by the hand I walked out the back and kept going. I wasn't going to permanently leave but I had a feeling I had to hide Leah.

I knew Leah was tired from walking and if someone was looking for her, they would have realized she was gone from the club already, I just hoped they wouldn't figure out what I was doing. Not wanting to stay in the town. I was worried in case they would report they had seen us. Making our way to the farmhouse Voncha and I had found earlier not far from here, I knew we were being followed except it didn't worry me who was following us. Alex was still mortal but slowly going through the changes. As Leah had explained not getting changed directly from a vampire, the change was more gradual, he was one of those who had stopped taking the pill only to find out the change could not be reversed, some it were not temporary as told, it turned out to be permanent, however, most it was incredibly temporary. Even Alex realized his days were numbered knowing Morris's real intent; he had no compassion or loyalty to anyone. With dust everywhere, I guessed no one had lived here for a long time. When we were out of the sun and inside the house Alex joined us.

"I need you to stay here with Leah and take care of her. I don't want either of you anywhere near the ceremony no matter what you hear from here. You should be safe here." Not wanting to take any more time I had taken off being careful not to leave a trail or give anyone any idea I had been at the farmhouse, let alone anyone on the grounds to know I had left in case they hadn't figured it out.

At least one thing would work out for us, the fact Morris was getting overly confident no doubt thinking no one was smart enough to stop taking the pills or would be brave enough to leave, especially Leah. He hadn't counted on me, at least not the fact that I was willing to take a risk. I wasn't the same shy person who kept to myself as he used to know me, I've certainly changed. I had to. If he was risking their lives, then I could certainly risk mine to save them. Making my way back up to the room I found that the door was already opened. A young man was looking at two different pieces of paper trying to decide which the right one was. Looking up at me frustrated he continued to shift through them without saying much.

"Where is Leah? Morris needs her." He more demanded than asked.

"She was feeling sick so she went and used the restroom downstairs; she was going to see Morris anyway to see if he could help her." He seemed more relaxed that she was not with me.

"Which is the one Morris gave you to memorize?" He had given up trying to guess which ones and now shoved the papers at me.

"All of them, why would I have any other ones? I didn't exactly move here with anything, as you can see, I'm wearing Leah's sweatshirt and sweatpants." Emphasizing the fact by pointing at them.

I had taken the papers from him as he gave me a strange look.

"Take them with you; Morris wants to see you also." Looking at me accusingly he stormed out of the room.

As soon as he was out of sight, I ripped up the original copy which I should have done in the first place except I had hoped to study them later to find out who had written them, I still doubted it had been Morris. Unfortunately, they were starting as soon as they could, using the dark clouds to hover over the area. There had to be another powerful shade here unless Morris was stronger than I was aware of. Looking around I had seen everyone even the one who had gone to collect Leah. I still had no idea what I was going to do especially if they questioned me about Leah. Coming in closer to the circle there was a young man I hadn't recognized kneeling motionless in front of the fire with his head down. His hands were tied behind his back, but he never once tried to get loose. Morris had made his way over to the podium to make his announcement.

I was standing in the center of everything next to the fire and next to this young man. The cages were also next to the fire, I could hear the change in the breathing from the others no doubt feeling effects from being so close to the heat. Morris started giving this long-winded speech about the hours and moon settings, while most listened I looked around when I noticed there were a few others who were paying attention to me, no doubt waiting for my move. I had no idea what I was going to do, we had a plan earlier but now it's too soon. I didn't want to risk the innocent getting harmed, with Morris being a shade I had no idea if I should injure or try to kill him. Looking at the young man next to me he had let out a deep sigh.

"How old are you?" I couldn't help asking him.

He looked so young I doubted he could have been over eighteen.

"Old enough to get wasted and have sex, definitely in that order. Unfortunately, the last isn't going to happen now." Looking up at me smiling for a moment before the smile vanished.

"You don't have to do this." I had hoped he wasn't a sacrifice or something to all of this.

"When Leah's baby couldn't be found I was elected, I'm the youngest in the group but I was hoping you might have figured something out. Most of us have been." If I wasn't feeling the pressure before I certainly was now.

I noticed Morris started looking in our direction as he spoke. I took a glance at the cages to the right side and decided this was the best time and no later. There was never going to be a safe time and certainly not having fewer people. It was do or die.

"I'm sorry this is going to hurt but I promise you will heal." Not waiting for whatever I was going to do he laid flat on the ground shielding his face.

Raising my hands, I had shot as much energy out from me as I could using the clouds almost as if they were a speculum. Lighting up the air it had felt so intense almost as if the sun had burst downward. I was sweating so bad, with the bright light many out of instinct had run for cover where there was darkness either inside the buildings or house. I made my way over to the cages quickly. While opening them I had a few come at me as Morris commanded the others to stop me. There were several who simply stood in their places or took this as the time to escape. Only a handful had come running at me. Again, using the energy forcing the winds to gust around me, I blew them back as the last cage opened. Morris hadn't seemed as worried while he still had his hands gripped around the vials of blood, he believed to be the real ones. My family and friends made their way out carrying Voncha and Jasper with them. Only my father, Kieam and Luthrow had chosen to stay behind. The other two I had met briefly at the tavern with my father. They had been two of the wolves who stood behind silently listening. The two who had betrayed my father and his friends, leading them right into a trap with Morris were there also.

"I can handle this, but if you're here I'll have to worry about you. It's easier to watch over one than worry if I might hurt you by accident while getting to him." Nodding I knew he understood but refused to move.

"I've raised you too much like myself. Accepting help isn't a bad thing. Morris can fry me to a crisp, but I can slow down any of the others who come at you." Being careful not to harm the others, we had already discussed the fact we would not attack the young people here who were just innocent ones who had been controlled by Morris.

Most of the others now were leaving simply because they couldn't handle the heat with the intense light being created. Leaving only four others and Morris standing there with a smirk on his face staring at me, I worried what he might be planning since I wasn't, just simply going by instinct. Wiping up the wind as strong as I could, spreading it out past the fire I had created a strong circle around Morris and I, closing everyone else out. I didn't want to risk anyone else getting hurt. The grounds were pretty secure as long as the fire didn't hop over the iron fence, it should stay pretty well contained.

I might not have been able to do too much; I could get the wind to feed the fire, the bright flash of light which didn't affect Morris. I had to use the little that I could. Now I was simply trying to figure out my next move. Morris was already making his next move, opening the vials Morris drank them all down as I watched feeling sick seeing him do this.

"I can still make you say the incantation. You just did me a huge favor by blocking everyone else out, there is no one to save you, and my sacrifice will be you." I had hoped to stall long enough while he spoke to me.

"I'm sure you could force me to read what's on these pages but are you sure it's what you wrote?" When I wanted time to speed up it always felt as if it turned into extreme slow motion. Now I just need enough time.

"It's alright. I remember the real words, all I needed was the victim to say them. Raising his hand curling his fingers and palm upward toward me I could feel slight dizziness except not as strong as before.

"What was Leah's baby for?" Still tried to stall for any amount of time I could.

"Fresh blood and she was the sacrifice until she couldn't get the words correct from the manipulation." Closing his eyes as he concentrated even more the flames rose slightly in a swirling motion.

133

"Sadly, you chose to underestimate Leah, I wasn't sure about her when I had first met her. She was smart enough to leave herself notes when she couldn't think for herself. She did even better than I could have." Smiling I knew he was curious what she had done.

"She's too stupid to do anything, gullible, naïve, she was the easiest to manipulate because she trusted so much. She is the reason there will be no more shades. Yes, I knew what she was, and I knew she would pass it onto the baby and my experiment worked. She did get pregnant. The baby only survived because of the shots I administered to her." Morris had sounded even more defiant as he tried to force me to walk into the flames.

Releasing powders and something else I wasn't quite sure of, a dark round sphere of some kind into the fire. I had taken a step back. At least this time I was able to control my own physical body. Using the energy around me I forced the winds to blow the fire away from me. Looking up frustrated no doubt not understanding what was going wrong, at least now I knew I had stalled long enough.

"When you drank the blood vials you absorbed quite a lot, those were not the vials you had before. I switched them with regular blood, and then Leah added her blood to it that had been tainted by vampire blood. You're now a shade who is infected and will very shortly be feeling incredible pain as the vampire venom kills off the remaining shade from you. It's one of the reasons shades hate vampires, if they are weak or infected the vampire side takes over, it's why they don't allow crossbreeding as they would put it. And as a gift, the liquid you had poured over Jasper, when you made me torture him, it was in one of your vials also." I knew I had him extremely frustrated, he might not have the gifts of a shade very soon, but he will have the traits of the vampire when it hits him.

Morris wasn't giving up, repeatedly trying to cast spell after spell. I hadn't wanted to risk staying around for those he hadn't needed shade gifts for. Dropping to the ground clutching at his chest I knew the hardest part had finally kicked in. His body wasn't strong enough to fight off the vampire venom. Soon I wasn't alone; several who had chosen to become vampires were now standing next to me. None were a threat to me but to Morris they certainly were. Most had been changed while under his control. The fact that living a normal life was taken without their actual consent, they would now have to learn to survive as the world constantly changes around them. Everyone they know is dying and worse having a harder time establishing who they were once they should have naturally passed on themselves. At least I knew my father well, he wouldn't abandon them. He had taken in Voncha and Jasper; I knew he would do the same for the others, almost creating a new family.

I could have ended all of this; while he was at his most vulnerable, I could have burnt him to a crisp sweeping him into the fire burning him except I just couldn't do it. No matter how horrible it was I just couldn't get myself to kill anyone. I still had no idea how I managed to harm Jasper when I did. As much as I knew this, they were still angry with Morris. It wasn't right for me to kill him, even though he had threatened my family and harmed them. These were already dead because of him.

Not wanting to stick around to watch, I already knew what they were going to do. My father had been waiting for me, thankfully now taking me home. When it was safe, and the fire had died down. The local fire department had been called in when they saw the entire place ablaze. They had no idea what was going on there or how it ended, they simply found a very unrecognizable, destroyed body next to the fire. Later father and his friends went to collect Leah and Alex from the farmhouse. During all the chaos, Leah had started having strong contractions, staying by her side Alex kept reassuring her she would be alright, that he would never leave her side until she told him to. Making it very clear to him, Leah never wanted him to leave.

There had to be a better way of curing the infection other than what Morris was trying to do but then he wanted complete control, which he almost had. He knew about the shades being infected and he wanted to be the most powerful being, no doubt to control them as well. What I was hoping for, and I wasn't sure if they would even know. If there was some way I could help rid the infection then Leah would be back to her normal self without having to worry about her own family dying off.

I wasn't sure how much my father was aware of or who exactly handed me over to him when my mother died; I just had this incredibly strong feeling she wasn't dead. I couldn't shake that feeling that my mother might still be alive.

THE HEALING
PROCESS

Not far from the house, dad and I could see how many
had already been waiting for us back at the house. Many of his
friends were standing outside along with the new ones from the
club. They were all discussing what had been going on while a
few were still disoriented, not sure what had happened in the last
few weeks. While they were all busy talking and I watched my
father join in, I slipped away unnoticed to check on Voncha and
Jasper. Leah was in the living room sitting and relaxing while Alex
went to get her a drink. At least she had someone to help look
after her for now. Walking down the hallway I peeked into
Voncha's room, he was still quietly resting. His face was so badly
bruised, bloody and swollen. Grabbing a washcloth from the
bathroom with a basin. I tried to wash off as much as I could
without waking him. All he had done was shift when I stopped.
Still sleeping I didn't want to wake him, for now, sleep would be
best while he recovers but for now he will have to settle with not
moving to much until he fully heals. Leaving his room to check on
Jasper, he was already sitting up against the headrest leaning
forward holding onto his head. As soon as I had stepped into the
room, he knew I was there but hadn't looked up.

"I would prefer you didn't see me like this anymore. I
hated it when you had to see me in the condition I was in earlier. I
should have been able to protect you and your father better. I

utterly failed." Jasper was still weak, cradling his head in his hands as he let out a sigh of disappointment.

"You didn't fail at anything. Everyone is alive and safe; you risked your life for us doing what you could. No matter how you look, I will always look at you as my hero and love you for everything you've done for me and my family." Sitting down on the edge of the bed being careful not to hurt him. I put my arms around him, hugging him.

"It was foolish for any of you to risk coming for me. Everyone could have died because of me and that's just not right." Lifting his head and removing his hands away from his face, he pushed me back slightly to look at me.

"If I had lost you because of Morris, I never would have forgiven myself. I was only targeted because he knew my mother; he knew I was living with vampires who were there to protect me. I think I finally figured out why he tested you so much and later with Voncha. Both of you had family traits of shades who like my mother, tried to blend in with regular mortals. Your blood wasn't tainted because you were changed by my father, it happened because the venom simply took over. The shades have an actual illness that not only weakens them but won't allow their body to heal itself putting their bodies into a permanent pause. They haven't turned into vampires; they are simply frozen in dormancy." The sad look on Jasper's face let me know he wasn't concerned about his past.

"Promise me you will never do anything like that again. Regardless of what happens to me, you are to stay safe. I can't afford to lose you." Jasper's voice came across as a whisper when he said, I can't afford to lose you.

"We've learned best by example; you would have done the same for us. You're just as important as the rest of us. My life would not be the same without you. You honestly can't expect me to let them kill you and do nothing about it. You must stay in my life. I need you..... I love you." Not having to say another word, he placed his arms around me hugging me very tight almost as if he was afraid to let me go. I hoped he never would.

"No one told me what happened to Morris, I don't remember much other than someone picking me up and moving me and Voncha to the house right away. I was worried when I caught a glimpse of you walking towards Morris." As Jasper said this his voice was shaky.

"He was destroyed by the mess he created." Not wanting to go into details.

A light knock at the door interrupted us as I moved back to see who was there. My father was standing in the doorway.

"I checked on Voncha; he still seems to be sleeping. How are you feeling Jasper?" Walking in the room further I knew my father was questioning my being with Jasper.

Normally he never would have given it a second thought except for the way I had treated and spoken to him at the lake house. He wasn't happy when he had first found out we were interested in each other beyond friendship.

"I'll be fine. Just more healing than I can start doing some research on the Golden Dawn, shade group. That way we will at least have some idea what else we will be facing." I knew Jasper wasn't that close to getting better except he was trying to distract my father's attention, not that it helped.

"We don't need to search for them; Leah knows where to find them. She can bring me right to them, the Rising Dawn that is." This was something I was already planning as soon as she gave birth.

"Are you out of your mind? They might want to kill you; after all of this you would think running straight to them would be the last thing you would want to do. You're not going anywhere near them." Jasper started sliding his feet out from the bed to stand up.

"If you remember I handled today just fine and the last few weeks. Besides, I don't think they want to kill me; they are just searching for a cure. If you go looking for them then yes, they will kill you." At least from what Leah had described to me about their hating vampires, they would.

"As your father, I refuse to let you go, you might be an adult, but you are still to respect my wishes. I have a few things to discuss with Jasper." The serious look had returned to father's eyes as he looked over at Jasper.

"I have something I need to discuss with you privately, it won't take long then you can talk with Jasper." Taking a step back I hoped father would at least take a few seconds with me in the hallway.

"That can wait until I am finished here." Turning his back on me it was his way of letting me know I was expected to leave.

"Alright then, I guess I'll see you later. I'm taking off with Alex for the Rising Dawn then." Turning I went out of the room when father was immediately next to me grabbing my arm.

Smiling to myself I knew how to get to him. Reaching out I had closed the door very determined to speak with father before he had his words with Jasper. I had a feeling I knew what he was going to say to him, and I wasn't going to risk it happening again. If he had taken a second, he would have realized I couldn't take Alex with me any more than I could have taken Voncha or Jasper.

"You are to do no such thing." Demanding as his voice boomed. I was sure everyone in the house heard.

"I wasn't heading out anywhere yet, I had to get you to listen. I don't want this to end up like last time. I know you told him to stay away from me. I understand you want me to have a normal, regular life but be honest. It's never going to happen because I'm not normal myself. How could you even think of doing something like that?" I felt hurt that he had, and I didn't hide it in my voice.

"I was doing what was best for you. It is still best for you." Not even attempting to look me in the face, my father kept staring at the door.

"If Voncha had been interested in me, would you turn him away also? Or any of the others who have been extremely close to me because they are not who you see me with? The two blind dates you had set me up on a few years ago. Remember those? The first guy tried to rape me and thankfully because it was my first date, Jasper had followed us on the entire date. He saved me when I needed it then and he's still doing it now. On the second date, he was just a horny pervert who had no respect for women, is that what you want for me? I know not all humans are like that but there are a lot who are." I knew he had felt guilty, even angry at the time when he found out what my experience with them had been.

"Not all mortals are that bad, there are some great guys out there, just give them a chance." I knew there would be nice guys out there only I had already found him.

"Why are you so dead set against Jasper? Is it because you can't see him past your partying buddy? He cares for me, loves me and you know I'm safer with him than anyone else. He without question will do anything for me to make me happy and to keep me safe. Look at what he just went through to protect you and me. I was forced to torture him to blend in so no one would realize who I was, he didn't respond to the pain hoping to make it easier for me." I was hoping to reason with him except I wasn't sure I was getting through to him.

"It's a matter of loyalty; he knew my rules when you were dropped off here. He's not mortal. I know things about him, from his past, what he is capable of and what exactly he has done. If you only knew you would turn your own back on him now." My father's voice was very deep sounding leaving almost an echo without having his own words escape between us.

"Don't make me choose between the rest of my family and you. As much as I love you, you're going to lose. Think over what you're going to say to Jasper." Turning around leaving him standing there in the hallway I stood behind what I had said.

Spending the rest of the day with Leah, she had already been experiencing a few labor pains. Before it had been Braxton hicks. It was nice seeing Alex taking such good care of her. Massaging her stomach when the cramping was getting strong or just getting her something to drink or eat to make things easier for her. It was nice watching the two while they were in love. Alex had already let her know how he felt. This is how it should be, simple, easy, nothing to fight over or be kept away from each other.

Giving them space I had finally gone back to check on Voncha to see how he was doing. Sitting up in his bed he hadn't looked any better than Jasper but at least he wasn't trying to hide the condition he was in from me. He seemed rather proud of his battle scars. As I came closer Voncha grabbed me around the waist lifting me off from the floor, flipping me over onto my back on the other side of him on the bed. Moving quickly, he was hovering over me smiling rather evilly.

"I heard your father's famous booming voice. What have you done now?" Smiling I knew he was joking.

"At least you're healing and feeling better. Dad is just mad about Jasper and me again." I didn't feel like going into details of the argument, especially with Voncha now that I knew he had feelings for me.

"Maybe we should make him worry we have all fallen for you? Think it's possible to die a second time from a heart attack?" Pressing down against my body I knew there was truth in his words as he was still being careful.

"I already suggested it to him. Unfortunately, he would run everyone off if he thought it helped. I don't understand why he's being suddenly protective of me; didn't he know this would eventually happen when I was younger?" I had been thinking about this ever since he sent Jasper off the first time.

"The vampire world is very different from what you've seen so far, this is the best aspect of it. There are traditions and rules we live by that to outsiders don't always make sense. For those of us who have been around for a very long time, they serve their purpose. Many rules that even I hope you never learn about." Voncha's voice lowered to almost a barely breathed whisper and a slight shudder.

"Both of you know me better than anyone else, every detail of my life growing up until now. My likes and dislikes, pet peeves, dreams, and nightmares, I've shared everything with both of you. Why would he think with that personal connection as I grew older, that an intimate relationship would never happen?"

"It's why your father told us to begin with, to never look at you that way and we didn't. At least not until you did get older; it just wasn't something we thought we would have a problem with." Voncha always spoke directly which I was thankful for.

"If father asked you to leave because of me, would you?" I knew it might have sounded strange, but I would hate to think my family would leave if simply asked.

"Jasper never would have left; he stayed nearby which is why he was around to protect your father. I would never dream of leaving you for any reason." Voncha started kissing my neck.

"I think I should get up." Starting to turn slightly Voncha stopped me for a moment pulling me towards him and kissed me on the lips.

"I'm always here if you ever change your mind." Letting go of me Voncha leaned back letting me go, I felt slightly light-headed.

"Jasper is your best friend. I would think you would be worried how he would feel?" Getting up from the bed to leave I had looked at Voncha one last time before leaving.

"He knows. We haven't kept any secrets from each other." That was the last thing I heard him say as I walked out of the room.

Standing in the hallway, Jasper's room was only down the hall slightly. I was worried he might have heard us through the wall. Pausing at the door before opening it I hesitated, not feeling like going in. Just how much did the two of them share, especially if they both knew they were interested in me? Turning the handle and opening the door, I peeked into his bedroom. Jasper's bed was empty. It had already been made with the chair no longer by his bedside. Leaning against the wall I felt sick to my stomach thinking he might have left if father spoke to him, if he could only be more definite like Voncha. Walking into his room I looked out the window to see my father speaking with a few of the ones who had joined us. As his friends left, each brought with them someone from the club to help mentor or as my father did when he changed Voncha and Jasper, to train and raise. Many vampires had assistants either with the family business or other means.

"What's so interesting out there?" Standing next to me peeking out to see what I was so captivated by.

"Your still here!" Turning I put my arms around Jasper hugging him as tight as I could.

"Of course, I am. Where did you think I went?" He seemed rather surprised.

"I thought dad might ask you to leave again." Not bothering to let go I was so happy he was still home.

"Did Voncha tell you that? You weren't supposed to know that. I didn't want you getting upset with your father, he had his reasons. Is that what you spoke to him privately outside of my room earlier?" All I had to do was nod my head.

"Voncha didn't have much of a choice, when dad and the others disappeared and we were being followed, we had to hide. I wanted to know where you were, he couldn't avoid telling me any longer." Which was true, I wasn't going to make another move until I was told about Jasper.

"The Golden Dawn, do you still intend on searching for them? They might not accept you since you take after both of your parents." I should have realized he wouldn't let this go.

"If I am a shade then I could learn from them instead of risking hurting anyone when I self-teach, they could teach me things I would never figure out on my own. Leah hasn't had contact with her family in a long time because of Morris, when we brought her here, she sent a message to her brother, he'll be coming soon to help either bring her home or set her up here. She doesn't know what she wants right now." I wasn't worried about my safety, I was positive the last thing they would want to do is hurt me since I wasn't tainted, but then that might be different after they are healed and because of who my father is.

"It's a hormone that you create in your bloodstream. None of their shades were carriers. If a shade is infected then later bitten by a vampire, the venom takes over. They lose who they were. Leah was infected so the egg didn't come from her, she was a carrier, it's hard to say how the child will turn out not knowing who the biological parents were?" I never knew shades existed and yet Jasper knew a lot more than he was letting on.

"I don't know if Leah even knows the little one isn't from her? No matter how it turns out, she's given life to it, loves it, and cares for it. That makes her as solid of a mother as anyone else. I assume they knew about me because of my mother? How did they know she wasn't infected unless she didn't know about them?" I had so many questions I just didn't know how much Jasper was aware of himself.

"They were infected after she left them, she never knew. Someone they had trusted was being used, they wanted to take control of this group and exploit their gifts except they didn't realize by infecting them made it impossible for them to reproduce or heal; by doing it they lost the power they wanted to control. They had to shut themselves off from others or risk becoming a rarity." I could hear the concern in Jasper's voice.

"Why do they hate vampires so much?" Jasper looked away as I asked.

I knew I wasn't going to like the answer.

"We've had a feud going on for years, it all started from something incredibly innocent. Because of it they started to look for fault with us, they felt that vampires were unnatural; they disagree with our consuming blood, the way we live, and certain traditions that are passed down. They tried to exterminate us, we defended ourselves and killed quite a few of them when they were not expecting us." Jasper seemed rather surprised when he mentioned they killed quite a few.

"I'm guessing they blame the vampires as a whole for them being infected?" I was curious who had infected them if it was someone they trusted?

"Yes, they blame us. It's difficult not to when the virus was created by a vampire only it was stolen and administered by a shade. The one who did it very unwittingly infected himself also. No one knew the full effects it would have other than what they had experienced so far. Ever since they have kept to themselves and we have left them alone, almost a forced peace." Sitting down on the edge of the bed Jasper ran his fingers through his hair almost as if he was relieved.

"Morris has been behind this for quite some time. If shades lived in colonies, how did they all get affected?" I couldn't imagine Morris being that well trusted unless they trusted him because he had been a shade at one time?"

"He had experiments going on for a long time before people realized what he was doing. He was finally ousted from the shade communities except he had already done the damage they can't repair now. He saved things from your mother; I think the egg might be from her. I don't know what your father has told you about your mother, how she died? Morris had her killed. There was no choice, it was all controlled by Morris, and it's why I didn't want to risk you anywhere near him, I....." Before I could get my answer there was an urgent knock at the door.

Leah had finally gone into labor; a midwife had come to the house that Leah knew to help with the birth. The entire time she seemed rather nervous to be surrounded by a group of vampires, it was easy enough to guess she was a shade, no doubt wondering what Leah was doing with all of us. She gave birth to a very wiggly baby boy. After the birth, the midwife left as soon as she could.

As soon as I looked at him, I knew Jasper was right. He looked so much like my mother, the porcelain smooth skin, bright blue eyes, and dusty blond hair. From what Leah had told me, all her family had dark fiery red hair and either brown or green eyes. Leah had dark green eyes and beautiful red hair. If I hadn't known, it couldn't possibly be her egg. I would have just assumed the blue eyes had been a recessive gene.

For a moment, my father glanced over at me no doubt curious about my reaction. Jasper continued to stare no doubt wondering if I would inform Leah, she just gave birth to my little brother? She was so excited and proud I had decided not to say anything. We would keep in touch, and I knew he would be taken care of and most of all very much loved.

A young man was standing outside not coming too close to the house. I had noticed the midwife stopped briefly to speak to him before she had left. Voncha and Jasper noticed also. I wanted to find out who this person was and why he was not coming up to the house. It wasn't until he had taken off his cap that I noticed who it was, Leah's brother. The red hair gave him away. Looking around I hadn't seen anyone else. Jasper tried to persuade me from going out, he had wanted to check it out himself, but I insisted on going with him. We were not that far from the young man; he took a defensive stance right away creating an energy ball in his hand no doubt to protect himself if we had wanted to attack him. The two of us stopped a few feet from him when he had done this, placing my palm upward I had mimicked his same action only staying relaxed to show him no harm. Not keeping the energy ball going I let it dissipate.

"You're a shade?" He seemed rather skeptical.

146

"Yes, I am, don't sound so surprised." I wasn't going to point out Jasper being a vampire since it wasn't necessary.

"Do you realize you're in a house full of vampires right now? You're a lamb to slaughter around them." His voice deepened as he sounded angry and did not bother to hide his disdain for vampires.

"If that were true, I would have been dead years ago. I'm perfectly safe in there, they happen to be my family. I'm not an infected shade but even if I had been I would still be safe. I saw the midwife speak to you; I'm guessing your Leah's brother?" Might as well get to the point, skip the small talk and find out why he was here.

"The midwife was from our colony. Leah is my sister. When I heard she was surrounded by a bunch of vampires. I came to check it out, I was hoping they hadn't changed her." Looking over at Jasper I think he was questioning if he was a vampire or not.

"You're welcome to come in and see her; no one is going to harm you." He hadn't said anything other than to nod in agreement.

From the expression on Jasper's face, I knew he wasn't thrilled but wasn't going to prevent him from coming in either. Making our way to Leah's room, Alex had still been standing beside her. The young man seemed relieved when he saw Leah sitting there talking to her baby but felt uncomfortable with the others around her. As we made our way in, we asked for the others to kindly leave to give Leah some private time with her brother. The young man was even more relaxed when Leah informed him the baby's father was a shade until he lost his natural-born gifts. At first, his fists started to clench as he looked at Alex no doubt angry, she was around a vampire, regardless of if he had been a shade at one time.

As soon as she noticed her brother getting angry, she started to fill him in on the man who had infected the clan, that he was killed by the vampires, this he seemed rather skeptical of. Closing the door behind them I could still hear them talking from the hallway. The house was getting less crowded as several more

147

departed. Eventually, it was only my father, Jasper, Voncha, and Alex sitting in the living room talking.

They were discussing what went wrong when they were captured. It had been a trap set up by one of his friends, who happened to be dead now, which he never went into detail on how. Alex had paced back and forth, no doubt worried about Leah, he hadn't left her once when we had moved her away from the others. After a while I could hear Leah calling for me, she seemed rather excited by the tone of her voice. Leaving the others in the living room I knew Jasper would have preferred to come in with me instead of leaving me alone with Ryan in the room. Leah's brother was holding the baby when I came in.

"I have great news; Ryan can take you to see the Golden Dawn if you're still interested? My family is well known so if you go with him, they will treat you well." Looking from Leah to her brother I wondered if he had volunteered himself or if it was her idea.

"This would help our people greatly. We could finally rebuild and keep those from ever harming us again." He did seem rather enthusiastic about my possibly coming.

"I am still interested in helping out, the only problem I have now is a confusing one." I wasn't sure if I wanted to share it since I hadn't made up my mind now.

"What could be confusing about being around your kind again?" Reaching over he handed his nephew back to Leah who frowned at him.

"The way you just worded your comment worries me, if I help the clan, they could start up a war against vampires again, which would mean my own family wouldn't be safe. If I don't help out, then an entire group would still be facing possible extinction." I wasn't sure what to do or if I could help at all.

"If they met you and knew you were raised by vampires, they might think different, especially since vampires are who killed the one who infected us in the first place. Plus, they could see what you've done for me." Leah tried to sound hopeful.

"What happened to the ones who were changed? Do they still live with the colony or were they forced out?" I kept thinking this over from the moment we finally arrived home.

148

"That's something we don't discuss; we are rather protective of our colony." The look on his face I knew I wasn't going to get an answer.

"When they still don't agree, and I change my mind I doubt they would let me leave willingly." I still had to think about my safety.

"I would make sure you get in and out safely, I doubt any of them would harm you but if you're able to help they would almost treat you as a god if you wanted, we can keep it a secret until you feel comfortable." He seemed rather sure of himself.

"I guess it can't hurt to try. Would be nice to have a natural peace with the two groups rather than a temporarily forced one, who knows, maybe this would be a good thing, I could meet a few others who share my gifts and maybe learn something from them?" At least I was trying to look at the positive side.

"Do you think the others will let you go? That one seems overly protective of you." At least I knew Ryan hadn't meant my father, he was interested in seeing if there was something more to it from the sound of his tone.

"Jasper and Voncha have protected and taken care of me since I was very little; they are extremely close to my father. I've learned a lot from them. It's not something that I want to discuss since it's still something I'm getting used to. Jasper and I have a very special relationship." I wasn't going to give details since there wasn't much to give.

"It sounds like a plan then; Ryan will take you there and I'll stay here with the baby. Alex will help me; I don't want to move around with him quite yet, especially since it's so cold outside with the snow. I don't care to travel in the cold anyway. Besides, I'm hoping if Emma likes it there, she might stay. Her little brother would love it." Smiling at us she returned her attention to the baby.

"I wasn't sure if you knew, I wasn't going to say anything." I guess now that she wasn't under Morris's influence, she could figure it out.

"It's not something I'll be sharing with my family." She had finished whispering it to me.

"What are you not sharing with me?" Ryan was curious about what his sister was keeping from him.

"Feminine issues." Smiling she waved at us to give us the hint she wanted to spend time with Alex and the baby again.

Ryan and I stepped out of the room, Alex had slipped in which made Ryan nervous until I reminded him his sister was in such good condition because he had looked after her, before I had even come there, he was slipping her vitamins for pregnant women since they hadn't been provided for her, he had also helped save her from Morris. While the others continued to sit Jasper stood up immediately. Walking Ryan to the door as he left, he whispered to me however it still wasn't low enough for the others not to hear him.

"I'll be back in the morning; I have a friend to visit this evening and then I'll take you. Make sure your ready it's a long hike since our shades don't exactly have speed like the vampires you're used to getting around with." Giving a nod of his head to say goodbye, he turned and left.

I was hoping he would have whispered it low enough; I didn't want to give the others enough time to think and argue over my decision to go. I might have been hoping for more than what was realistic except I had hoped I would learn more about my mother. She was part of the same colony as Leah and Ryan. I wanted to learn more about being a shade since Jasper knew the most except, he wasn't willingly giving out information about it anymore. He even started to stammer getting incredibly nervous.

Jasper never finished his sentence, and I knew there was something he was going to say except he was interrupted by Voncha's knock at the door when Leah went into labor earlier. I could already tell my father was angry that I was even considering it; I could feel Voncha's frustration and Jasper's worry. Sometimes I wished I wasn't so connected to everyone. I blame that part on the shade part of me, I wasn't sure if being a shade had any control over it, but it felt good having something to blame.

Instead of making eye contact with any of them, I had simply walked up the steps, down the hallway, and to my room closing the door behind me. I had a lot to pack if I was going to get ready; I wanted to make sure I was prepared because there was no coming back for a while. I wasn't sure just how long I would be gone. I was having a hard time deciding just how much to pack if it was a long way, I would have to carry it all, but I didn't want to risk forgetting anything. I finally settled on a small backpack filling it with a couple of shirts and pants that could be worn repeatedly, a small shawl in case I did get cold, a few personal emergency items, and a few Wiccan items wrapped in purple cloth.

I hated to admit it, but it would also give me a chance to get away from everyone and have a chance to think about my relationship with Jasper, how I was going to react around Voncha now that I know how he feels. I wanted Jasper except I had such a close relationship with Voncha. I was worried I would lose him when I didn't choose him. I know I hadn't lost him yet; he had let me know he was still there for me, just not in the way I would have preferred. As I was packing Jasper quietly let himself in the room. He startled me when I turned around to find him standing right next to me.

"I don't trust him, he's hiding something. You're not going alone." Jasper had his hands crossed over his chest

"I don't fully trust him either, but it is my way in. Who could I possibly have come with me that you would trust? It can't be another vampire or you; they would kill either on the spot. My supposedly living a normal life and the fact I have no friends to show for it, not that I would want to risk dragging any of them into this, I know I'll be safe." I understood he wanted to protect me except there were no options available.

"I'll take you at least halfway there and follow the rest of the way. I'll stay back far enough not to attract their attention and if you need either of us Voncha and I will be ready." Jasper was still determined.

"What if this turns into a trap like the last one?" I knew he couldn't talk his way out of this one.

"We will be prepared this time." Speaking before he gave it thought. I knew he was reacting emotionally instead of thinking it out logically the way he normally would.

"Shouldn't you have been prepared last time?" Putting a sarcastic tone to my voice.

"Your right, we should have been prepared instead of waiting for them. You don't have to go, this group if it's important enough could have sent someone other than a message, I feel it's a trap." Jasper wasn't amused by my comment or tone.

"It would shorten the travel if you and Voncha took us at least halfway, but you can't go any further, neither of you can risk coming closer. If this was a trap, I'm sure they could come up with something much better than this. Besides, they really can't risk an attack against them, they might react immediately when they see you before they find out there's nothing to fear from you." At least Jasper had to agree with my reasoning.

"Did he give any explanation where he was going tonight?" Jasper seemed to be curious why he hadn't stayed here with his sister if he was so worried about her.

"Ryan said he had a friend to see before we took off. My main reason for giving him the benefit of the doubt is solely based on Leah's confidence in her brother. I should be safe, I can take care of myself, I've learned from the best." Smiling at Jasper he hadn't been too thrilled.

"I know you can protect yourself; I just hate the thought of you needing to. Flattery will get you nowhere." Standing closer to me looking down Jasper kissed me on the forehead.

The plan had been to take off in the morning even though I would have preferred traveling at night so that neither Voncha or Jasper were caught in the sun. Ryan assured me that we would be traveling through mostly forest areas and the weatherman promised a cloudy day. I wasn't sure if I would get that much sleep, I was nervous about my trip not that I wanted to share that with Jasper, or he would try to talk me out of it again.

"We won't have much time to talk before we leave tomorrow. Mind if I watch you sleep?" Not so much as a question it seemed more like a statement when Jasper sat down on my bed.

"I always sleep better when you're around." Knowing Jasper didn't sleep did creep me out now that I knew, I didn't mind him watching me sleep it was just the concept that he never needed sleep.

With Jasper at the head of the bed, I had rested against his chest with my arms wrapped around him. The house had been kept warmer with the baby being here so feeling the coolness from Jasper felt great. It hadn't been long before I had found myself dreaming; unfortunately, they hadn't all been pleasant dreams. At one point Jasper had woken me up which I had been thankful for. I was dreaming about Morris and in the middle of a battle we were suddenly whisked away somewhere else I hadn't recognized before. Voncha was laying on the floor dead, not vampire dead but no more return. I had woken myself up from that one crying. I swear I must have scared Jasper.

"If you're so nervous why force yourself to go tomorrow, you can stay here, and eventually they will send a messenger." I was sure Jasper was correct except I didn't want them around my family.

"I'm not nervous about tomorrow, it's just that I'm finally feeling safe and relaxed that the past few weeks have caught up with me. I'm just glad you're here." Giving Jasper a tighter hug I had let myself drift off to sleep again.

Father wasn't happy with the idea of me leaving let alone with Ryan and intentionally going to a shade colony. He had even tried grounding me, which at my age was a little late for that type of parenting, but I admire him for trying. Waking up in the morning much earlier than I had planned. Voncha knocked on the door to let me know Ryan was waiting outside. Voncha hadn't liked the fact Ryan wanted to wait outside instead of being polite and waiting for me inside. Jasper had waited up all night, slipping off from the bed, from beside me I grabbed my bag and wore the clothes I went to sleep in for my first day of travel. Meeting Ryan downstairs he seemed very eager to leave, not that he knew our new travel arrangements. After explaining them to him he seemed reluctant to take off now, which hadn't helped either of Voncha or Jasper's worry.

"I'm not traveling that way; I don't trust you either." Pausing between words it seemed as though he was looking for a way out.

"They are only coming with us halfway, to help speed up the travel. They won't even come close to where we are going to, it's not as if I want to risk their lives. You will be safe with us; they won't harm you. It's just like a piggyback ride." I tried to reassure

153

him as much as possible, but the way Voncha and Jasper were acting, it wasn't easy.

"I need to see my sister before we go." Now finally heading into the house Ryan walked straight to Leah's room opening the door.

Ryan had wanted me to come in with him. Following behind leaving Voncha and Jasper in the living room wondering what he was up to, he closed the door behind us. Leah was excited to see him as he leaned over hugging his sister and kissing his nephew on the forehead. Pulling out two small boxes from his pocket he handed Leah one. As she opened it excitedly she pulled out a delicate silver necklace with a heart pendant attached. Her name was etched on the front, on the back were the words, "my inspiration." The second box he had held firmly in his hand, turning to me he handed it to me.

"This is for taking such good care of my sister and for protecting her when she needed it." Ryan had sounded very sincere.

Opening the small box there was a similar delicate necklace with a pendant heart, only the front didn't have my name on it, Ryan's was etched on it with the words on the back, "to new beginnings, hopes, and future." I had never felt strange about a gift given to me before, but then I never felt like there was an alternative meaning to a gift like this one had. I knew if Voncha or Jasper were to see this they would be even more on edge and distrustful of him, not wanting to risk leaving me alone, not just for my safety but also out of jealousy. Holding it firmly in my hand I had hoped to slip it into my pocket before anyone else saw what I had done with it, I didn't want to risk wearing it.

"It wasn't necessary, I considered it a privilege to get to know Leah, probably Morris's worst mistake but then he hadn't recognized me at that point, however, thank you for the gift, it was very thoughtful." Hoping this would appease him he had kept smiling waiting for me to put the necklace on.

Walking behind me and reaching out for the necklace, Ryan had insisted on helping me put it on. As he did the locket had fallen inside of my shirt since the chain was long.

"I guess we will have to find a shorter necklace or just wear lower collars." Smiling he knew I was uncomfortable wearing it. I just hoped no one else noticed or Jasper would never let me leave.

"Are we ready to leave? We should get going before the sun comes up." Jasper hadn't wanted to start but he did want to skip traveling as much as possible with the sun out.

The forecaster had mentioned cloudy skies all day except they hadn't rolled in yet even though we could see them in the distance.

I guess it was a good thing Ryan had gone to visit with Leah before we left. I wasn't sure how she managed it; she talked him into trusting Voncha enough to let them take us halfway. While Voncha was giving Ryan a ride, Jasper had been mine. As we took off, I could feel the wind rushing past us leaving the house behind, we could no longer see Leah or dad waving goodbye to us. The scenery rushed by so fast I hadn't bothered to see or watch for anything. I could hear Voncha breathing next to us as he kept up to Jasper. Resting my head on Jasper's shoulder with my eyes closed. I had breathed in his scent. I never told Jasper how long I would be gone, not that I could plan that. I was hoping only for a few months, just for a moment I had felt sick. The idea of leaving Jasper so soon, I didn't want to let go. I knew this was something I would miss, not just traveling this way but his scent, he was incredibly intoxicating.

Not that I wouldn't miss Jasper himself, but the scent always brought back an instant image of him in my mind which is why I had packed one of his shirts he had worn the day before. I hadn't told him but I'm sure he would figure it out when he found it missing. We had been going for quite a while when Jasper started checking to see if I needed a break, shaking my head no in response, we kept going. It was already going to be hard enough to say goodbye when I knew all I had to do was tell them I wasn't ready, and they would bring me back home. Uncomfortable or not, there were many reasons why I wanted to go, that I needed to go. I just wished I had someone I knew with me, unfortunately, Ryan didn't count since I hadn't known him at all.

I could only tell we had passed certain areas by the feel in the air or the obvious spray of the water as we passed it, I would have tried to catch a glimpse, but my eyes were never fast enough to focus to see where we were. During our trip, we had only stopped twice, mainly for Ryan and me to sleep. Ryan had rented two rooms insisting that I sleep in the same room and Voncha and Jasper in the other room, he still hadn't trusted them. Jasper and Voncha not trusting him had insisted on adjoining rooms with the door left open the entire time.

After traveling for a couple of days we had reached our destination which had been out of the country and far enough from home. This would be the first time I had ever been this far away from home and gone this long. I was thankful to have Voncha and Jasper take us this far otherwise it would have taken us a few months traveling by foot, Ryan didn't believe in using a car even though he had no objections to a boat. Shades were not gifted in the way of speed the way vampires were. As Ryan and Leah had informed me, usually they had pets that they rode however couldn't take them here so we went to where the coldest region was located that very few people even bothered living that they could get away with their travel. It helped; they were also able to cloak much of the area to keep anyone from seeing that the shade city had even existed here.

There was rumored that a couple of other shade colonies existed except for protection reasons, they certainly kept their locations just as secret and concealed which made me wonder if they were infected also? If they were not, why couldn't they find each other if they could find me? It was like searching for a needle in a haystack. Jasper reminded me vampires were easier to find since they were more habitual and certain aspects made them stick out if you knew what you were looking for.

Slowing down until we had come to a stop, Ryan looked relieved to finally get off Voncha's back but then I also think it was rather mutual. Neither Voncha or Ryan tried to talk during the trip, not that I had talked with Jasper, not an easy thing to do at that speed, and the wind dried out your mouth if you attempted to speak. Ryan hadn't experienced travel like this so it would have been disorienting for him, I know it certainly was for

156

me when I found out and had my first trip with Jasper. At times I had to remind myself that all of this was still new to me even though now when I think back there were certainly clues or times they had slipped up, I just never caught on because I never believed in the existence of vampires. I had decided never to say I didn't believe in something until it could be proven it didn't exist. The world suddenly looked so different to me now.

"Are you sure you don't want us to follow you further?" With his arm scooped around my waist I knew Jasper didn't want to let me go yet.

"I'm positive, besides I'll be safe I don't want to risk your life. I know you are both capable of staying hidden but there's no point in taking a chance if it's not needed. Hopefully, I won't be gone for too long." I was hoping I wouldn't start crying when I said goodbye to Jasper and Voncha.

Kissing Jasper on the lips and tight hug I started to think he wasn't going to let go of me. I then moved toward Voncha, giving him almost an equally tight hug since I knew I wouldn't see either of them for a while and I wasn't sure how our relationship was going to be affected if I had decided to date Jasper and get serious with him when I came back. Kissing him on the cheek, we had finished saying our goodbyes.

Standing there watching as Ryan and I had started our climb up the side of the mountain, most of the walk would be over the top, the highest I've ever been. No wonder they were not worried about outsiders seeing them up here. It would be too difficult to get up here let alone for someone not to know you were coming. I hadn't looked back once since I knew I would never leave. Following Ryan as he made his way to his home, he kept clearing a path with his hand using the energy to heat the path melting the snow along the way.

TRUST ME

After walking a while, we stopped near a cliff resting our feet, I wasn't used to this much exercise. I might not have been out of shape but then I never walked and hiked this much either. Ryan and I hadn't talked too much but then it was difficult when I was busy trying to catch my breath. The altitude was getting to me. Listening to my breathing Ryan had decided to stop and let me get acclimated to the height we climbed. At least for a little while after this cliff, there would be a long straight path before we started going up again. He promised that we were getting much closer and not that much further to walk. 'Not that much further' seemed to be his favorite set of words he used to get me to take a few steps more before asking, almost as if we had been in the car and the kids asking, 'are we there yet.'

"How are your feet?" Ryan had sat down on the rock next to me.

"I'm not sure, numb but I'm not checking them, or I might never get my shoes back on." I was busy rubbing my legs, they had felt like they were cramping slightly.

"We don't need to go anywhere right away, there is a cave we can sleep in, that should give you enough time to acclimate to the lack of air. The shade colony provides its protection and air climate." Ryan seemed distracted when he explained this.

"What are you looking at?" He seemed rather fixated with something on the ground.

"Stay where you're at for now." His tone of voice deepened which worried me.

I could see a little red where he was standing. Melting away the snow around it, he reached in pulling out a sock that was stained pink. The snow had dissolved most of it except both of us knew it was blood. Looking around in the same area he had found a lump, not a rock as we first suspected. It had been a tennis shoe. Grabbing me by the hand we started walking slowly around the cliffside. We would have taken a different route except this was the only way up. Ryan wasn't sure if there was a vampire up here, it figures he would blame a vampire first before thinking it was anything else.

"This is the only pass along this rock to get where we need to go. Something has killed up here, there is fresh and old blood." Still looking around for more clues, we kept walking.

"How can this be the only way up?" It seemed as if they would want more ways to get to the colony.

"It keeps others out who shouldn't be up here. The other two sides are flat rock, with no open crevices or areas to hold onto. If we had climbing gear and you were experienced, we could do it. With there being old and fresh blood, I don't think whatever did this has moved on. I'm guessing you're wishing your vamp boyfriend was here?" Ryan had only glanced at me while he was still paying attention to the trail ahead.

"It would be nice if he was here." There were so many other things I could have said but truthfully, I hadn't thought about him since we left him and started hiking.

Pain sort of won on that one, I felt guilty thinking it should have been one of my concerns. Now that Ryan had brought him up, I couldn't get Jasper off my mind. I was curious what they would do if my father was still upset with me leaving and most pressing if we would run into who left the blood or caused it? There's nothing better than the danger of forging an immediate friendship. For the first time, I caught a glimpse over the edge as we walked by. My stomach dropped; I could only see the tips of the trees from the forest below. I wasn't sure what we would do if we had run into anyone. I was hoping Ryan did since he insisted on continuing. I was busy looking over the edge when Ryan stopped quickly, I ran into the back of him.

"I didn't think you wanted to get that friendly?" Whispering to me smiling he looked back towards a sound that was getting louder.

Putting his hand over mine, I was about to respond except he cautioned me not to. We were not alone. Not knowing who else or what else was out here was getting scary. Someone was walking towards us crunching down the snow. We were about to back up until we had seen what sneaked up on us from behind. Only taking a glance back we realized there was nowhere to go. A person was blocking the pathway down and now two more blocking the pathway in front of us.

"I suggest you follow without fighting or I promise you will fall to your death, no doubt helped by us." The man behind us spoke first.

Neither of the men seemed to be dressed for the cold weather. Short sleeve shirt and jeans with blood spattered on them. The one standing behind us was broad-shouldered with scars on his face. The two other men looked rather like him, only one had a beard and mustache which was overgrown and dirty. The two in front of us started following the path expecting us to follow, it looked like we didn't have much of a choice. The man behind us had taken out his gun in case we tried to either escape or trick them somehow. They had taken us to the cave we were originally going to spend the night. The closer we were to the cave we could see more blood on the ground.

Instead of going into the cave, they had us sit outside along the wall, we were just at the tip of the cliff where it had finally started to widen out. I would have tried doing something if we hadn't been so close to the edge. Tying our hands behind our back would have made it difficult to do anything. I was thankful not to go into the cave, I already felt like throwing up when I had seen the dismembered leg on the ground in front of the cave. Now I was worried about what they were going to do to us. I tried not to panic; Ryan had still held onto my hand occasionally squeezing it. Even though I wished Jasper and Voncha were here to protect us. I was thankful not to be alone. Then Ryan leaned over to me to whisper something when the others back was temporarily turned to us.

"Don't worry I'll be fine. I want you to stay put and do absolutely nothing no matter what sounds you hear or what happens. I just don't want you to panic when I do this. You'll need to trust that I know what I'm doing. I'll come back for you" Waiting for a second for my response I wasn't sure how to respond to this.

"Alright." That was all I could think to say? Was he planning on leaving me here?

Waiting for the three of them to be busy, they were putting body parts they had dismembered into a body bag. Only one of the men had checked to see if we were still tied and leaning against the wall, then he went back to the others to discuss what they were going to do with us. The longer they spoke the sicker I was getting. I was beginning to think they were worse than Morris had been. The group of three men were not vampires or shades, it was something I was unfamiliar with. The normal human form except they had long dirty nails, their eyes would get a glint of light flash across them occasionally. I would have guessed werewolf except there were too many things about them that hadn't quite fit the description, at least from tales or stories I had read. Ryan had whispered to me that he guessed they were experiments, which could have possibly belonged to Morris. He had worked on creating monsters for quite a while and lost a few up here when they ran off on him.

At least we didn't have to wonder what's been happening with the missing hikers. Not feeling comfortable with us watching them, every so often one would take a glance over at us. Taking that moment when the one had looked over, Ryan stood up brushing himself off. Looking at him in amazement I wondered how he was able to get his hands untied? Catching the attention of the three men, they were prepared to attack Ryan if he tried to take off or attack them.

"Not to worry, I'm not going to ask who the dead or mutilated bodies belong to, why you, or if you did or did not kill them. Heck, I don't even want to know what you have planned for us but there is one thing I would love to do before I die." Ryan wasn't waiting for them to respond even though they did seem surprised he was asking for the last right.

Before they could ask him what he was planning, Ryan swiftly shot across to the two of them surprising them both at his speed, the wind whipping around him knocking one of the men off the side of the cliff as he grabbed the last two men leaping off the cliff disappearing. I felt as if I was in total shock, did I just see him jump over the side with them? How did he move so fast if shades can't run fast like vampires? There was so much wind rushing past him I felt plastered to the rock wall when he first took off.

I wasn't sure how long he expected me to just stay here not knowing if he survived the fall himself. I wasn't even sure how far of a drop it had been. After waiting what felt like forever, I finally stepped forward to peer over the ledge to see to a horrifying sight. The tips of the trees still being several feet down while the side was very rough rock not giving much hope. There were clothing pieces from the previous victims stuck in the branches. The last thing I wanted to do was explain to his family how and why he died, and I lived. Deciding not to wait any longer I made my way down the path. I had hoped to find some way down to the ground below so that I could find out if Ryan was alright or not. I figured if Ryan could get out of his ties, then I should be able to. At first, I hit a blast against the side of the rock breaking a piece hitting myself with it. Then I tried something much simpler. I rubbed the rope against the jagged rock that now jutted out from where I blasted a small hole. Walking down the bumpy, uneven path was much easier with my hands-free.

Pushing much of the bushes and overgrown brush aside so that I could still see the path, a figure appeared immediately in front of me. Following instinct, I lashed out and hit the person as hard as I could, I had only assumed it was an attacker since they hadn't said anything or tried to announce themselves and Ryan was at the bottom of the deep ravine. When the person had fallen backward hitting the ground is when I realized who it was. Ryan was holding his bleeding nose smiling back at me.

"I am so sorry I didn't think it was you. I hope I didn't break your nose?" I felt sick that I had hit him, especially after what he had just been through.

"If the fall hadn't broken it, I doubt your punch would. Besides I have good news." Smiling still Ryan stood up.

"What news?" After what just happened I doubted there would be good news to tell me other than the fact Ryan lived but then I could already see that.

"Good news is that they reached the bottom," waiting for a second the expression on Ryan's face changed, "I guess that's not good news since they fell over the edge and hit a few rocks," waiting another second before finishing, "but they also hit a few jutted-out ledges on the way down and didn't land on their feet on the ground the way I had. I'm pretty sure the laying on the ground looking mangled not breathing is a pretty good indicator they died. At least they know what their victims felt like. Guess they shouldn't have dealt it if they couldn't take it either?" Acting as if he was surprised Ryan kept smiling, which in a way both creeped me out and impressed me how calmly he handled all of this and so quickly.

"You have a seriously twisted sense of humor." I was still surprised at the way he explained it to me let alone was standing in front of me alive.

"No, not twisted, just determined to be positive." Not losing his smile once he reminded me of Leah when he answered.

At least four more hours of walking and only Ryan knew how much longer we had until we were there. I had no idea if we were even halfway. Ryan had kept up his same pace while at times I was getting winded from the altitude, something I just wasn't getting used to. It wasn't until I finally had a bloody nose that Ryan stopped. Pulling out what looked like a tied-up umbrella, he slowly opened it to reveal a small pup tent that we had gone into. I wasn't thrilled being this close to him, but it was nice to get out of the wind. The snow on the ground had still been just under my knee, I hoped it wouldn't get much deeper or I was going to have a problem keeping up. I started to think maybe it wasn't a safe idea to come with Ryan. Pulling out of his pocket a handkerchief he handed it to me to squeeze my nose until the bleeding had stopped. Laying back I had felt dizzy until at some point I fell asleep. Ryan let me sleep for a few hours before waking me wanting to make sure that I was still conscious enough to finish traveling.

"I'm sorry I'm pushing so hard for us to get there but if we had walked slowly on our own, we would have come through after the storm, now we need to keep ahead of it." Giving me a hand up, we started walking again.

Again, we hadn't talked much even after the encounter with the strange men. The wind had been picking up off and on drying my eyes causing them to water. Ryan had only looked back a few times to check on me. Once he had looked around almost as if he had picked up on something but then stopped looking for it. I swore I had seen Jasper once when I had taken a double take thinking he was standing by a tree, my heart raced with excitement thinking for one second it might have been him. There wasn't anyone there, it was better that way, at least he wasn't putting his life in jeopardy again. The sky was rather eerie, behind us I could see this sheet of water coming down, the exact line where it was raining and where it wasn't. The rain was almost following us. Looking ahead to see where the snow was in the distance, I could see exactly where it had ended. There was this large open field of green that had looked untouched by the snow.

Stopping for a moment I had one foot where the snow had come up to my knee and the other foot placed on the side where there was no snow other than little streams of water from the melted snow. Then we walked into an interesting area, there was steam all around us. I could feel the heat coming up from the ground. It felt so good on my cold feet slowly warming them up. I found out why there was no snow. There was also a small vent in the center that let out a lot of heat.

"I wouldn't recommend getting too close to that vent unless you feel like cooking your hand." Ryan had caught me trying to figure out where the steam was coming from.

"What do you mean there's a vent? Do you know how deep it is?" Ryan had told me there were vents, announcing this as if it was perfectly normal.

164

Looking around. The ground looked very different in a few areas, where we were standing it had looked rather normal. The strange spots had more rock, almost as if they had heated up and melted together. The steam could be seen rising from a few spots and now as I noticed there were small holes that peppered the area. We had walked closer by one where the ground sounded crunchier than normal, almost like shale when it's stepped on. The dirt was much darker in this area, peering over at the one spot where the steam was coming out there was this deep, dark-looking hole.

"If you hadn't noticed, the mountain we just climbed had an old volcano, there are lots of old lava tubes that are empty, only a few still have water in them and it's still hot so they produce steam." Stopping for a moment Ryan looked me over.

"Are we standing on an active volcano?" I had never been this close to one before.

"We are standing over an old abandoned mine which would lead into an old volcano. I don't know if it will ever be active again, just be thankful it's not right now." Ryan was somewhat distracted while he was digging through his backpack.

"Have you ever been in them?" I was curious how much he knew about it.

"A few of the shafts that are higher up, the mines that were left from the old mining days were easy to get into except some were nasty and have caved in. There is a volcano down there; the steam comes up from it, just nothing that is actively spewing. I'm sure before I existed there was a volcano here, everything interesting seemed to happen before I existed." Ryan seemed rather frustrated when he thought about it.

"Too bad you couldn't have found out about things like I had, life is interesting enough for me now." Learning about the existence of special creatures, vampires, and shades. Life wasn't basic anymore

Ryan had smiled at me, no doubt understanding that I was still absorbing everything that had changed. It wasn't a matter of fighting a dishonest boss but finding out vampires and other creatures existed, that I was a shade and had gifts. There were so many things to take in, I had rarely left the little town we lived in. I used to think going to the one state over was a big deal. Now I'm on the biggest adventure of my life. We had walked for two more hours when Ryan pulled out his pup tent again. Getting inside I was going to ask just how much longer it would be.

"We can stay here for the night; we won't have to worry about a fire. The steam from the volcano will keep us warm." Unhooking his backpack, he unrolled a sleeping bag.

"I hate to sound like a broken record or the annoying kid who won't stop asking, how much longer until we get there?" Asking as I sat down pulling out my makeshift sleeping bag, unfortunately, it attached to the outside of my hiking gear so when it had rained it wound up wet. Instead, I pulled out a small blanket I was going to sleep on.

"Is that what you're going to sleep on? Not much of a sleeping bag, you can share mine it's large enough for four." His voice sounded sincere with no ulterior motives.

"It's alright I'll be comfortable with my blankets; I didn't know how long we would be gone. I hadn't planned on it being far out here in the wilderness. Why is there a volcano way out here? Just seems rather strange, just doesn't seem like a typical area for a volcano to form." I admit I was baffled by it.

"Centuries ago, volcanoes carved out lava tubes and other caves around here, most of its gone, the steam is being generated by the shades. We took over most of the lava ducts up here, so we will be home by tomorrow night." Slipping into his sleeping bag Ryan only zipped it halfway shut.

Lying down on the two thin blankets wasn't very comfortable but I wasn't about to get into the sleeper with him even if it had seemed softer. Laying there for a few hours I had concentrated on the constellations that I could find in the sky, even watching a shooting star going by making a wish as quickly as I could on it trying to distract myself from the cold. Steam or not I still would have liked a fire. Shivering slightly, I heard the zipper from Ryan's sleeper open. Getting out he slid over to me.

"I'll switch with you since you don't want to share with me, I hate seeing you cold." Moving aside he motioned for his sleeper.

"We'll compromise; I don't want you to freeze especially since you were the one prepared. We can use my blankets as a buffer then we can both share it since you said there was enough space for four?" I hoped he wouldn't think I was being childish for insisting on a separation between the two of us.

"Sounds fine to me." Climbing back in Ryan lined up my blankets.

Climbing in I settled in right away, the heat from both of us as well as a thick sleeper helped greatly. It might have been warmer than anywhere else because of the volcanic-like heat but it certainly wasn't enough to stay warm. I never woke up for the rest of the night; I was comfortable on the ground. As many times that I had gone camping with Voncha, we had stayed in sleeping bags they were never this comfortable. It was almost as if we were sleeping on air. Instead of giving it any further thought, I let my mind drift as I slept very comfortably until the sun woke us up in the morning, something I wasn't used to. Most of the house had always been dark.

One thing I couldn't stop thinking about and had even dreamed about, were the possibilities of how Ryan had survived the fall if the others died? I knew he was injured slightly but it should have killed him also, how did he survive it? I need to start paying attention to these little details, there were so many things going on, obvious things I should be questioning, and I wasn't. It was almost as if I was a little kid again where I just trusted everything and felt if it happened there was a reason, I just didn't question things then, this is different, and I needed to start finding out why instead of just accepting. Was it a shade thing? Would I be able to jump off a cliff and survive if I needed to? I started obsessing over this to the point I was finally starting to wake up.

Feeling a little pressure on my side I lifted the sleeper just to see Ryan's arm sloped over my waist with his hand dangling in the air. Looking back at him he was still sound asleep until I had moved and woke him up.

"Sorry, I'm used to gypsy my sheepdog sleeping on my bed, sometimes I tend to put my arm on him, can't help it since he's so fluffy and cuddly." Ryan blushed just a little.

167

"I'm not mad; I doubt you planned on hugging me in my sleep. I think it might be time to get going, it's already morning." Nodding his head in agreement we packed everything up.

Ryan was suddenly talkative now that there wasn't much snow to walk through and no winds gusting at us.

"How long have you lived with vampires?" Ryan slowed down to match my walking speed.

"My father is a vampire and he raised me, Voncha and Jasper are his best friends, almost like brothers and they helped raise me after my mother passed away. I've been around vampires my entire life, not that I was ever aware of it. Because of Morris the whole family secret just slipped out." I felt strange for telling someone this.

I hadn't even told Jasper how I felt learning all of this. I always told Jasper everything.

"How could you not know your family is a group of vampires? Didn't they think you would figure it out when you came into your powers? I bet your mother would have told you the truth, vampires can't be trusted it's why they lie to us." Ryan seemed shocked that I hadn't known about my family.

"Dad didn't know I would have gifts at all, he had no clue that we grew into them. My mother certainly trusted him, or she never would have been with him or had me left with him, besides she decided to keep all of it a secret from me." Ryan seemed upset that my mother chose a vampire over a shade.

"There are laws in our community that are set to protect us; one of them is never to have a relationship with a vampire." Speaking as he gritted his teeth.

"At least I won't have to worry about any of them getting interested in me then, I am half vampire still." I almost felt like I was gloating. Truthfully, I didn't know if I carried any traits or not.

"That's something we won't be sharing with the others. As far as they need to know is that your family has died off and you've been a loner ever since. Who knows maybe you might like it enough to stay?" Ryan sounded more than hopeful.

"I highly doubt that I will, I have too much back at home that I could never leave permanently." I couldn't hide the sadness in my voice, I missed my family already.

"At least enjoy the adventure while you're here, something of a downfall at times for our shades, we thrive on excitement, curiosity, and passion." Giving me a wink as he started walking faster

We started to walk along the last open cliffside, at least Ryan had promised the rest of the way I wouldn't have to worry about slipping to my death, and he still hadn't explained how he survived the fall? Looking up I could see the mountain still jutting out, it wasn't that it was such a tall mountain but wide. We had started to walk where it was slightly colder again, most of the snow stayed up on the mountain with barely any frost underneath us. I had heard a sound I wasn't familiar with when I felt Ryan grab a hold of me pushing me up against the rock. He also leaned as close as he could to the rock as I could feel some crumbles of something falling behind me almost dusting my hair until I felt a sharp scrape on my back. It hadn't lasted very long; it was a minor rockslide, but we hadn't wanted to stick around when the rest of it had decided to come loose. As soon as we were on flat ground again, we stopped. Pulling out his first aid kit, Ryan stood behind me pulling my shirt. Feeling it stick to my back I could only assume the piece of rock that had hit me cut my skin leaving blood to stick to my shirt. Cleaning off the cut with an antiseptic wipe, adding cream, and then the bandage. I hated to think what my shirt looked like.

"Not always easy to predict when rockslides are going to happen in that area but usually it doesn't take long to get through. The only thing I would be envious of a vampire is the fact when they lick their victims, they could heal small wounds if they wanted to." This was the first time he had said vampire without deepening his voice.

"You can't heal with your hands?" If I was a shade and they couldn't heal then how was I able to unless it was the gene that my body produced that made me different?

"There are some shades that can heal, only minor healing like broken bones, cuts, and scrapes. Nothing too major such as

169

diseases or some birth defects, I haven't met one who can heal minor issues let alone major ones, yet I still think it's more a myth than anything. Who knows maybe when our people are not infected, they will be able to manipulate the energy in the air much stronger than we do now?" Ryan seemed to be contemplating the possibility.

"Your sister introduced me as a shade who could heal? Do you believe that I can't?" I was surprised to find he didn't believe shades could heal, maybe it's been much longer than I realized, or my mother is older than I knew she was.

"No, not really but if it makes you happy believing it then maybe it might happen someday?" He sounded hopeful but made it clear he didn't think it was a power they possessed.

"What is the shade city like?" Now I was curious how it might be laid out or look.

"It's something you're just going to have to be patient and find out when we get there. I promise you when you do see it, the place will just amaze you. I grew up there and I'm still in awe of it." Ryan seemed rather confident and proud of his home.

I was beginning to doubt whether we would make it to the shade city by this evening since we had been walking for so many hours.

I could hear water running in the distance, rather thunderous from the sound of it. We finally came up to a huge ravine not that I could see the bottom with all the frost-covered trees on either side, what I was missing had been the noisy river that went straight down the center of it. I had shot Ryan a dirty look, he promised no more cliffs, and I guess this wasn't exactly a cliff since it looked divided far enough with no way across. Looking over the ravine Ryan had walked over to a few trees that lined the upper edge, pulling at a rope that caused a chain reaction. At first, it had looked as though bundled rope shot across except by pulling on it, the rope had lowered and now was in a rather strange looking shape across the long ravine. Then I realized what Ryan intended on doing. He meant for us to cross the barely-there rope bridge to get over to the other side.

I had been frozen in my tracks and no doubt had a look of horror. I could handle cults, vampires, or even demons, heck I could even deal with walking past a cliff, but heights were not one of them. If I fell there was nothing I could do but fall straight down to my death, something I wasn't ready for no matter how brave I thought I was. If shades embraced excitement, then this rationale of reasoning of mine must come from my father's side. Walking over to me when Ryan realized I wasn't following he tried his best to persuade me.

"Only way there is across the bridge, it's much safer than it looks; helps keep out what doesn't belong. Vampires are not afraid of it, but most humans or other creatures won't cross." He was right and I certainly didn't want to cross after looking at it.

"I can't get across there, it's way too high and flimsy looking." Trying not to look down, I swore I lost my stomach already.

"I'll be holding onto you the entire time. The bridge is safe; I've crossed it a million times, I've only fallen off twice." Encircling his arm around my waist making sure he had a firm hold; I was almost feeling light-headed.

"That's not very reassuring!" For a brief second, an image of a movie flashed through my thoughts that Voncha and I had watched. The girl was saved by the pilot; she fell in love with him instantly even though she only knew him for about an hour, "I never understood how people could get turned on in situations like this? In a movie, where they might lose their life or be injured, and they start making out." I knew I was stalling but then I had so many images running through my head, especially of me falling to my death I had the right to think irrationally.

"Don't worry that will never happen." Questioning it for a second, I had to ask.

"Getting turned on or falling?" I knew my comment was strange, but I wanted to make sure he meant the second. At least for right now I wanted it to mean not falling.

"Don't worry no matter what happens I won't let you drop, at least not alone. Just trust me." Holding me tightly he tried to prove he could move me along if he needed to without my having to do anything.

Not even using the side ropes to balance, I slid one foot in front of the other never once being let go as he helped me across.

Halfway I had slipped but without missing a second his arm was still tight around me as I no longer felt the ground beneath me until he set me down carefully on solid ground. Balance was never exactly my strong suit. We were on the other side away from the bridge when I let out a deep sigh. Turning around to thank him for helping me across, he pulled me towards him kissing me quickly on the lips. Frustrated I had pushed him away from me.

"I was about to thank you but not that way." He knew I was involved with someone why would he make a move on me unless he thought the comment earlier was flirting?

"I thought I would let you know what it could be like if you were with others like you, a real shades life rather than being stuck with a bunch of heathens who could not possibly appreciate your talents." Never once raising his voice I knew I should have expected this that shades would never accept my being in a vampire family.

"Don't forget I am half vampire myself. They are not heathens; most happen to be my family and are at times better educated than shades so watch your tongue. You insult them you insult me and that won't get you anywhere. Just remember when we get there to introduce me as a simple friend of Leah's, I don't want them knowing exactly who I am yet." Frustrated I turned leaving Ryan behind me slightly laughing knowing he had gotten to me.

I wished Voncha or Jasper could have been here, the trip would have been so much faster, but I also wanted to keep them safe, so I knew this was for the best, it was sad I had to keep reminding myself why I was doing this and why I wasn't with Jasper right now.

Thankfully we didn't have to walk too much longer after the flimsy bridge; off in the distance, I could already see a part of the city. Ryan was right, I was in awe of the place already and I had only seen a very small outer piece of the city. As we came closer part of the rock slid back revealing an entire city behind it. The ground along with the ceiling looked as though it had been frosted by ice except there wasn't even any snow or ice around. Touching the edge as we were closer to the wall, it felt so smooth to the touch almost as if someone had used an electric sander to clear out the rough edges. The walls also felt very warm to the touch. Ryan had watched me the entire time as I inspected the surface and ground around us. Ryan was enjoying my reaction to the little piece of the city I was seeing. It wasn't glass or ice; I couldn't tell what material it was, but I loved the way it felt on my fingers.

"Not far behind the walls very hot water runs through it, most likely why it stays so warm." Ryan tapped the wall to emphasize his point.

"At least now it makes sense why there's no snow way up here when it's surrounded by it." I had to admit I loved the way the place looked.

The only thing I could do without had been all the people staring as we walked through the guarded gates, each of the guards gave a slight nod of the head to Ryan as we passed through. I felt so self-conscious when everyone kept staring at us, not even bothering to pretend not to or to look away when I noticed them. Following Ryan, he kept heading towards his home. I was hoping we would be there soon since I was feeling extremely uncomfortable having this much attention and I wasn't sure why. The lower ground had looked like a lush garden with play areas for the kids and a few areas where adults were playing games or simply sitting and chatting, at least they had been talking until we walked by and like everyone else continued to stare at us as we walked past. Tapping the side of a tree a very thick green vine lowered itself to the ground. At first, I wasn't sure what Ryan expected from it but then he stepped onto it holding his hand out for me to join him.

"It's not easy the first time you use it but after a while, you will get the hang of it, our city is above the ground in tree houses. Some shades still prefer to make their homes in the rocks and others live below the ground." Ryan seemed rather excited at the moment as he explained.

Stepping onto the vine next to Ryan the same way he had, I tried to hold onto the vine. Ryan was right it would take some time getting used to it, my balance on the vine wasn't so great. I had to hold onto Ryan for balance. I just hope I wouldn't pull him off with me, if I did, I intended on landing on him. The vine lifted us so smoothly I never once lost my balance. Leaving the ground behind us the leaves from the trees became much denser so I could no longer see the ground or the people who had been staring at us.

When we had stopped there were plank wood floors everywhere. The town had been built above the ground only better than simple little tree forts. Most looked like huts and a few exquisite buildings stood out, but they all looked amazing. Stepping off the vine Ryan was already making his way down a particular path as I followed. Even up in the trees, there were several who had stopped just to stare at us which Ryan still hadn't paid any attention to. After turning down so many wooden paths we had stopped in front of a very simple cottage as Ryan entered, I had taken a moment to enter. I wasn't sure who else would be in here. Looking around inside it looked like any other simple quaint little cabin, very cozy. Very small for the first floor but then I could guess the personal rooms were upstairs, but then if he lived here alone, he probably didn't require very much space. Leah had mentioned her brother liked taking off on his own to travel, which is why she hadn't been able to get in contact with him when she first needed help.

"When I'm here this is my home, my family lives next door." Looking around at his place Ryan seemed rather proud of it.

The place had an eclectic look about it. The unusual artwork on the walls resembled the furniture. There were so many odd little pieces I had no clue what they were.

"Very unusual decorating." Commenting as I noticed the oil painting with unusual symbols on the wall.

"Friend of mine made that, the words are not meant for others to know, sort of a personal message." As he spoke his voice lowered almost sounding sad.

Before Ryan could show me the rest of the place a knock at the door interrupted us as a young man walked into the room with a huge smile on his face, Ryan certainly seemed happy to see him.

"This is my younger brother Evan, next year he'll finally be old enough to come traveling with me if he wants to." Evan had closed the door behind him.

"Figured you were back, from all the gossip floating around, guess they were right you did bring a girl home, usually what you bring home isn't breathing." Evan seemed to be giving a slight hint as he looked at us both.

"This is Emma; she's a friend of Leah's who is visiting." At first, it sounded as if Ryan wasn't sure how to introduce me.

"The council won't like you bringing a non-shade here, she does know what you are doesn't she?" Evan seemed worried now.

"Yes, she knows what I am and she's a shade herself." About to say more Ryan stopped rather quickly.

"What shade city are you from?" Now that he was comfortable with the fact, I wasn't a regular mortal he wanted to know more.

"I'm not really from a shade city; my parents raised me independently of them, so I was curious what Ryan's home was like." I hoped this might satisfy his curiosity.

I could have told him my mother was originally from this colony except I wasn't sure how the others felt about her before she died or if they knew she had a baby or about the vampires?

"Everyone is curious about you; it's all they are going to talk about until they find out. If you didn't want to be noticed, you could have come in the back way, it's longer but you could avoid the staring." Evan had gone over to what looked like a chair, a brown hollowed-out wood piece. It reminded me of an ice cream scoop.

"Does the town have rules about non-shades visiting?" Now Evan had me curious about a few things. I knew they didn't like vampires but mortals?

"It's to keep vampires out or those mortals who would expose us. It's also to attempt to keep the city clean from outside illnesses." Ryan kept his eye contact with the floor as he explained.

"Why are vampires hated so much, it can't be just the infection? That had been administered by a shade and he stole the serum from a vampire, not sure why the vampire created it in the first place, but I doubt it was to infect shades? A single vampire and the whole race of vampires are blamed and one shade that was involved and he's left blameless? Doesn't sound fair?" Looking over at Evan I could tell this wasn't a conversation he wanted to be a part of.

"It's much harder for a shade to kill another shade; we've lost too many to the vampires when we were at war with them. I have to get going, mom and dad are going to be curious about you, and you're invited for dinner tonight." Standing up giving us a nod of the head Evan let himself out.

"It's best not to discuss vampires here, follow me upstairs to your room. You'll be staying in Leah's old room; she's spent more time living here than I have." Speaking lightly Ryan went up the stairs.

There were three rooms upstairs; mine was at the far end. I could guess Leah decorated the room since it hadn't matched the rest of the place, and it was more her style. The room was dark black with purple, yellow, and red accents, everything was incredibly frilly and feminine. Leah's bedroom had been the complete opposite of the downstairs where everything had been creams and beiges, very neutral.

"I have to go out for a while; when I get back, we can go over to my parent's house early so they can have a chance to get to know you before we eat. I'm sure they will have lots of questions for you so be prepared." I couldn't help but feel it was more of a warning than a statement.

Ryan hadn't stuck around long; he almost seemed more annoyed having me around now. I know we didn't agree on vampires but why hold a grudge against an entire group when it was only one acting for his selfish benefit? I had come for one main reason, not really what Evan now believed. I came to find out if it was worth trying to cure the shades, even Ryan didn't know I was the one they spoke of, it might be why they hadn't found me when they came searching for me, after all, why would they look in a house of vampires for me? There was only the rumor they were looking for me. It's hard to know if I should help a group that if they are cured will only go out and war with those

I love or if I let them die this group of shades will cease to exist. Sitting down on the bed looking around I did start to wonder if I should have come at all. I doubted I would ever be ready mentally to be put in this type of situation. It's the right thing to do but not if it's to fix something so they could cause harm. Does it make sense to fix a killer's liver if it only means he will go out taking the life of others?

I never really knew any other shades and so far, the close-mindedness wasn't making me wish I wanted to know them. All the new things around me and people I kept wondering how Voncha and Jasper were, if they were still waiting at the end of the clearing or if they would wait back at home? I was more curious if Jasper was thinking about me? Would he be more direct and confident about us or realize with separation, he might not want me. Feeling too tired to unpack a few things from my bag I just left it on the floor. I changed my shirt so it would stop sticking to me and laid back on the bed. Feeling comfortable I stared at the hand-painted ceiling until I fell asleep.

Time passed by much faster now that I had slept. Slightly nudging me Ryan woke me, standing at the end of the bed giving me a rather strange smile. I sat up when he moved his other hand out from behind his back with a bouquet, honeysuckle, and lilies. I was surprised he knew my favorite flowers unless Ryan was good at guessing. Taking them from him smelling them the sweet aroma from the lilac was amazing, my favorite scent.

"I thought you might like these; I bought mom the same only with white roses added, they happen to be her favorite. If you're ready, we can leave now." Ryan still seemed proud of himself.

"Yes, I'm ready we can take off." I felt strange taking the flowers with me, I would have preferred leaving them in the room, but Ryan insisted on bringing them with me, at least show his family.

We didn't have to go very far, just outside the door we probably only took about ten steps to the right of his door. One thing I missed about home was the space. We didn't have another neighbor for several miles of the house and the cabin we went to was about the same. Here everyone was so close together.

"All of the families here in the city live relatively close to each other, not that we have that much space above ground, some under the ground have more distance. Up here there is much more space to move around where underground it's a very long passageway. I've always found it depressing. We have nothing to hide from each other, everyone knows each other but then that's what you get with families who live a long time and are living this closely." Ryan seemed to easily pick up on how I was feeling or thinking unless from his traveling he became used to these thoughts himself?

His family, although smiling looked very uncomfortable, I could only guess they were not used to newcomers like the rest who lived here. The house was immaculate and certainly not decorated with anything like Ryan's place. Dark green with grey as the color scheme, very open and comfortable looking with oak furniture, Ryan's mother was the first to introduce herself and of course state what I had just been thinking.

"Ryan doesn't normally bring outside friends' home with him. My name is Joyce, and this is my husband Peter along with Evan who I believe you met earlier." Evan was the only one who had looked relaxed waving over the couch, not even taking his attention away from the new game Ryan brought him.

"How did you two meet?" His father seemed apprehensive, apparently not trusting why I was here.

"I knew Leah first and then she introduced me to Ryan. She's staying with my family for a little while, not sure if Ryan has updated you or not but I think he should be the one to say." I wasn't sure if he wanted to discuss it yet, except eventually they would either find out or ask.

"You've seen Leah? How is she?" Now we had everyone's attention.

"She's doing just fine, very healthy and happy. I think it would be better if I discussed the details with you later." Now Ryan seemed nervous.

"I guess I wasn't the only one who should have been prepared." I whispered my comment to Ryan so only he could hear me.

I just hope I hadn't started something, I thought it would be safe to mention that I knew Leah. No one had pushed the subject; my family never would have let it go until they had all the facts.

The next few hours had been relatively quiet until Joyce and peter asked about my parents. I could tell from the look on Ryan's face he was hoping I would leave the fact that my father was a vampire out, except I just couldn't do it. I could never deny who my family was no matter how much those around me might oppose it. He's my father and he raised me after my mother passed away, why should I deny him that right of acknowledgment? He did his best. Trying to stall what Ryan felt would be a massive upset with his parents he announced louder than needed that supper was ready ushering everyone into the dining room.

SHADE LIVING

Once evening came, Ryan's family was feeling much more comfortable around me even though I knew the question would eventually come up again that Ryan tried so hard to avoid. Something his mother picked up on right away no doubt causing her to wonder if I was a shade or to her fear, a vampire.

"Where did you grow up? Not that often do we run into other shades out there, we know they exist, but their locations are usually kept rather secretive, unfortunately, we know that many are infected with the same problem we have. The problem spread from one group to another. They felt it would be safer if we kept separate in case a group was attacked by vampires or as separate groups, we would preserve ourselves better this way." Joyce was holding it in except I could tell she had so many questions she wanted to ask me.

I had sat down next to Ryan on the couch with his brother Evan on the side. His parents sat down on the love seat across from us; instead of having a television facing their couch the way we had at our home, they had both of their couches facing each other with a coffee table in the center. I hadn't seen any television sets since I had been in their home. I kept feeling Ryan bumping into me no doubt trying to remind me not to let out the fact I had been raised by a vampire. I had already made the personal choice that if it had come up I wouldn't deny who my father was, if they were to find out later they would not trust me because of lying to them. First I decided to start with the easy side of the family and hopefully, it would put them at ease, not that I knew too much about my mother, she passed away when I was three years old. My father did have several pictures of her which he put into a photo album for me.

"My mother was a shade except I never knew what group she had belonged to, she died when I was just three years old. I take more after my mother, my father's traits never really showed. My father was devastated when she passed." I tried to think how best or rather delicately to tell them about my father.

Trying to change the subject Ryan started filling them in on his travels, what he had seen and where he had been. Then finally came up where he found Leah getting herself into trouble, apparently nothing new to the family except this time when he mentioned Morris's name, the coloring vanished from their faces. Explaining all of the events and occasionally I interjected to fill in the missing pieces, they seemed relieved Leah had gone home with me since I had been protecting her along with the others until they were told they were vampires. Sitting straight up both of his parents looked at me accusingly.

"How did she pass on, was it the same infliction our people suffer from?" As soon as she asked Ryan jabbed me in the ribs rather roughly that everyone noticed. I knew they were thinking my father or one of the other vampires must have killed her.

"Stop jabbing me, I know you don't want me discussing it, but I refuse to keep it a secret, I'm not ashamed of my background, only you are." Standing up in a huff Ryan didn't hide his feelings at all.

"Fine but it's your funeral." Walking out of the room he slammed the front door behind him leaving me sitting on the couch with the rest of his family.

I had to admit I was worried about how they would take it when I told them, but I felt there was no reason to deny my father.

"You're a vampire? You have no right being here in the shade city and no doubt holding my daughter hostage poisoning my son's mind." Peter stood rather quickly.

"My father is a vampire so I might have some dormant traits from him, my mother was a shade and so far, I take after her. Leah isn't dead; she's still a shade and very healthy. She can come and go any time she likes; she's even gone for a walk with the baby so if she wanted to leave, she has the opportunity. If it were not for a group of vampires your daughter would be dead along with her son." Then I realized I had let slip the last piece.

"Who is the baby's father?" Sounding stern and ready to attack, I didn't want to tell them.

"The baby's father was originally a shade before Morris took control of him like many others." For the first time since being here, I felt I was in danger. There was a sound rustling up next to me.

"Mother, relax the baby is perfectly healthy and so is Leah. They are safe and being well cared for, it's true they would have died if it hadn't been for the vampires. I've met them and unlike the stories that get told here, not one of them ever spoke Ill of the shades and they never attempted to attack me once." Ryan couldn't stay gone long since he knew how his parents would react; he left out the fact that the baby's father was a vampire.

"Who knows that you're here? Does anyone else know you have a vampire for a parent? We can't risk the council finding out or they will kill you." Joyce was extremely nervous but hearing her say they would kill me made me even more nervous.

"I haven't met anyone else here other than your family. We haven't spoken to anyone since we got here. Why would they kill me because I have a vampire as a family member?" It seemed extreme to kill me for something someone else was.

"They would feel it allowed a breach, a way to be attacked. The other colony didn't allow the ones changed to continue living with them. Instead, they set up a colony for them to exist together. Our colony's different, if your all shade it's allowed but if your half or even related to one or worse yet one yourself then you are killed, supposedly to protect the colony. We don't agree with it but there is nothing we can do about it." Joyce's voice shook as her husband stood embracing her trying to help calm her.

"We can't exactly have you leave, or the rest of the colony will know something is up. Just avoid the question altogether if they ask then say you are from an independent colony. They won't know the rules you follow and won't ask, out of respect. We need to make this look like a normal visit and then you need to leave." Peter had sat down with Joyce, not that I could hear some of their conversation they were whispering quietly to each other.

"We need to make this look planned; otherwise, this could mean our lives also. What possessed you to come here, didn't you know you would be killed?" Joyce seemed shocked I hadn't thought about this possibility.

"I only learned recently that I was a shade myself, it was something my father hid from me at my mother's request. I didn't know about your rules, and I wish Ryan had told me it was that strict. I was just hoping to learn how shades lived and possibly learn how to use my gifts better, so I don't hurt someone by accident." I didn't want to say the real reason or expose I wasn't infected.

"The only way you could learn here is if they thought you were abandoned, you would have to lie to them. If you were my child, I would have you out of here now, it's just not safe." Joyce had taken a rather deep breath after saying her comment.

"Knowing the rules, you're willing to live here even though everyone here is already infected, is everyone at risk of venom taking over, or do they need to be bitten? I'm not sure how that works?" I wondered if everyone had it and would end up becoming a vampire why not just kill everyone now?

"The tainted blood only prevents us from using our full gifts and completely prevents other things such as reproduction and healing. I had my children before I was infected." Joyce had given her husband a rather strange look then motioned to me, which he nodded.

"If you trust us, we can say you are my niece, they will believe it since you already look like my side of the family. All of my husband's family and our children have fiery red hair, mine has dusty blonde with blue eyes." Joyce looked hopeful that I would say yes.

"I could do that, that way when I leave, they can just assume I've gone home." At least that way I could still learn.

"Ryan can show you around for a while unless he was planning to leave right away?" Joyce had given him a rather interesting look.

"I wasn't planning on going anywhere for a while; I wanted to see how Emma did here. Besides, it might be fun introducing my 'cousin' Emma to everyone." Ryan had given me a wink when he said 'cousin.'

"I'm sure we will be approached by the council soon, I'm sure they've heard about your being here. It doesn't take very long for them to respond to rumors, especially ones like this." Peter had let out a sigh.

"I take that as your hint for us to leave." Ryan had tapped me on the shoulder expecting me to follow him.

At first, I had thought we were going back to his house except we walked right past it and past a few others until he had grabbed a vine urging it for a ride. The thick green vine slowly lowered itself down stopping for us to get on. Again, helping me not to lose my balance Ryan held onto me as we were lowered to the ground. Not as many people were staring at me this time except there were still a few. I never did care for it when people would stare not taking their eyes off of me, especially if they didn't know me or did not intend on saying hello. I had waved at one thinking maybe I could get them to crack a smile but then they only looked angrier.

"What is the problem with people? They look so pissed off I'm here? Was I supposed to check in with the council before I came?" I would have preferred staying in Leah's bedroom instead of dealing with this.

"It doesn't hurt; people here haven't seen anyone from the outside in a long time. They don't trust what they don't know." Ryan had kept up his pace walking past everyone ignoring their stares.

I wasn't the only one getting the glares; they had even done the same with Ryan except he acted as if he didn't notice any of them. There were fewer houses where we were at now other than an opening to a cave. Walking in, lights were streaming along the top, lighting the way, it had opened into a large room with the most beautiful garden I had ever seen. The trees were full of lush color, carved stone benches, a waterfall, and bright sensual flowers with an incredible aroma. This place had reminded me of pictures Voncha, and Jasper had taken during one of their trips to the Butchart Gardens in Canada. Walking over to the stream running through the center, Ryan slipped off his shoes and sat down at the edge sliding his feet into the water.

"Anytime I go traveling, I always come here to relax first, this time there was an exception. This is the best place to meet others our age. It was built to keep us busy and out of the way of the older ones." Ryan had tapped the ground next to him indicating he wanted me to join him.

"If you travel a lot, do you have very many friends here?" I had been curious since it sounded like he was gone quite a lot or rather his mother didn't expect him to stay.

"Don't get me wrong, I love it here except I get tired of being packed into such a small space. So many of the shades either don't mind or don't know anything different. I used to travel with my mother quite a lot until Peter prevented it. People have never accepted me but then I'm from another colony." Stopping quickly Ryan looked as if he regretted telling me.

There were quite a few young people, even a couple of older ones sitting on the benches. At first, they had been curious except they hadn't stared anywhere near the way the others had. Not one person had come over to introduce themselves or to see who I was. Everyone seemed busy with their agenda. Not paying attention to it Ryan had lain back on the grass with his feet still in the water. Mimicking Ryan I had taken my shoes off, putting my feet into the water and laying back. The ceiling was just as beautiful, it might not have been the natural sky outside. The sun had broken through the smallest hole above reflecting off the wall displaying little rainbows all over. There wasn't glass on the ceiling; I had concentrated on them getting Ryan's attention.

"Yes, they are diamonds. The sun reflects, even the moon has an amazing effect on them. One of the rules is that we cannot mine diamonds, rubies, or any other natural gem like that. If someone is building their home or adding space underground, they must get permission from the council first. I prefer having my freedom, no one to answer to. I get tired of everyone knowing how I wipe my butt." Frustrated Ryan had covered his eyes with his hands.

"It's probably why my father and I have always preferred living on the outskirt of town. I know it's not the same; even the city has more privacy than here. I've never seen anything this close. I think I would want out also even if the people were friendly." I couldn't understand how anyone would want to live like this. I would rather live out in the open than live in fear and packed in.

"Leah always looked forward to me bringing home gifts for her, it's why she was in the situation she wound up in. It was my fault that she even left the city on her own." Running his fingers through his hair almost looked like he wished he could rip his hair out.

"How could it be your fault? Neither of you could have guessed that she would be grabbed by Morris?" I had sat up waiting for him to respond.

"She never would have left if I hadn't told her what it was like on the outside. She was content here. She would have been safe, never used, and certainly never would have been pregnant. I know I'll love my nephew; I hate the fact she's with vampires and not safe out there in the world, but I truly hope she decides not to come back here." Ryan was now sitting up and closer to me.

"We should probably get back before mom wonders if I drown you instead of introducing you. I would introduce you if there was anyone worth meeting." Standing up avoiding my question, Ryan had picked up his shoes not putting them back on and started to walk away.

Grabbing my shoes and trying to get them on my wet feet quickly I had caught up to him catching everyone's attention. I had decided if Ryan was able to ignore their reactions then I could also. Taking the vine back up we had walked to his home, asking me to wait there he was going to let his parents know we were back. Sitting in Leah's room I looked around trying to find a clue, I wasn't sure to what but something that would at least explain this place so it would make sense. I heard Ryan come walking into the home. Knocking on Leah's door even though I had left it open, I could see him.

"Mom wants to spend time with you; she'll take you past the tavern to the training grounds to learn." Not saying much Ryan had left the doorway going to his bedroom.

Getting up I followed him; he was only one door over. He had dropped his shoes in the living room, shirt in the hallway, not worried about where they lay. Ryan was lying on his bed with a pillow over his face. Moving it slightly he heard me standing at the door.

"Trying to add to those who watch me?" Smiling slightly Ryan hadn't made the slightest move.

"Not interested in watching you wipe your butt; I just have a few questions. Do you trust me?" I was beginning to question this.

"Sure, why not, is that your question?" Ryan set the pillow down now, leaning over he had sat up to look at me.

"What did you mean that you're not from this colony? Is Peter your father?" I hoped he could at least answer this.

Not moving and not looking at me, Ryan had stared at the ground almost as if he was looking for an answer there. His silence spoke more words to me than if he had made an excuse why he didn't want to answer.

"No, you don't trust me." Not bothering to wait for an answer to my statement or not I had turned walking into Leah's room closing the door behind me.

Laying down on Leah's bed I started to get homesick, I missed my father, Jasper, and Voncha. I missed my bed, the old familiar scents, and friendly people. I wondered how the wedding was. Did anyone notice I had been gone? Did they clear up who supposedly killed Beth, not that I know where she had gone after she left Morris's place? I had seen her in the building that one time and not again after that. Even when the ritual had started, she was nowhere to be seen.

Looking around the bedroom I noticed Leah's diary. As curious as I had been I was never one to snoop through someone's possessions. Even with the nap I had taken earlier, it was still a long day, and I was thankful to finally be off my feet. Not even noticing when I had fallen asleep, I had some incredibly restless nightmares.

Morning came with a knock on my door; I hadn't even bothered to change before I had gone to bed. I slept on top of the comforter when Ryan opened the door coming into the room. Not bothering to wait to see if I had responded to him or not.

"The council is at Peter and mom's place; they want to speak with you. They want to take you to the council's chambers to ask questions away from prying eyes and ears. No Peter is not my father, and I was born in another colony not that I'm accepted there." Not waiting for me to say a word he had done what I did the previous night, just walked away.

"At least it's a start." I had shouted after him before he left.

I had packed rather light keeping it simple, getting dressed in a clean pair of clothes, simple jeans, and a white, short-sleeved shirt, slight embroidery of a wolf's face on the front. My shoes had dried so thankfully my socks won't end up wet. Walking over to his parent's home there wasn't anyone outside; I had tapped on the door before letting myself in. On the couch were three members of the council and Peter and Joyce sitting on the couch next to each other.

"Did Ryan know we needed to speak to you? Almost appropriate you're wearing that shirt; it fits your family." Not looking at the others they walked past me expecting me to follow.

I had flashed a confused look at the others as Joyce simply waved at me to get going. I wished one of them would have come with me. I might have been an adult, but I was in a situation that could be very dangerous. The only assistance I had was with Ryan coming down the vine with me helping me as he did before. Making an excuse that he was simply coming down to go to the garden he thought he would ride down with me. At least they wouldn't see I didn't know how to balance on the vine on my own. One thing I had noticed going through town this time. Not one person looked or even glanced in our direction. We had walked a long distance before coming to the chamber. There was this large glass building we entered. I had noticed I couldn't see in, but I could see out.

Following the three we walked into an incredibly exquisite-looking building. The flooring was white marble along with the walls that didn't have glass. The deeper we went in the less glass and more marble. Strange they prevent others from harvesting things like this without their permission, but they had so much of it? We finally came to a room that was even more breathtaking. The ceiling was completely open to the outside, the sun was fully out shining down on the marble floor and as I looked over the flat ground, it led to a drop-off. We were directly on the edge of the mountain; their private balcony except it didn't have any railings along the side to prevent you from falling over. I had a rush of panic feeling that I had just been talked into my doom. Were they going to push me over?

"Make yourself at home; we have a few questions to ask you." The older Lady had sat down a little slower than normal. Looking at her she looked very frail.

"Not to worry child, we are simply interested and want to get to know you better. Ryan has never brought anyone into our colony before, he certainly seems to enjoy his traveling, and do you like traveling?" The other gentleman had asked me a question not that they told me their names unless they assumed I already knew?

"I'm not sure; this is the first time I've left home." I had kept my answer short and to the point.

"No need to be shy around us, we are all family." Smiling at me I was sure he was only trying to either relax me or get me into a false sense of trust.

"We hear you know who Morris is?" She didn't need to list the last name and I knew who she was talking about.

How was I supposed to answer that one? Not personally but I saw him get killed, I just worked for him but there wasn't anything personal there? Any question could lead to my family being vampires, how was I supposed to answer that and be Joyce's niece and never once left the colony until now?

"I see we confused you. My name is Joraih; I am the eldest council member. The ones you have spoken to are Lithiana and Gerigino. We are not the only council members however this is

189

one of the assignments we handle as council members." Joraih was the last to sit down.

All three had been dressed in the same robes, nothing different and certainly nothing colorful. With a place so vibrant in color I had expected their clothing to have more personality.

"We see you share the same love for wolves as your cousin. Perhaps an easier way of handling this would be to allow you to ask us any questions you might have." Joraih had a pleasant smile except it still didn't help me relax.

"I'm sorry I didn't ask to visit; I wasn't sure about the visitation rules you have. I didn't mean to be disrespectful towards them if I broke any." I had hoped by sounding sincere this might help. I couldn't ask them any questions I had, or I would be in serious trouble.

"That's why we are here now; we would have met you before you came up here. Joyce has told us that you are her niece, from the same colony as Ryan. Wouldn't that make him your brother?" The look on Joraihs face looked rather strange now.

"I'm pretty sure I would have remembered him being my brother if he had been, he's, my cousin." That felt like a strange question.

"Answered quite well, we have the same basic rules other than harsher punishments; they are set in place to protect everyone. Have you ever been bitten by a vampire?" Lithiana leaned forward when she asked me.

"No, never been bitten. I've been sliced by falling rock; I still have the scab from that one but no, I've never been bitten, lucky my dogs haven't bit me either." As soon as I had said that I had a feeling I shouldn't have.

"We know other colonies allow different things; we do not allow dogs here. No animals other than bees that come naturally to the greenery, we do not need animals." The way Gerigino made his comment, it sounded more like a threat than anything.

"How do you feel about vampires? Do you have any contact with any of them or know any?" Lithiana certainly didn't have a problem getting to the point.

How could I say no if I knew Morris? He was one just before he died not that they would have known that. He supposedly created some vampires and other experiments like the three we ran across on the pathway here. I was about to say I didn't understand the question, one of the lamest ways out except I didn't get the chance. Glass behind us broke as a very familiar man came rampaging in. He was one of the three men from the hill, how did he survive? This one had been knocked over by the wind unless Ryan was only able to kill the two, he took with him. Standing up much quicker the council members stood ready to attack the intruder. There were also several more members dressed in the same clothing joining them. With their combined effort they were able to contain him for a short time by funneling a wind surge around him. It only lasted a short time until he started to move forward against the pressure, it had almost looked like he was laughing. None of them seemed to notice he was looking directly at me.

I had seen a flick of a flame shoot into the air now swirling gusts of fire around him. At first, he had screamed from the fire, his skin burned bleeding from the ordeal. This still hadn't stopped him. Raising his hands up and to the sides, he yelled something I didn't understand. Two of the council members were blown off the side of the mountain while the others were thrown into an adjacent room. The three members who had been questioning me were still trying to fight him off, with shards of ice, fire, drenching water, wind. They had simply burned, bled, and soaked him. The look on his face was so deranged it scared me.

As he passed the three, he came towards me. I wasn't sure what else to do other than close my eyes, focus, raise my hand, and yell 'no' at the top of my lungs. The fear alone I could feel pulse through my body. I had found the more terrified I was the stronger the light burst would be. When I had opened my eyes all I had heard were gasps from all around me. Looking straight ahead where the creature had been, there was barely anything that resembled him. It was almost as if I had liquefied him to the wall. There was no coming back from that one. The members who had gone over to the side were now slowly floating up. Now I understood how Ryan could prevent himself from dying if he could use the wind to cushion his fall. Now I was surrounded by all the members. The looks in their eyes had me speechless and glued to my spot. I had done it this time.

"Welcome to the family, you're welcome to go back to your aunt and uncle now." Lithiana sounded rather calm and impressed. At least I didn't have to answer their vampire question.

Nodding my head, giving a slight wave goodbye I slowly walked out. I felt the urge to run except I didn't want anyone questioning me or wondering why I was running. I had made it back to the vines. Ryan was there waiting to have the vine come down to bring us up. Riding it up Ryan kept looking at me wondering how it went with the council.

"How did it go; you have the strangest look on your face that I haven't seen before?" Ryan did look surprised.

Not able to answer, I couldn't even blow the smallest of breath. I was having a difficult time breathing and felt incredibly dizzy. Making my way to Leah's room as quickly as I could, I sat in front of her bed putting my head between my legs trying to catch my breath. Ryan had come in trying to figure out what was wrong with me. Placing his hand on my back he started to rub my back reassuringly.

"It couldn't have been that bad. They didn't kill you?" Not that it was helpful, but it did make me to laugh.

"I was lucky; one of the men you didn't kill made a surprise visit. Just as they had asked me the worst question, he dropped in. They were fighting with him, and he seemed to resist it. I can't believe I killed him. I don't know if I should be happy or disappointed in myself?" I was still feeling light-headed.

"I wondered what happened to that one, after the fall I couldn't find him, so I came back up, mom and Peter wants to know how the interview went, they've been pacing and driving Evan and me crazy. Just don't tell them what you told me." Before I could say anything, Ryan had left to tell his parents I was back.

At least I didn't have to worry about Joyce and Peter killing me if they didn't like what they heard. Getting changed quickly I made my way out the door. An older couple was walking along the path, it had been the first time I'd run into anyone on this pathway. Smiling at me they had waved, said a friendly hello, and kept walking by. Stopping in my tracks for a moment I watched them as they left. It felt strange they suddenly were being friendly to me let alone speak to me. Why are they treating me differently? If they were friendly to me then they should be treating Ryan much better unless there was something I wasn't aware of? The front door had swung open as Joyce pulled me in. At least everyone was smiling except Ryan.

"Your interview must have gone wonderfully; we haven't heard any complaints. Tell us what they asked you? I'm sorry we didn't have much time to coach you, they must have accepted your answers." Joyce brought me over to the chair directly next to the couch as she sat down.

"I didn't say much, they asked a bunch of questions except they seemed to be preoccupied with their private matters?" Other than this there wasn't much else to say other than the part Ryan told me to keep to me.

"I already know about your protecting the council members from one of Morris's loose experiments, everyone is talking about it." Peter seemed rather proud as Ryan decided to leave.

"He doesn't like to hear about these things but then it also doesn't help that it came here because of him. They used to be crazy people who would just walk the streets or eventually die off around the mountains. Now that they see him, they have followed him up higher and usually one or two of them follow him all the way. He swears none were following." Peter's voice sounded angry.

"He means well but he doesn't pay attention and it brings danger to the colony. Since he hasn't broken any rules, he's not dealt with but someday I won't be able to protect him. They lost a council member five years ago because of an attack. These experiments were meant to destroy us. Unfortunately, many of them are stronger than we are magical, they can't produce magic, but they can absorb it." From the sound of her voice, I knew Joyce was defending her son.

There must have been much more than what Ryan was telling me, no wonder why he never accepted Peter as a stepfather when Peter views him in a certain way. If any of them had come and gone they would have the same problem, I wasn't sure If I should feel sorry for Ryan or wish he was more careful.

"Ready to go train? We have an entire day before we need to be back to celebrate, it happens to be Evan's birthday."

TRAINING

This is what I had been waiting for. Soon as I could learn I could finally head home. We had traveled for over two hours away from the shade city following a much worn-down stone trail leading to the training grounds. Every shade had been trained here except recently because the gifts they had were not that strong. At one time it would have been dangerous training in the city and now with their gifts not being as strong as they used to be they trained at home. Most of the skills were no longer taught because of fear of dying. There was no one there who could heal so some had even been outlawed. On our way to the training ground, Joyce had let me know the very act I did when I was in the presence of the council was exactly that, a skill that had been outlawed.

We were directly next to the lake with a rounded half-dome behind us. The ground was half gravel and half grass that had managed to grow through. There were dark markers all over the rock where a fire had been thrown or chipped away at the rock. Different colors marked different areas of the training ground. The first thing Joyce had done was to teach me proper hand motions. Each one would allow me to either shoot a fireball a short distance or further. How to properly control the fire, I couldn't create the fire except I could control it, or the better part, pull fire from the elements around me. If there was moisture in the air, I could control the water making it rain over something. It was the same with controlling the elements around me; I couldn't start them however I certainly could manipulate them. I was enjoying learning this. At least now I knew if I was in a romantic situation, I knew I wouldn't lose control and accidentally blow the person up or set them on fire. It might have been a strange concern but one I thought about.

After practicing for several hours Joyce was still ready to teach me more, how to float myself down from a mountain using wind. Controlling the flash that had come from my hand, the fact it was a symbol of those who could heal. I was beginning to get exhausted, so I finally just sat down. Joyce had smiled at me getting the point, she had come over sitting next to me.

"How do you like it here so far?" Joyce was curious if I liked the shade city more.

'It's alright, how can you stand it when they treat your son so crappy?" I would have a hard time being friendly to those who were outright mean to my family.

"He was never meant to be here. We can train more tomorrow if you want. Evan's birthday party is tonight, and I still have enough time to finish up and get ready for it." Joyce was about to leave me there with more questions.

"No, I'm tired of no one answering questions and just leaving. I have so many questions that I don't know the answers to. For some reason either out of embarrassment, not trusting, or something I'm not getting answered." I had pretty much shouted this at her. For once I was getting angry.

Giving me a strange look, first looking around almost as if she was expecting someone, she walked over to me grabbing me by the arm leading me away from the training ground. She didn't seem to be angry but then we were not going anywhere near the trail we had taken when we first came here. We walked along the steep side of the mountain; the shade city wasn't in sight being blocked off from the trees. We followed along the lake and now down to a deep ravine. Standing in the middle of it there was a tremendous wind rushing through. Motioning she wanted me to control the wind; I wound up creating a funnel around us. Standing next to me so that I could hear her with the noise, only the two of us would hear any of the conversations now.

"What exactly do you want to know? Keep the funnel up in case they are questions that we cannot afford others to hear." Joyce was very determined to keep this private.

"Did you ever have a relationship with a vampire?" If she had this would almost answer my real first question.

"Yes, I did, I'm not proud of it. I had been working with Morris until I no longer agreed with him. The entire shade city thought he was a god and the only way out since I didn't know anything about the outside world had been to stay with a particular vampire." Joyce had sat down looking sick.

"I thought you were in love with him?" From the stories my father had told me it sounded like they were unless it was just my father.

"How do you know anything about my relationship? I was young at the time. I met him when I was nineteen. I was already in a relationship, but I wanted to get away from the shade city, I no longer felt safe." Now she was giving me a rather strange look.

"Your relationship with Robert was just a matter of convenience and the baby you had with him meant nothing?" I knew I had found my mother, now I was starting to wish I hadn't.

"I don't know how you know about it, but you are never to say a word to anyone about it. If you know him or the girl, I don't want to know about it. I had been under Morris's control when I first met Robert, I wasn't thinking clearly. I thought it was what I had wanted. The council thought I was visiting a family of wolves; they think the same thing of Ryan when he leaves. They are humans who transform themselves into a certain animal from their family heritage. My husband is a part of the council, if he knew I had a baby with a vampire he would have me thrown out. My family tried to kill Robert and the baby. They didn't want anyone to know; since I was dating Peter no one questioned it." Joyce had sat down on the ground looking defeated.

"If you're not infected then why don't you heal everyone?" I felt stunned to find out the real situation behind their relationship.

"The person who was protecting my baby was killed by Morris. He wanted her since he couldn't get to me, I had been the

197

last one not infected by the poison. He didn't feel he needed me because he had my daughter. Morris had her at his home, and I wound up getting infected when he caught me, and that's when I was injected. He thought he could still control me. It wouldn't have mattered I would have been too weak to heal anyone. I had been bitten by a vampire while I worked for Morris. Morris used to keep their secret, no one knew of their existence, and they trusted him until he had killed an entire group of them. Robert, Jasper, Voncha were the main ones I had known, they managed to escape with a small group." Joyce looked incredibly worried now that she was telling me this.

"If Ryan isn't Peter's son, then who is?" I know I had been asking all the questions but at least they were getting answered.

"He's not my son and Leah isn't my daughter. Their families had been killed when they turned, I took them saying they were mine, that was when the colonies were being separated. Evan's parents never came back, it's never been confirmed but we can only guess they had changed and left to avoid being killed along with their son. Not everyone agreed those infected should be killed for something they had no control over. Many of us would love life to go back the way it had been before the council took over. Unfortunately, none of us are strong enough to do that." Joyce had let out a huge sigh.

"Are there any questions you would like to ask me? Why am I not infected or the fact I can heal? Who I am?" I watched Joyce stand up.

"No, it's best I don't know much about you for now, maybe in the future." Motioning with her hand the wind died down a little.

Letting go of the wind around us; Joyce had left me standing there. Sitting on the hill waiting for us had been Ryan. I just stood there watching as Joyce disappeared. Walking over to Ryan and lying next to him on the ground I felt deflated. I had always hoped to meet my mother one day I just never thought it would end like this.

"Wish I could have been in there for that one if she didn't want anyone to know what you two were talking about, was it about the council members? The fact most of them are experiments of Morris's. Or the marriage talks? I'm assuming from your reaction it's none of these." Ryan turned to his side facing me now leaning on his arm.

"Can the council members be healed?" Looking over at Ryan I finally made my choice.

"Not really, they are just experiments who are controlling the shades, and they are too blind to notice, at least they don't want to realize how serious the situation is." Standing up Ryan offered me his hand.

We had walked about halfway; I kept running over what we had talked about causing me not to pay attention and walk slower. Ryan had noticed when he was far ahead, and I hadn't caught up yet. I had been staring at the ground until I walked right into Ryan. Being bumped out of my mental world I looked up at him. We were in the caves leading to the back of the shade city. Thin vines hung all over the sides while moss completely covered the walls. Standing close to me Ryan leaned against the rock wall.

"Life here isn't the greatest; I would stay gone from here if my family didn't need me. If I could find a way to protect them I would but for now you have to just learn to let it go." Standing in front of me he leaned in and hugged me.

"I'm going to need your help doing something, but we can wait until after the birthday party, we will need some time to figure out exactly how we are going to do it." I had made up my mind." I was so absorbed in my thoughts again I had only felt pressure as Ryan leaned against me.

Looking up at Ryan, his face was within inches of mine; slipping back a little I was now against the rock wall. Leaning in further he placed his hand on the side of my face leaning in kissing me. His lips felt so warm, the way his body felt. I could swear I heard his heart beating faster. The image of Jasper had flashed in my mind. Pushing Ryan back, I was angry he had tried this again. Leaving him standing behind me I walked as quickly as I could back to Joyce's home. I wasn't sure how I was going to handle this. I knew one thing that had to be done; unfortunately, there were not many opportunities. For the rest of the night, I pretended to enjoy myself. I couldn't wait to lock myself in my room. When I had Ryan kept knocking on my door trying to get me to come out so that he could apologize to me. Opening my door quickly letting Ryan fall on the floor, I knew he had been leaning against it.

"Never try to kiss me again." Walking away from him I had written down a few words on a piece of paper handing it to him.

"Everything is known." Writing down on the paper in response to my question.

I had asked him if we were to speak would anyone hear it? Ryan let me know writing things down was still safe, if we destroyed it when we were finished. In writing, Ryan had let me know for years someone has tried and they had failed attempting to get rid of the council members. There was no way to vote on final decisions they made and certainly no way to object, if you had it only meant you died faster. The colony used to be rather large and now it's much smaller than it once was. If they were not made prisoners, they simply vanished with no explanation, and you certainly didn't risk asking or you would be next.

It might have seemed rash or quick that I had come to this conclusion except I felt it had to be done. I wrote down that I wanted to kill the council members. I wasn't sure how Ryan would react to this. Nodding his head, he let me know he agreed. Taking out his lighter he burned the pieces of paper letting them fall onto the metal incense burner. Ryan had grabbed a box out of Leah's closet and now took it into the living room. Following behind him I was curious what he was doing.

"I keep hearing how this person who happens to be a shade will be able to help get rid of the infection, how exactly are they expecting this to be done, by a ritual or something? No one ever really says unless it's supposed to be a secret?" After hearing the conversations this evening, it sounded as if everyone knew about me, they just didn't know I was the one they spoke of.

"No ritual, it's simple really. Just a drop of the shades blood on the palm, it's supposed to burn off the infection." Hanging up festive lights along with the fireplace mantle, witches' broom by the side with mini pumpkins on top of the mantle.

"What are all the decorations for?" The only time I had seen lights strung up had been around all Hallows Eve time.

"It's almost all Hallows Eve; we don't get cold or snow in the shade city, it's warm here all year long. Without the changes of the trees, it's difficult to gauge the time going by. The trees we have here are not the same, they were specially created." Looking back at me Ryan looked worried.

"Shades celebrate Halloween?" It had looked more like Christmas decorations than Halloween.

"Can you think of any other time shades, vampires, werewolves, or any other creature can be around mortals and just be ourselves? When we use our natural-born gifts people assume we are just doing a great magic trick. That and it's fun to dress up." Ryan reminded me of a little kid who loved trick or treating for fun.

"I missed the entire summer being sick going through the changes and then being stuck at Morris's and now I've been here for six months. I only planned on being gone for two at the most. My family must be thinking the worst right now." They must be panicking knowing they couldn't come up to see me.

"I was hoping you might have just fallen in love with the place, being around others similar to yourself and not wanting to leave." Ryan sounded disappointed.

"I need to try something; if it works then I will do it to the others. It may be nice here, but I miss home, I have loved ones still there. Your sister Leah is still there." Nodding his head in agreement he had missed his sister wishing she had come with us except she insisted not traveling with the baby while he was still small, besides it was safer for her to stay there in case anyone found out the father was now a vampire.

Looking around the room, searching through a few drawers until I checked out Leah's old bedroom, I pulled out a needle, Ryan had been watching no doubt curious what I was searching for and what I would do with the needle when I had found it. Walking directly over to him I intended on experimenting with him first.

"I need to test this out on you first." Looking hesitant Ryan closed his eyes puckering for a second as if he expected to get kissed.

"You're not getting kissed or poked with the needle; you won't need to close your eyes." Reaching out for his palm I turned it facing upward.

"What are you doing then?" Ryan looked on curiously.

"You'll see." I knew even Ryan wasn't aware it was me.

Poking the tip of my finger until I had seen a tiny drop of blood come out, I held my finger over Ryan's palm letting it drop onto it. As it did my blood immediately absorbed into his skin as he watched rather shocked that it hadn't just pooled on top or dropped off to the floor like so many experiments had done in the shade city in search of the right person who possessed the healing gift. His skin began to turn an off-white almost flushed as he started breathing heavily. Before he could collapse on the floor, I helped him walk to his bed, laying him back and covering him with a sheet as he began to shiver.

"What did you do to me?" Barely able to ask above a whisper since he was still shivering so much, his teeth clattering against each other.

"If it is expected to work then it will burn off the infection otherwise the whole waiting for the right shade with the healing gift that is not infected is more of a myth than any childhood story I've ever heard." Sadly, I really couldn't think of anything to compare it to without offending him.

"I feel like I'm on fire, I told you I was sorry for kissing you." Almost sounding sarcastic he laid there twitching until he had finally laid still.

I worried the second he stopped twitching. I hadn't expected him to lose consciousness. Peter and Joyce had stopped by to visit; I had told them Ryan was sleeping. I had used the excuse I kept him up all night. I wasn't sure if Joyce had believed me, but she accepted it for now. I had hoped he would be awake by the time they expected us over for dinner. I kept checking to make sure he was breathing. His heart was still beating, and warm air was coming from his lips. At least he was doing well, I had decided to check out the area the council members had taken me for the interview. I hoped I might be able to sneak away to get some help dealing with the council members.

A couple of people were looking over the side enjoying the view. One couple had spoken to me as they left while one other continued to stand on their own looking over the side. I had hoped no one would be here. Looking over the side I wondered why more don't break in here, at least something other than the experiments unless it's because they take that long to find it? This would be the perfect place except how would I lure the council here? I never planned on staying here this long; I wanted to be home by all Hallows Eve. I used to throw a huge party for Halloween transforming the few acres plus the house into a haunted home. I would have to stay here two more weeks; it would be the only time available that everyone would be assembled here. According to Ryan, they had all Hallows Eve tree lighting event here. The lights were already strung up with a tree ready to be decorated. Each family would add a piece to the tree. There were already pumpkins everywhere with various carvings.

"How do you like it here?" The stranger spoke never looking at me.

He had a hood covering his head, a full-sized, long black cloak. The same type of long black jacket Ryan had worn.

"I've enjoyed visiting my aunt." I knew it couldn't be Ryan and the scent was horrible almost as if he rubbed himself with a dead skunk.

"Aunt? That's the excuse you're using? I borrowed Ryan's jacket he left at the house."

"Voncha? What are you doing here?" Looking around I wanted to make sure no one noticed.

"We were worried since you were gone for so long. Jasper had come up earlier except he's seen that you've moved on. Not exactly the way I would have preferred. Your father wanted to know if you were planning on coming home."

"I never saw him; how did you even get in?" How could they think I had moved on?

"It wasn't very easy; this was the only way we could get in here. If anyone wants to scale down a slick side can do it now, plenty of places to hold onto. He saw you kissing that kid, so he left. Don't count on him coming back to visit, the rest of us will always be available to help you." Giving me a hug Voncha had turned to leave.

"Voncha, wait, please." Walking over to him wrapping my arms around him, "you don't understand. I wasn't kissing him. I pushed him away; he must not have seen that. He made a move on me when we were walking back, I was absorbed in my thoughts at the time, and I know it sounds horrible but I'm not doing anything with him. Did Jasper leave to go home?" Looking at Voncha in the face I hoped Jasper hadn't gone far.

"You'll have to convince him yourself." I knew Voncha was right.

"I need both of you on all hallows eve during the witching hour. Come with me." I had grabbed Voncha's hand making sure no one saw who he was even though I think most ignored him thinking it was Ryan.

Bringing him past the training ground and down into the ravine where Joyce taught me, I had taken control of the wind coming through whipping it around us. I needed to make sure no one could hear us. I know Voncha was wondering what I was doing let alone how I was doing it. I had never practiced in front of him before; this was my first time showing him now what I could do.

"I need to kill the council members; they are experiments of Morris controlling them. The shades here don't have the power to fight them, and most are fearful if they do, they will die because of not being able to heal or what the council members might do to their families." I hoped Voncha would understand.

"That's a pretty strong action to take. Once you kill someone you can't bring them back, it's not like myself turning someone into a vampire, they become immortal with drawbacks." Voncha always preferred avoiding wars unless there was no other way around it.

"When we were attacked earlier by the outside monster, he had something in his hand to blow the others away from him. He didn't care what the others were doing to him he was coming right for me. Only two of the council members seemed to have slight powers, the rest held the same piece in their hand that he had; only theirs were not as strong. Joyce and Ryan have told me a little about them or rather it slipped out." Maybe I was getting involved in something I shouldn't?

"Joyce? Sorry, it just felt strange when you said her name, that was the same as your mother's name. Find out more information about the council members, leave a message in the first dug-out hole along the wall, I'll collect it later. Jasper, your father, and I will decide if we should do anything. Have you healed anyone?" Voncha was curious since this was one of the reasons I had come up here.

"Only one and that was just a few hours ago, he hasn't regained consciousness yet, he blacked out." Now I was starting to feel bad for leaving him for so long.

"Was it the kid you were caught kissing? If so, then Jasper has nothing to be jealous of or to worry about. You never left his side once when he was injured. You should probably go back and check on him to make sure he's alright. I'll be back later to check on you." Looking around to make sure no one was watching Voncha leave.

I had made my way back rather quickly to Ryan hoping he might be awake or feeling better. He wasn't sweating any longer; neither did he have a fever or shake. His skin had a healthier glow to it. Breathing was no longer labored but steady. Sitting down next to him leaning over to listen, Ryan surprised me. Grabbing me throwing me over to the other side of the bed, I had slightly hit the wall. Ryan flipped over on his side smiling at me.

"I have to say I have never felt better, when it first kicked in for a second, I thought great the crazy vampire-loving chic is going to kill me. Where did you go?" Ryan was in a better mood.

"I went out to look around. I was hoping to be back before you woke up. I have some questions that need to be answered. How would I get one of the council members to speak with me?" I know before I was nervous about talking to them and now, I intentionally wanted to speak with one.

"You can always speak to Peter, he is safe. I just make him very nervous it's why we don't get along that great." Ryan had looked at me strangely.

"I almost forgot we are supposed to go to your parents for dinner, they came over earlier, but you were still out of it. I told them I kept you up late last night and you were still sleeping." Climbing across him to get out of the bed I started to pull his arm to get Ryan to sit up.

"Keeping me up late? Were we busy being intimate? Because if they ask that's what I'll say." Smiling Ryan knew he angered me.

"You do and I'll hurt you, we need to get going or they will think I've already killed you." It didn't help Ryan was still wearing the same clothes from the day before.

Anytime I was invited over to someone's for dinner I was used to bringing something, something my father had taught me to do out of proper respect. Ryan had absolutely nothing in his fridge to bring. Grabbing him by the arm and now pulling him to their home. At least we had made it on time.

"We were about to send Evan for the two of you. Come sit down, we are just setting dinner out." Joyce had called us from the kitchen.

The dinner went quick, Joyce grew all her herbs and had a vegetable garden. There was a large garden for all the shades in the colony to grow their food. Desert was like nothing I had before; it had the best ingredient, strawberries, and rhubarb. I think Joyce was worried about the dinner and if I would like it since it was vegetarian. Something I was already used to since my father really didn't eat anything but then neither had Jasper or Voncha. I would have considered myself vegan if I hadn't liked milk, eggs, chicken, turkey. So no, I was not vegan.

"Tonight, is game night, any suggestions?" Peter asked looking around the room waiting for a response.

"Do you have scrabble?" I wasn't sure what kind of games they would have.

"We have something like it but only two can play." Peter sounded disappointed.

"That sounds great, peter and I will play my version of scrabble and maybe you guys can play spoons?" Voncha and I used to play until I found how sharp his nails were and we quit.

Evan pulled out the pieces needed for all our games. Peter and I sat down on the couch while the others played at the kitchen table.

"What is your version of scrabble?" At least Peter was curious now.

"You'll see." Grabbing the pieces and separating them I had Peter confused.

Instead of using the normal board to place the handwritten letters, I had arranged them easily so I could grab the ones I needed. The first words I had spelled out were, "you're a council member." In response, Peter laid out the letters, "yes." Then I proceeded to ask, "how many are shades." Giving me a strange look before glancing at Joyce he answered, "four." So far, his responses only had to be short ones. Clearing the coffee table every time making new words helped, I just wished I had more letters. Taking a moment to think I started to lay out the next words. "Are shades safe from the others?" This was when I wished I could use a question mark. Laying down only two letters he spelled out, "No."

"How are you two doing over there, you're being very quiet?" Joyce sounded worried as she looked over at us questioning how we were playing the game.

"We're learning a new way of playing the game. I found out Emma is fascinated with lava rocks; I'm going to show her my collection real quick." Standing up Peter gave me a nod of the head to follow him.

Standing up I wasn't sure if we would have to go far to get to his office, thankfully it was off from the living room. Closing the door behind us and flipping on the light switch Peter went and sat down. Pointing to the chair opposite him I sat down waiting for what he was going to say, he didn't have any lava rocks out to show.

'No one can hear a sound from here, you could scream in here and Evan, Joyce, or Ryan will never hear you. You figured out that the council has every place tapped so they know everything that is going on or being said. Who are you?" Peter leaned forward resting his chin on his hands.

"Yes, I have found that out, it's why I wanted to talk to you with the paper pieces. I originally came here to learn to control and find out what gifts' shades have since I recently found out I am one myself. Except I am also here for another reason that I'm having trouble with, it's hard for me to help one group who is on the brink of extinction when they might turn around and just wipe out another group." I wasn't sure how to say it, but I hoped to ease into it.

"Originally when the council was started, we helped protect our people, it had been set up by Morris. We had only continued it after he left since we thought we were still protecting ourselves from others and Morris, we never thought for a second, they were not shades. We found out they were experiments of Morris's. They were to resemble and act like shades only their task wasn't to protect us anymore, it was to eliminate us. For now, we serve a purpose, we are stuck here doing anything they ask until they feel like killing us all." Peter sat back dropping his hands to the sides of his chair.

"Why doesn't everyone leave?" It seemed simple enough.

"We are not safe on the outside. None of us want to become vampires, we know of other creatures that exist and we are very weak. We would be like mortals. The creatures hold something dear to us, family, that is held in cages. We mess up and they get killed." Peter's voice was saddened when he said this.

"How do you know they are not already dead?" I thought it was strange Joyce hadn't brought this up when we had talked.

"We are allowed to visit, to feed and clothe them except they are not allowed out. They are kept underground. "Standing up Peter grabbed a piece of paper and started drawing the city on the paper with all of the tunnels leading down.

The one he marked with arrows leading to the prison.

"If your family could be free and you had the power to fight the other council members, would you?" From the look on Peter's face, I could tell he thought I was joking.

"What could you possibly do? We tried to rise against them except they are far too strong. We can't afford to lose any more of our people. Do you honestly think you can take them on?

I heard what you did to that one but there are eleven of them here. It would take a miracle." Peter shook his head in frustration.

"Then I believe I'm your miracle. I've already healed Ryan, he's no longer infected. I also have vampires who will help, provided you don't try to kill them." I knew I had his attention then.

"Vampires would only take the advantage to kill us off. There hasn't been a vampire in our colony in over a hundred years. At least we could heal others; I only assumed you were infected like the rest of us. I just couldn't explain how you did that feat earlier killing that monster. They came to the conclusion you had a device they couldn't see." Now pacing Peter's mind was racing.

"Your opinion of vampires has been clouded by Morris; he started as a shade. He was stopped and killed by vampires. When my mother died, I was raised by vampires, they never bit or harmed me. They did everything in their power to protect me. This group you can trust. Besides I've had two vampires visit today already." I decided to tell him the truth about myself.

He seemed shocked as he dropped to the floor still watching me.

"If you and your vampires could take care of the council members then the other three and I could release our family members who are being held. I just don't know how to get them out?" Peter let out a deep sigh.

"I'm sure we can figure something out. I want to check this out." Picking up the map he drew, I followed Peter out of the room.

"Did you like the collection of rocks?" Joyce had looked us over.

"Yes, I did, it was very interesting." I was ready for today to be over.

"I'm sure everyone is as tired as I am, I think it's rather late and we should get to sleep if we plan on getting up early." Peter had waved goodnight while Joyce kissed everyone on the cheek before turning in.

Evan looked rather confused but went to his room. I had grabbed Ryan's arm pulling him out the door and to his place.

Showing him the picture Peter drew he understood what I was getting at. I wanted to check out the place tonight but after I left the letter for Voncha to collect.

"I live for this." Had been Ryan's only words.

Wearing all black we tried to blend in with the shadows, taking lesser-used areas not that many were out right now. Most were asleep in their homes. Most of the lights had been turned off while the moonlight barely reached through the treetops. We made our way to the ledge, laying down on my stomach I looked down and could see the first gouge Voncha or Jasper had put in the side rock. Rolling the paper that contained the situation the shades were caught in and our possible idea to handle things, I had tucked it in firmly so the wind or anything else couldn't blow or see it. Getting up we had left quickly, not wanting anyone to wonder why we were here so late.

There were so many tunnels that if it hadn't been for Ryan I would have been lost. The city felt so small, to begin with, even though they had a few areas that were in the open air along with certain parts of the mountainside. If situations had been different, I probably would have fallen in love with the place. Ryan was right even if they were not having new shades born there was still limited space. I had started to think about him, even if I did cure everyone here. They might be the only colony left. No one had heard or seen anyone for years from any of the others. Many they had lost touch with and had no clue where they were located anymore.

Twisting around so many turns and going incredibly deep I began to wonder just how far down we were going to go. We had come to the end of the last tunnel leading us into one gigantic room. The ceiling had to be fifteen feet high. There was a rather nice size ledge and a little island in the center of the pond. Only one bridge went across to the island. The bridge was high up, not anywhere we could grab it. Ryan had no problem soaking his feet in the water and yet he wouldn't risk swimming in this. He motioned he didn't know how to swim. What was it with shades and vampires? Why do they hate the water so much? I know I never liked water that I couldn't see the bottom too but at least I knew how to swim. My neighbor had taught me how to when I

210

was little. Taking off my shoes I tested the water. I was expecting the water to be cold, instead, it was warm so I lowered myself in slowly to test it out in case only the surface was warm, and the rest of it could have been hotter since I wasn't sure what was heating it. So far nothing, I pushed off from the side swimming over to the little island in the middle. Leaning on the edge I pulled myself up. Dripping wet I looked for the opening, there weren't any visible doors except I had found a very small latch. Pulling at the latch the center opened revealing a very small hidden door that was covered with moss.

This wasn't what I had expected; the little building that was covered with moss couldn't have held everyone in it. When I stood inside there was just a small size room almost the same size as a small closet. There was a small round cover similar to a manhole cover. As soon as I had removed it out of the way I had investigated the deep hole, pulling out a flashlight shining it down the light had revealed steps going straight down along the wall. Following the steps down, there had to be at least twenty steps before I came to the first four rows, the steps continued to lead downward.

Getting off the steps on the first floor there were hallways in each direction, each aisle had people contained on both sides. Each cell had a couple of people in them packed like sardines. Looking over the cell doors they were lined with an electrical line. I had guessed if they chose to, they could electrocute them to death. There were no off switches nearby that we had seen and no levers out in the main area. I was guessing there had to be something in their main chambers kept away from everyone. Somewhere that Peter and the other three were not allowed.

The people inside were rather surprised to see me in there, apparently, no one visited this late at night. From the depth of these rooms, I guessed the water was only to appear deep to keep anyone from getting across, otherwise, there might be something in the water I didn't want to know about. As I was about to leave, I heard this very light voice. Looking around to see who was saying it, the others were pointing down one direction. Following the path along the wall, the voice was coming from the furthest back part. An older woman had put her hand between the cell doors. As soon as I was standing in front of her, she moved her hand away and replaced it with a much younger hand. The young girl standing next to her simply let her do this out of trust.

"I know who you are, I may be old and feeble, but I know a true aura when I see one. Please heal her, even being trapped in here it helps to heal oneself, if they decide to electrocute us to death, she can keep herself separated from the cell and survive." The woman's voice was very hopeful.

"You're wasting your time old women; no one can save us anymore. It would be better they put us to death and get this over with instead of suffering down here." The man was two cells down from hers.

Not wanting to start an uproar or bring attention, I had used my fingernail to cut into my skin. Letting a drop of blood drip into her hand, she closed it and went to lay down. The old woman was incredibly happy sitting next to her explaining to her what was going to happen. I repeated this with twelve other hands. Just a drop of blood hadn't taken much. Now they were urging me to leave, there were enough of them once healed they could reach out to their cellmates next to them, helping them.

Closing the door behind me and swimming back to the other side, Ryan was standing there acting nervous.

"What took you so long?" Grabbing my hand, we started to walk out right away.

"It took longer than I thought; an older woman recognized what I was. I healed the little girl in her cage that she asked me to, I healed twelve others while I was in there. If we can't get them out in time at least they will have a way to protect themselves." When I finished, I heard something to the side of us.

Still holding onto Ryan's hand, I pulled him back, stopping him from going any further, we went back down to hide. Someone was coming down the path. The only thing we could hide behind had been the large black box that handled the bridge in the morning. Crouched down behind it we watched to see who was coming. There were two members of the council, the experiments. They had a large bag with them that seemed rather heavy. They had put their hand on part of the wall pushing it open revealing a door. As soon as they were in I had run over to the door they went into. Pushing the door open I didn't see them other than a hollowed-out room with another two doors, only one of them was open with a light on inside. We had never seen the door outside since the walls were covered with vines and moss.

Getting close enough so that I could see in, I peeked around the door just a little. The look on Ryan's face let me know who they had. Pulling a body out of the bag and setting it on the table. They were making drawn lines on his body. What shocked me had been the freezer with the glass cover, inside had been Morris's head. They were trying to reconstruct him. Backing up before they realized we were there or before more came down, we made our way up and out of the tunnels as fast as we could. Not slowing down for a second until we had come to Ryan's home.

Grabbing a piece of paper to write on, Ryan handed it to me with the words, "the body they had on the table, he went missing over a year ago. Everyone thought he might have been grabbed by the wondering experiments outside of the colony. It's another reason most don't leave, their afraid of running into those things." Burning the paper and setting it on the incense burner until it was nothing more than ash.

Stopping for a moment I smelled something, that unmistakable scent. I was sure Ryan worried maybe someone had seen us possibly setting a trap in Leah's room. Grabbing him by the arm pulling him back I shook my head no.

"I'll see you in the morning." I had hoped to make it clear enough.

Looking at Ryan he had grabbed one of his baseball bats holding it over his head ready to swing downward with it. Taking it out of his hands and throwing it back into his room onto his bed.

"I can sleep on my own just fine." Shoving him into his room I opened and closed my door rather quickly.

Not that it was needed; I had felt a hand cover my mouth no doubt assuming I would have screamed. Standing there not even fighting it I knew who it was. Letting go of his grip on my mouth I turned quickly to see him. Jasper had been standing there with a panicked expression on his face. At least it would be easier to speak with Jasper than it was with Ryan. When I was little,

Jasper had taught me American Sign Language. Jasper had started signing to me, so I knew they had received my note.

"Where have you been? I've been waiting several hours for you." Jasper signed emphatically.

"We were checking out the tunnels down below where the prisoners are being held."

"Voncha said you were in extreme danger and injured." Jasper stood back looking at me surprised but relieved.

"How did you know to come here?" I was curious how he found us.

"I followed Ryan when he came out of that tunnel, I thought he was with someone else, you were both wearing hoods. I can see you don't need me." Jasper had made a move to go out the window.

Grabbing him before he could leave, I wrapped my arms around his waist as tight as I could. Hugging him for quite a while before he forced himself to turn around now looking at me, his expression looked so sad. His left hand brushed through my hair then leaning over kissed me on the forehead.

"He fits you; I saw how content you were with him. I think it's best you stay here; you'll be much happier with him." Jasper did not attempt to hold me.

"You only came because you thought I was injured? If I had been, then what? How could you possibly think for one second that I would choose Ryan over you? Voncha told me you caught Ryan kissing me. He made a move on me; I wish you had seen me push him away. I've always trusted you, why don't you trust me? I love you, Jasper." Staring into his eyes begging for him to understand.

"I can't stop wanting to protect you, but I also shouldn't stop you from moving on with your life. I'll be here to protect you as always, but I can't be more than that." Not another word and Jasper was gone out the window.

Dropping down onto the floor, I could barely breathe. Hyperventilating I tried to gasp for air, my ribs and lungs hurt. The tears flooded from my eyes and for the first time, I wanted to die. I was suddenly aware of the air in the room; at least it had felt like there was a lack of it. I felt as if I had been crushed, left for dead, the only problem had been I wasn't dying, at least I would have had some relief. I couldn't feel the wall behind me any longer as the room darkened. Eventually, I had simply passed out; it was too much to take.

The next few days didn't go any better. I stayed in the bedroom not moving from the floor. Ryan tried his best to get me going, to give me something to live for. For the first time, I had realized I made a mistake leaving, that I should have stayed home. I had always waited every year for Jasper and Voncha to come. I had known he had feelings for me since I was seventeen. I knew I was too young, and I just wasn't ready. I never said a word to him because I had honestly thought he had a crush; he couldn't possibly feel that way for me. He never took advantage of me or hinted. I had only caught a slip-up and overheard him talking to Voncha. The one who had surprised me had been Voncha and how he felt. I was so thrown off; I knew how I felt about Jasper even though coming here made it easier not to deal with it. I didn't want to hurt him. I just didn't feel that way about him.

I knew Jasper preferred being single, coming and going when he wanted. I was busy with college, making plans for the future that neither of us let the other know. Then he kisses me so passionately before he's caught. All I could do was think about him, risk my life to save him and my family. I finally had him and now I've lost him? I guess he didn't love me as much as I thought he had.

When I had come to that realization, I knew I needed to get control of myself and finish what I had planned on doing. I would build a mini army in secret; we would wait for the annual, all Hallows Eve event after all the others on the council would never see it coming. Everyone continued to live as they had before I came. My only plan now had been to fight and then go home to my father and Voncha. Ryan had decided once his family was safe, he would finally move out himself. Ryan was going to come home with me for a while and help Leah with the baby.

Voncha had visited twice before to make sure they knew the plans and if they needed to be aware of anything. He also tried to explain how broken Jasper was except I couldn't deal with it right now. At least not after the way he had left it.

ALL HALLOWS EVE

Voncha had been preparing for weeks ever since we had finalized our plans. Jasper hadn't been around the house in weeks, I hadn't been the only one disappointed in him. There had been two days before my father, Voncha and a few others were going to come rid the shade colony of Morris's final experiments and free their families. Over the next few weeks, I would sneak into the holding cells, I had cured every shade that was trapped in there. I just wished I could have removed them from their cells, I just couldn't find the controls to do it.

The best way of killing off the experiments would be to tear them to pieces. We wanted to make sure there was no way they could come back from the dead in any way. It wouldn't be easy since they were incredibly strong and able to withstand quite a lot. Vampires were better at destroying compared to shades who used the elements to attack with. There were a few shades on the outside of the cells living with the rest of the colony that were brave enough to get healed and fight for their cause. Many were aware there would be vampires there fighting with them, that they were not to be harmed. The shades were being oppressed enough they were willing to fight alongside vampires not even complaining about it.

Practicing his fighting moves, Voncha had seen in the distance Jasper streak across in such speed no doubt hoping he wouldn't be noticed. He wasn't going to let him get away with this one.

Quickly following Jasper to one of his favorite retreats, where he would go to relax and forget for a while that the world existed. It was a rustic cabin similar to the one they had owned together, except only Voncha and Jasper knew about this place. It looked worn down on the outside, moss, and brush growing all around it. Almost as if you could blow at it and it would collapse. The inside had looked completely different. Red hardwood floors and cabinets with a Jacuzzi, a bar filled with every liquor there was made with a few extremely old vintage wine bottles. Voncha followed him in not that Jasper didn't know he was there. Grabbing a drink from the cooler, he sat down and simply looked at Jasper.

"Are you going to be there when we strike?" Jasper still hadn't told Voncha if he planned on helping.

"I'll be there to protect and then I'll be gone, I don't plan on coming back here." Jasper had made his comment short and to the point.

"I swear I could destroy you right now. I didn't bother stepping in because I knew how much she meant to you not that she meant any less to me, I did it out of respect for our friendship and the simple fact I knew how happy she would be. I've known for a long time she was in love with you, and this is the crappy way you treat her?" Voncha's voice was rising as he spoke.

"I never asked you to." Jasper had shown no reflection or feeling in his voice.

Shooting across the room Voncha had grabbed his long-time friend by the neck lifting him into the air shaking slightly from anger.

"I swear if I get a chance, I'll prove how much I love her, and I won't hold back. I never thought you would do this, you actually had her!" Voncha's voice boomed.

"What do you expect me to say? How much do I love her? The fact I would still die for her. That I can't eat or wished I could drink myself to death because I know that I hurt her? If I didn't let her go then I wouldn't be allowing what should happen naturally. She's where she belongs, once this danger is out of the way, she

217

will be safe and around others like her. If you love her as much as you say you do, you'll do the same and let her stay there." Pushing past Voncha, Jasper knocked him to the ground, not bothering to look back.

Brushing himself off still feeling angry with Jasper, Voncha went back to his exercises. Not wanting to miss any opportunity, Voncha wanted to be as physically ready as he could get. After preparing for battle, the time had finally come. They were going to sneak into the colony without being seen staying there until All Hallows Eve when the tree lights were lit, the costume judging won't be happening this year, not that anyone knew that but the few who were coming for the fight.

Everyone knew exactly what was expected of them. Coming up to the side of the mountain Voncha, Robert, and the others were led into the city by Peter. Robert and Voncha stayed with Emma while Jasper, Kieam, and Luthrow stayed with Peter and Joyce. There were six more vampires who insisted on living in an empty home next to Ryan's, they didn't want to share a space with anyone else planning on leaving as soon as it had been over. They simply volunteered to repay the favor of us saving their lives recently. My father had been told about Joyce still being alive even though he wasn't sure how. It had been reported that Morris had killed her; it was why he thought her family wanted revenge on my father.

Not as many vampires had volunteered to help as I would have liked, most I think we're still worried whether the shades would stick to their truce and not kill them. However, with their help and those who have been healed now, the fatalities should be kept extremely low. With all of us, there had been thirty ready to fight. We didn't want to get overly confident with our number in case they had their experiments. The only part that had changed since I had last talked to Voncha had been when we found Morris, so we had filled everyone in on the fact they were trying to reanimate Morris.

Outside of our home, everything was moving along just like any other ordinary day. After watching the decorating, I was thinking I should visit next year during this holiday. They celebrated it; unlike anything I had ever seen. Various painted pumpkins hanging everywhere. Broomsticks were on every door. There were several different sizes and shapes of cauldrons decorating the pathways with either candles or torches set next to them. They had celebrated this day as their greatest freedom; dressing up, had been the only day they didn't worry about experiments or other creatures attacking. Many shades were natural witch doctors having years of family heritage that healed the sick, protected mortals during childbirth and illness. One day their rituals and gifts were not ridiculed or persecuted for.

To prevent ruining the surprise we had made sure everyone understood how important it was not to speak, that way in case we were being overheard it would sound as if we were going on about our daily lives.

The colony had been busy decorating and getting ready for All Hallows Eve. It almost seemed fitting that we would be having a bloody battle on the day of Halloween. Anytime I had given thought to Jasper being so close by and not with me I had felt incredibly sick. Not wanting to let anyone know I was having a hard time with this I excused myself to my room saying I wanted to get myself ready mentally. They celebrated in the shade cemetery. Everyone from the colony including the council members would join in. It was amazing looking. Almost as if a wedding, Halloween, and parts of Christmas had collided.

Sitting on the floor in front of the bed I wondered if I should live here. If I did, I would miss my old room, my things. I knew I could bring those things here but then it wasn't as if my mother wanted me yet. She didn't want to know. Ryan planned on leaving for good and I would greatly miss my father. If I were at home, I would see Voncha, maybe I could convince him to stay more often than just to visit on my birthday? I had been lost in my thoughts for a while when I heard a slight thump. Voncha was trying to get my attention. Closing the door behind him, he started to sign to me, he said,

"How are you holding up?" As he asked this, Voncha sat down next to me.

"I just don't want to screw up, there is so much depending on this working." I knew what he was asking except I preferred to avoid it if I could.

219

"You know that's not what I mean. Afterward, are you staying here? Do you want to? If you do, I promise you won't lose your father and me. We will visit you." Voncha rested his right hand on my shoulder.

"Sometimes I think it would have been nice to stay but I don't have any reason to. Ryan is leaving, other than him. I don't have any other reason to stay. Besides, I prefer to come home." Leaning slightly, I rested my head on Voncha's shoulder.

"Everyone is resting, go ahead and sleep, if you like I'll stay here or I'll leave, whatever you're comfortable with." Voncha kept running his fingers through my hair.

My hair was growing out and thankfully the temporary dye I used was washing out. My hair still wasn't as light as it used to be, I think it was slightly darker because of the dye.

"Will you lay in bed with me while I sleep? Like when I was younger when I had nightmares?" I knew I didn't have to say anymore after this.

Voncha laid down at the back of the bed while I lay resting my head on his chest. Looping his arm over my waist lying very close I had felt safe and comfortable. There was so much that still needed to be done and I couldn't get my mind to stop thinking about these things. What concerned us the most was the simple fact we had not found a way to release the prisoners. There were parts of the council chambers that had been guarded at all times. We never had a chance to poke around looking for something that controlled the jail cells down below. It didn't matter how tired I was I just could not fall asleep. Leaning me forward just a little Voncha started to rub my neck and massage my back. I could feel my body no longer feeling as stiff as it had been. Laying there feeling much more relaxed I had finally slept for a few hours.

When I woke up, I was now laying on my back looking up at Voncha who had been watching me sleep. For a brief second, I had forgotten where I was when it flooded back. As soon as this was done, I planned on going back home. Hopefully, life would go back to the way it was for a while. Knowing that I wasn't a normal mortal was just fine with me not that I had to act any different, just meant I now had a different way of looking at the world. I still owed Janice and her husband a wedding gift.

Smiling at me I knew Voncha had something on his mind. He had looked at the door for a moment before he signed to me.

"Did you sleep well?" Voncha seemed to be looking excited over something.

"I slept well, are you looking for something?" I couldn't help being curious, he was acting as if he was up to something.

"There is nothing better before a fight or anything for that matter than to get the endorphins going." Voncha started smiling even more, very close to an evil and devious smile.

"I'm not having sex with you." What was up with him? Honestly, it was the only thing that wasn't running through my thoughts.

"No, I wasn't planning on having sex with you. Not that I would turn it down if you wanted me to. I'm just going to be straightforward about this. You know how you feel about Jasper. He's in the other home not far from here, he's not planning on coming back with us. You know how you feel about me. All I want you to do is give me a chance; if you don't feel anything for me then I won't make another move on you." After stating this, Voncha waited for a response.

I just felt more confused than anything. Jasper didn't want to be in my life anymore, Voncha and Ryan had. I've known Voncha for so long so maybe he was right, so many things changing who knows, maybe this wouldn't be a bad decision? Not having to wait very long before Voncha made his move. Leaning into me he brushed his fingers through my hair sliding his hand down to my neck. Leaning forward, brushing his lips over mine until they were firmly pressing against mine. Sitting up he had wrapped his left arm around my waist lifting me into his lap. As his lips moved away from mine, he continued to hold me firmly close to him. Tipping my chin upward, kissing me again, and lingering each time. This would be so easy to accept, it had felt good. I felt light-headed as I let myself try to get caught up in the moment. Releasing me from his embrace, Voncha finally moved back looking at me.

"You can't tell me you didn't feel anything for me." Whispering slightly to me as he continued kissing my neck, still holding me close.

"I will always feel something for you. I've known you my entire life, I've already loved you. I just don't love you in that way. I'm sorry Voncha." It was hard turning him down.

"At least I can't say I never tried." Squeezing me tighter before Voncha let me go.

Leaving Voncha in the room I figured I could relax more in the living room with the others except I hadn't expected Jasper to be standing there. We had only caught each other's attention for a split second before Jasper tried to pretend, he hadn't seen me. At least until I walked by him, and he looked at me as if he was trying to figure something out.

Voncha was right, it certainly was a way to get the endorphins going except I would have preferred not feeling like this and then seeing Jasper. Walking past my father he had grabbed my arm, both he and Jasper were looking at my neck rather strangely. It didn't help that Ryan started to laugh hysterically out loud falling off the chair onto the floor. Looking into the hallway mirror I saw what they were staring at. Grabbing a pillow from the couch I went and threw it at Voncha. Voncha had signed he 'was leaving me a loving memento in case he died tomorrow keeping me safe, this would remind me of him until it went away.' He wasn't the best trying to cover up things like this. My father wasn't ignorant, and neither was Jasper. At first, Jasper had grabbed Voncha slamming him into the wall. There was going to be a huge dent left from it.

Slapping Jasper on the back getting his attention, I had signed to him. "This is what will draw attention; besides you made it clear you don't want me, Voncha made an offer, and I told him the same thing I told Ryan. I'm not interested. Not that it's any of your business." Moving away from both, Jasper was acting like a jealous teenager.

Not wanting to deal with either of them I had sat down on the couch near my father. Ryan's laughter had finally cleared up a little and now turned to hiccups. Joyce had dropped off food and brought in the flier that was being handed out to everyone. The exact time for the lighting of the tree, what time the costumes would be judged, and a few other minor activities that were being held, at least now we didn't have to wait that much longer. The hard part was about to begin. One at a time Peter had come back to collect different ones to help get them ready. We were positioning ourselves in different areas, that way when the attack began, we would all be in different places trying our best to control the fight, I just hoped no one on our side would end up seriously injured.

We all had different costumes except they had a similar theme so that we would know who was helping and who needed to be escorted out of the way so that they would not be caught in the middle of the fight. We all had a dark slash of red through our outfits. I worried when I saw my father, Jasper, and Voncha leave. I knew this would be dangerous except it couldn't be avoided, the shades needed our help. I had hoped by doing this with the vampires, by giving them their freedom and saving their family members might make permanent peace between the shades and vampires?

It was finally All Hallows Eve; there were so many outside and surrounding the tree. We were out in the huge open space where the beautiful view of the mountain was seen. As some had called it, the edge of the shade city, a favorite place for many to come and look out at the world. The only place you could get wet from the natural rain or see the sunrise and sunset. The tree had been positioned at the opening; the first sight anyone would see was the tree. There were a few vending carts with snacks and drinks. A few of the vendors I had recognized in their costumes. Many of the families had kept their little ones near the tree. The apple bobbing events, baby crawl, and ring toss games for the little ones had finished. Some of the smaller ones had left before the rest of the evening's events. Most of the children and families had stayed near the side of the tree, the easiest area to take off once it became dangerous. There was rather festive music and a few couples dancing to it under the moonlight. Confidant his costume covered him, Voncha had pulled me onto the dance floor. Jasper was still acting jealous, I felt he deserved it after the way he had treated me. At least he can see what he was giving up.

Lithiana, Gerigino, Joraih, and Peter had excused themselves in front of the other council members; they were taking gifts and food down to the prisoners in the cell, something they had done every year. Peter seemed to think he knew where the release was to let the others go. It had left us with a few shades and vampires to finish this. The music had now been turned off, Joyce stood next to Ryan and me. Evan had excused himself now going back home saying he wasn't feeling well. At least it was the excuse we wanted him to use to keep him out of the way. The rest of the council members now stood in front of the tree. I wasn't sure how I hadn't noticed it until now, even the look of their skin gave them away. They had brownish-green skin, each wearing rather impressive robes for the event tonight.

Normally they would have given a speech except they never put out the podium. Instead, they all stood in front of the tree, something was different about this, and I had that moment of panic come over me. The tree had been fully decorated and ready for the bright lights to be turned on. Instead, one of the members had pulled out a match, lighting it, the tree had gone up in one huge fireball.

"Normally this would be a day for you to celebrate family, to celebrate the gifts that you will no longer have. Thanks to your missing family members we have finished building our own family that is much superior to any of you." As he spoke several more, however, much more hideous-looking creatures came out to stand behind them.

They had plans of their own; at least I understood why they picked this day. Everyone would be here feeling safe in such a large group knowing there had never been a creature attack on this day. We were not the only ones using that to our advantage. As they moved out to attack, we had closed off the exit heading back into the shade city. The cemetery where everything was taking place had been on the far side of the councils' chambers. The training grounds were off to the far-right side of where we were at. We were in a rather large open area to the outdoors; they could have bolted getting away except they had planned on killing the surviving shades tonight. They hadn't planned on giving up their goal until it was completed.

I hoped they hadn't set up a trap downstairs when the four had gone down to help them. Letting out the families and those who were not participating we now had the others cornered. They knew we were ready to fight. Not wasting any time one of theirs had made a run at Jasper. Jasper had told me once he always preferred the others to make the first move when he was in a fight; he said it gave him the upper hand. The rest of us had joined in; I was amazed at my father. I knew he had a temper, but I never knew he fought so well. He had already taken out one of them moving on to the next creature. I had to stop myself from watching everyone else and get into it myself. I wasn't looking forward to killing anything even if it was an evil creature and I had already killed one earlier. I was only trying to protect myself, not kill it.

When he came at me, I didn't have a chance to get any shots in. Getting knocked to the ground with a huge gash across my chest I started bleeding right away. Leaning over me going for the killing blow. I had managed to get my palms facing upward blowing him straight upward as he came down. I controlled the winds with the fire from the tree striking him from the front and the back ripping him apart with the force. I had noticed even though I was much stronger with the elements, the others I had healed who hadn't either been taught or fought like this before, were catching on quickly. I was rather proud of how determined they were. Not fighting far from me and keeping an eye on me was Jasper. I knew he was watching even though he would look away quickly dealing with his fight.

Out of the corner of my eye, I had seen something come whizzing at me. Ducking down quickly out of automatic response, looking upward as an experiment head went sailing over me. I wasn't the only one surprised by it; Joyce who had produced the lethal blow was just as amazed at what she could do now that she was no longer infected. At times we found ourselves being attacked by more than two at a time. At least I could control my attackers by blowing the extra that I couldn't handle away from me while I dealt with the one. A couple of times I had blown away the extra ones who were attacking Jasper, Voncha, and my father. Joyce had been taken by surprise getting knocked down to the ground and now unconscious. Kieam had pulled one of the monsters off from Joyce killing it and now moved her to the far side of the room to keep her from getting further harmed while she was unconscious.

It felt like fireworks were going off with all the chaos being created by the shades and fast blurs that the vampires were creating by moving faster than what I could focus on. Looking up I had been hit by something, I was drenched feeling sopping wet. Lying on the ground I raised my hand. There was so much blood on me. I didn't see anyone else on the ground, for a brief second, I had thought maybe it was from me. My head was throbbing from hitting the floor so hard. I felt blood coming from my skull. Concentrating the best, I could I felt my hand get hot as I started to heal myself. Jasper had been watching me when I hit the ground; it had almost cost him his life paying attention to me instead of the monster he was fighting against. Voncha had pulled him off before he could have easily taken Jasper out when he was distracted.

On the right side of me, there was a finger. I was hit by an exploding body. For the first time during this battle, I had wanted to throw up, I was feeling so nauseated and sick from the blood and stench of death. There were a few vampires who had been wounded but nothing that couldn't be fixed. The last two experiments had been killed by Ryan and his old childhood friend Brent. Voncha had come over to find out how I was doing. I was lying in a pool of blood. My body hurt from being slammed into the ground, the blood on my chest had gelled. Moving slightly, I could feel my rib, it had been broken. I thought we were supposed to be able to heal bones. No matter how hard I tried, I couldn't heal my rib.

"You had a pretty strong wallop from that dead body, looked nasty as it splattered on you. How do you feel?" Kneeling next to me Voncha had a strange look on his face.

"I already healed my head; my rib is broken. For now, I'm fine, is everyone else alright?" I wasn't sure what he was getting at.

"Your clothes are a mess, make sure you get cleaned, don't need you getting an infection from those things. I want you to stay laying down for a little while, Jasper thinks you're worse off than you are. Jasper thinks you're dying. I'm going to have Ryan hopefully heal you. Just play along." Waving over to Ryan to get him to come over.

"Why would he think I'm dying? I didn't lose that much blood and I just broke a rib, yes it hurts but I'm not dying." From the devious look on Voncha's face, I knew he was up to something.

"I told him you were, that Ryan might not be able to heal you." Giving me a wink, he took a glance to see if Jasper was watching.

My father and a few of the shades were looking around making sure no more experiments were around. Going into the room hidden in the corner to see what was in there, only a couple of people were left in the main room with us. Jasper was now standing near me as Ryan had rushed over dropping to his knees. Pointing to the area that had needed healing he positioned his hands, concentrating his hands lit up almost burning my skin. The bone was healing except my skin was burning. Stopping before he damaged the skin anymore, we left the bone knowing if I gave it the time it needed, it would finish healing on its own.

The room that the others had checked only had a few other experiments that were hiding, one they had left alive. There was something about him that didn't feel dangerous, something just indescribable. Letting him leave unharmed the others came back to join us. Jasper was kneeling by my side. He seemed almost afraid to touch me in case he was to hurt me further.

"Is there anything I can do? Let me know and I'll do anything you need." Jasper had been shaken by the idea of me dying.

"Jasper. I'm sorry Voncha told you I was dying, I'll be alright. It's not anything that won't heal. I just want to go home." At this point, I was so tired and in pain, I felt like crying and I hadn't hidden the sound in my voice.

I couldn't stop the tears from flowing. I knew I would be alright. I even knew how the others were doing. The ones who had been in the prison cells down below were now out walking around free, emotional reunions and best of all the moon had cast its glow over everyone truly making this a magical night. Reaching out I had hoped Jasper would at least hold my hand. Trying to sit up Jasper was right there giving me support even though at first his arm put pressure on the rib that hadn't finished healing yet. Lowering his arm, he helped me stand up. The pressure was sending stabbing pain. I might have been the one who was slightly broken except the way Jasper kept looking at me, he looked far worse than I was.

"Let me take you back to the homes, you should rest, if you want Ryan can take you." Jasper's voice sounded shaken.

"Did you mean you would do anything for me?" Standing there while Jasper held onto me, he couldn't even answer other than to nod his head in agreement.

"Take me back to Leah's room just don't leave me once we're there." I had hoped he wouldn't assume that because I was resting in Ryan's place that he would take that time to leave."

I won't leave you." Jasper had made his promise.

I could have walked except Jasper picked me up from the ground carrying me back. We had been thanked and congratulated so many times on the way there by others I was beginning to think they were stalling, or we just wouldn't get there. Walking into Ryan's home I realized I didn't want to lay down like this. I didn't have Leah around and didn't know my mother well enough to help me in the shower. I had decided to have a final talk with Jasper; I only hoped it wouldn't be our final talk.

Placing a towel on the bed so that I wouldn't get bloodstains from the battle on her bedspread I had looked at Jasper. Taking in a deep breath I wasn't sure how to start this, but I couldn't stare at him forever.

"I have known you my entire life; I don't ever want to lose you again. I always thought I would end up with you except I barely thought I could live after you left me the first time. Why did you think I wanted Ryan over you? Why did you think I would be happier here? No matter where you are is where I'm happy." I never thought it would be hard to tell Jasper of all people how I felt.

"I thought I lost you; I knew Voncha was lying to me that you were dying. I can always tell when he does, except the thought of losing you, seeing you laying there in pain. Voncha was right, Ryan might not be able to protect you any more than I could. I just wanted what was best for you; I didn't want to be the one who held you back from being happy. Ryan is more like you; he could make you happy and give you a life I can't. I threw all of this on you at the worst time not even giving you time to decide if you wanted me." Jasper's voice had started to trail off.

"I've always known what I wanted; I knew I had wanted to wait for a short time when I was younger, I knew where and who I wanted to be with later. Every person who has sex for the first time regardless of if they are mortal, shade, vampire, or anything else remembers that person, even if it wasn't good or if it was amazing. Centuries down the road Voncha still remembers his first. That one moment you share such an intimate moment with another. I've always wanted that one person to be worth remembering, my entire life with you has already been like that moment. It's not like all the birthdays I've celebrated, this was one thing I wanted to be done right, you're worth remembering forever. Promise never to leave me, not just until I've finished healing but for the rest of my life." Taking a deep breath, I said everything I felt, I just had to wait for Jasper's answer.

"I have always trusted you; it was difficult for me to see you be kissed by him, especially when Voncha kissed you later. I honestly thought if he were to make a move you would have chosen Voncha over me. You two have such a unique connection. If I have made you feel that way so far then the only thing I can promise to do is love you with my dying breath, never leave and hopefully make sure the rest of your life is better than anything you've ever experienced." I didn't think it was possible to love Jasper any more than I had, he's already lived up to his past, I loved him even more.

Lifting me off the bed cradling me in his arms. I placed my arms around his neck leaning into him. His lips pressed against mine. Just the feel, smell, this is how it was meant to feel.

"Let's get this blood off from you." Still holding me tight, I expected to go into the bathroom to get washed off with Jasper.

Instead, he started undressing me leaving the bloody clothes to the side. His own clothes rested on mine.

Turning on the shower and leaving it at the last setting I had. It felt strange being carried into the shower, lowering me to my feet as my toes touched the cold water that pooled on the floor of the shower before it warmed. I leaned into him as the water poured over me, it felt incredibly good and would have been more romantic if the floor of the shower wasn't colored red from blood. Looking up at him, Jasper kissed me softly then rested his forehead on mine. I couldn't help but feel excited, he was mine and I was his. I knew he was safe, and all of this was over. Now I was curious what our future would be like. Jasper and Voncha would always leave a week after my birthday, now I wasn't sure what to expect. Would they still disappear for three months? Would Voncha continue to come back for my birthday? I had been busy with my thoughts as Jasper caught my attention.

"Are you ready to go home?" Jasper spoke softly to me.

"Eventually, but first I want to stop at the cabin." I wasn't in a rush to go home anymore.

"Did you leave something there?" Jasper sounded surprised.

"I keep expecting someone to walk through the door and the last place I want to be intimate with you is in my childhood bedroom or here at Ryan's home." I knew we would leave but I hadn't wanted to leave his arms.

"We should see if everyone left yet and then we can stop at the cabin." Kissing me on the forehead, Jasper held my hand leading me back outside.

Drying off and changing my clothes. I couldn't help but peek at Jasper as he dried off and got dressed. Leading me through town, the majority of people returned to their homes, very few were outside and if they were they seemed lost in their thoughts relaxing on the benches soaking in the nighttime air. My father and one of his friends were talking with a shade who seemed enthralled by them asking so many questions.

"I don't know about any of you but I'm tired and ready to start heading home, it's been an overwhelming day and will be a while before we get home, we should probably start now, I was hoping dad might start first. I wanted to make sure everyone makes it safely." I knew from the look on my dad's face he was being nice but wanted a polite way of getting out of the conversation so he could leave.

Leaving the colony behind, I doubted I would have a reason to visit again. If my mother wanted to contact me, she knew where to find me. When we were at the bottom of the mountain dad stopped when he realized Jasper and I were poised to head off in another direction.

"Where do you think you're going? Home isn't that direction and you have work to return to, that and find out if the authorities have come to any conclusions over your boss's death." I didn't miss the look my father gave Jasper.

"You seriously can't still be having issues over my being with Jasper. This isn't a fling and he's not taking advantage of me. Who better for me to be with than someone who truly loves me and has already proven he would do everything he can to protect me? I love you dad but give me one good reason not to." Jasper looked at the ground as I asked.

"I know what he's capable of. He's not the sweet patient person you think he is, I've seen his temper." My father kept hesitating as if he didn't want to tell me exactly why.

"Like your temper? I doubt that he is like you. Yet my entire life you had Jasper and Voncha watch over me, be a massive part of my life, and left me in their care because you trusted them because you didn't trust anyone else." I didn't want to keep having this argument with my father and I honestly didn't believe anything Jasper could have done in his past would get me to turn him away.

"There's always a room waiting for you at home." My father gave me a quick kiss on the forehead and took off.

"We can take this slow; he's going to need time getting used to it." I wanted to reassure Jasper, but I knew he was still worried.

Getting on Jaspers back, we made the trip back to the cabin. Nothing changed so Voncha hadn't stopped in since. Jasper looked around worried and slightly blocked me from going in further.

"It's been cleaned, kind of a strange thing for someone that broke in. I think someone might be living here not that I sense any new smells." Jasper looked confused.

"After everyone went missing, Voncha took me here to stay safe while we figured out how to get into the compound. I slept in your bed." I knew no one else had been here.

"I hope it never happens again but if it does, you're not to risk your life for me. That scared me more than anything else when I saw you. I knew you needed to protect yourself when you cast the spell on me, I kept hoping you would find a way to leave but when I kept seeing you, I was worried he might have had control over you and there was nothing I could do to save you." Jasper's voice shook slightly as he spoke.

"I can't make a promise I know I can't keep." Half of me regretted wording it this way.

"I made a promise to your father, and I broke it. He's right, I'm not who you know me as. I have so many secrets from you, many unforgivable. Much of it I hoped you would never know." Jasper brought me over to the couch and sat down.

"You've kept every promise to me. I don't need to know about your past unless you want to tell me." I wasn't sure if I wanted to know since Jasper was determined it was so horrible.

"There is so much I need to explain, and a few things can only be understood if I show you but I'm not ready to have you look at me that way yet. We'll take it slow but for now, I think it's important you get some sleep." Brushing my hair away from my eyes and kissing me on the forehead.

"Then I'll get comfortable here for now." Leaning into Jasper as I always have and resting my head on his chest, nothing had to be finalized right now.